LOVE AFTER LOVE

Love After Love

ALEX HOURSTON

FABER & FABER

First published in 2018
by Faber & Faber Ltd
Bloomsbury House
74–77 Great Russell Street
London WC1B 3DA

Typeset by Faber & Faber Ltd
Printed and bound by CPI Group (UK) Ltd, Croydon CR0 4YY

'Love After Love' from *The Poetry of Derek Walcott 1948–2013*
© The Estate of Derek Walcott, 2014
Reprinted by permission of Faber & Faber Ltd

The right of Alex Hourston to be identified as author of
this work has been asserted in accordance with Section 77
of the Copyright, Designs and Patents Act 1988

A CIP record for this book
is available from the British Library

ISBN 978–0–571–31693–9

FSC
www.fsc.org
MIX
Paper from
responsible sources
FSC® C020471

2 4 6 8 10 9 7 5 3 1

LOVE AFTER LOVE

I

I fell in love with a laugh, though it was not the sound, which was not beautiful – it held the suggestion of phlegm, for he was and remains a smoker; a filthy habit, kissing him stinks – but the laughter was for me and it carried in it delight. I fell in love and found myself altered in the most profound way.

I looked like shit, that's for sure; straight off a flight, though it was only internal, my eyes dry, my hair just fuzz and the seat of my trousers bagging. I was acknowledging all this in a wall of mirror, waiting to check in to my mid-grade hotel, when he joined the queue behind me. He smiled, and I was struck by his height. If you drew a line out from his shoulder, it would skim the top of my head, just. Then:

'It is,' he said. 'It's you. I thought so,' and I turned to him and there was the laugh, though it didn't work at once. He tipped his head back to let it out and I saw his teeth, the pink inside of his mouth, heard that final throaty catch. A rushed shave, perhaps, for he had left a little square of stubble beneath the curve of his chin. He put his hand up to the place as I noticed it.

'Hi!' I said and I knew that I knew him, but had no idea from where. I felt his appeal though, already. I remember that.

'I always wonder who I'm going to bump into at these things,' he said. He wore his hair a little longer and less considered than most of the men I know, and his style of dress: a well-washed shirt and ancient shoes, told me nothing.

'Me too,' I said, which was a lie. I avoid my colleagues for the most part – too much jockeying for position, too much need – then he hugged me and it was immediately retro; smoke and wool, the warmed remains of a lemony cologne, and I had it. Adam. University. The Masters year. Very much on the edge of it all. There was the obvious satisfaction at placing him.

'Are you speaking today?' he asked, when he'd let me go.

'No.' I said. 'Just here to listen. You?'

'This afternoon. In fact I need to go and prepare. It's lovely to see you, Nancy. I hope we can catch up later.'

His stride was long and flat-footed and his shoes made slapping sounds as he left.

I found my room three floors up and midway down a thin dim stretch of corridor. It was mainly TV; a huge flat screen angled over the bed which showed a soundless picture of the hotel at night and a menu that the remote control didn't influence. There was a desk set into the wall with a spray of hotel stationery at one end and at the other, a kettle, a cupful of worn tea sachets and a circle of UHT pods overlapping like the petals of a flower, which pleased me. The bed itself was queen-sized and wrapped tightly in a throw of chocolate-selection purple. I opened the window the inch that it permitted and took a few deep breaths. There was silence, save for the rumble and clatter of someone else's room service.

I love a university town. Dump me in one and I swear I'd know it just from the feel. The cycle of term is so comforting; you are always so definitively placed. I told him all of this, later.

'Which is your favourite?' he asked.

'Hard to say. I'll need to do some research.'

'I suppose there will be the perfect size?' he said.

'Most likely. Let's make a study. Write a book.'

At that, I imagine, we kissed.

I straightened the room; loosened the sheets and put the throw in the bottom of the wardrobe with my case. I hung up my suit, shook out my underwear and laid my nightclothes on the pillow. The shower was tiny, and sputtered, and I turned carefully in the thin hard beams of chalky water for the time it took to wash the soap out of my hair, then changed into a dress I'd never worn before; a tea dress from a catalogue that had seemed too whimsical when it arrived but was perfect for a brief stay in a new place that I'd likely never go back to. It all felt sufficiently strange as I set off bare-legged in the cold sun of a late spring. No destination and unsure if this was a problem or a gift.

It got warmer, out in the streets. I walked up to the castle, rode a tram and tried to see it all as an adventure. The sleeves on the dress were cut high and I was distracted by the sight of my own bare arms. I thought perhaps I'd shop, and ten minutes on, had bought another dress with a tight waist and full skirt, and a tailored blouse, both with some woman other than me in mind. I checked my watch – two more empty hours – and this felt tricky all of a sudden, so I slotted in amongst the workers in the window of a noodle bar. The waiter brought me a bowl of thin scalding broth whose first sip skinned the roof of my mouth.

The email had said to meet in the lobby for introductory drinks. I took the lift alone, smoothing down my front anxiously as I dropped and when the doors opened, saw straight away a good-sized crowd. It took a little time to cross the floor, time enough to realise that I knew no one. The lady who had checked me in stood now behind a long low table of laminated name badges. Next to her, a sheet of paper rested on a music stand, reading: 'Welcome to Edinburgh, Therapists!' above a clip art image of a brain.

'Are you a delegate?' she asked.

'That's me,' I replied, and pointed at my name. His was a couple of rows across. She handed me a cloth bag with a lot of information and a bottle of water inside. By the refreshments – rows of upturned cups on saucers and silver platters of custard creams – I looked through it all, for something to do. In due course, we were taken in.

Adam was on second, and when he walked up to the podium, I thought straight away of the big bad wolf, cartoon-mean, sitting up in Grandma's bed. He looked uncomfortably tall, narrow-faced and muzzled. His smile was wide and toothy and showed appetite. He introduced himself as doctor and a teacher and held a little deck of notes before him that he didn't use. He spoke well; his subject was digital dystopia and I saw that he had found himself a niche. He was lucid and funny and sincere and I felt the room warm in response to him. The woman next to me leaned across and whispered:

'God. He's rather twinkly, isn't he?'

Each laugh of the crowd broke higher, and when he was done, the clapping was fast and there were even the rumblings of a cheer. He laid a palm on his chest in acknowledgement and I felt a little pleasure of my own at his success. Towards the end of the applause, we made some sort of brief contact across the space and he took his seat at the end of a row in front of me, held aside with a card reading RESERVED. I watched him fold his long legs underneath him, and as he turned to hang his coat, he gave me that smile, which was beginning to do its work. My neighbour saw it too, and showed her discomfort with a lengthy excavation of her bag.

The afternoon was long and overheated and artificially lit, and I spent it watching the back of him. He settled himself askew, his spine a shallow bracket, one shoulder dropped. He might have been asleep but for the scribbles he made now and then in his book. It made me feel bad for my own lack of attention but I couldn't fix on what was being said. His jumper was a tactile mossy green; looking at it made me want to sleep. When he lowered his head, a strip of skin was exposed between the collar of his shirt and his hair. The air in the conference room thickened and staled. My contact lenses set solid on my eyes.

He found me later at the makeshift bar. Our corner of the lobby was beginning to feel like home; the same girls who had poured the tea served white, red or lager now, off the stained table-cloth, and an afternoon spent together seemed to have made friends of us all. I stood with a woman, Sue, about my age, who practised out of Loughborough but had plans to teach, and Chloe, newly graduated.

'Now the thing I always ask,' Chloe said, 'is do you prefer the term "patient" or "client"? I really can't decide. I mean, I get the whole point about not medicalising the process, but don't you just find "client" so transactional?'

'Shall I get us another?' I said. 'Here. Give me your glasses.'

Sue handed me hers, sighed deeply and began to answer.

'Hello,' he said and the two of them stopped.

'Nancy.' He kissed me twice, his hair a whisper on my cheek and I realised I'd been waiting for him.

'I think that's the end of the free booze actually,' Chloe said. 'They only give you two, you know. It says so on the bumph.'

'There's always the bar,' I said, then somebody suggested tapas. There was a loaded pause, and people began to say yes.

We were twelve, in the end, out of maybe sixty. Ann took charge. She'd been the last on the programme to speak, and had done it well, if mechanically, on the subject of her book, several copies of which she carried, clamped against her side. She was a tiny woman with a thick curved bob and a pair of men's brogues. She would have looked good in the shirt I'd bought earlier.

'Anyone need to go back to their rooms?' she asked. 'In fact, no. That'll kill it. Let's get out of here. I'll leave these with the concierge.'

She moved her books from under her arm. I had read as far as: *The Real and the Actual in Therapeutic* – on the uppermost, when she flipped them against her chest with a coy smile.

'Back in just a mo,' she said.

I went to the loo and made a little empty chatter with the other women as I took the shine off my face and darkened my eyelids, though I went no further than that. The men waited outside, five to our seven, and as we walked towards them they paused from their chat and looked up at us in some gesture of appreciation or respect. I smirked at the oddness of it.

'I know the way,' Ann said outside and we set off after her. The restaurant was a short stroll in warm weather. The first few roads were narrow and empty between tall old yellow buildings. Strange pockets of sound reached us from groups in adjacent streets having better fun and we quietened at that, pulling apart into a straggly row. Adam walked ahead, listening to Ann. His trousers were too long and had frayed at the bottom. Ann talked about tapas. 'It's so sociable, isn't it?' and the way that, at this place, which was so good, the specials changed twice a day. He knocked his elbow against his side now and then in a funny little tic, and I thought I remembered that from before. I heard someone at the back ask: 'What do you call a group of therapists?' and laughed with the rest, though I hadn't heard the punchline.

Then we arrived and straight away I loved the place, which was dark and low and uninhibited. The table was a squash, with one long bench running along the wall side and a row of wooden school chairs on the other. People filled the seats first and when it came to me, I took the bench. I edged down to the mid-point, the wall cool and uneven at my back and stopped across from him, one spot down. Luke, a shy man with rimless glasses and a restless manner, probably twenty-five, took the place to my left. 'Hi again,' he said, out of the corner of his mouth and moved his napkin to his lap. Chloe, on my right, said: 'Blimey. Isn't it dark in here? We won't be able to see what we're eating.' She lit the torch on her phone and bounced its tiny beam between our faces, like a country copper or a kid telling ghost stories.

'Look,' she said, at the space next to my head. 'People have written on the wall.'

I turned. Under my hand, the plaster leaked moist cold, though when I felt my palm, it was dry.

'Secrets!' she said. 'How about this? *It was me who told my best friend's husband*, she read, and looked back at the rest of us with a salacious delight.

Behind me, I heard Adam speak. 'The therapist's stock-in-trade,' he said.

'What?' someone asked.

'Secrets,' he replied. 'That's what my wife says.'

'Anything else?' said Luke.

Chloe knelt on the bench and moved the little cone of light along.

'It's in Spanish, this one. Anyone speak Spanish?' she asked.

'I do, a bit,' said Ann but when Chloe read it out, she couldn't help.

Then: '*My boss is stealing and he knows I know.*'

'Interesting,' said Luke.

'No. Bollocks,' said Ann. 'Wish fulfilment, or else the staff just make it up. Let's get some food.'

I wanted to say that it didn't matter; that the messages signalled transgression and charged the room, but I let it go.

They brought us sherry first; a couple of inches in tulip-shaped glasses that smelt of tar and raisins, and bowls of under-ripe green olives whose meat was tender and bland. There was a short chaotic discussion over choices until it was agreed that Ann should order for us all. She shouted up her selection to the waiter and I listened to the fast Spanish guitar and thought about the way it drove the pace of the place and reached in and sped my pulse.

'So you two already know each other then, do you?' Chloe asked in a lull, looking between Adam and me. 'How come?'

'We studied together,' I told her.

'Oh?' she said.

'I retrained. I was a mature student,' he replied, good-natured. 'Both Londoners up north.'

'And you hung out? We have a load of mature students too, but we don't exactly . . . get that involved with each other.'

'Ah, Manchego,' called Luke, as the first of the food arrived. Thin, pale slices of cheese, arranged in a wheel. I took one, stippled with holes.

'No, actually it's Mahon,' said Ann. 'It's presented differently, do you see? Nancy, you don't have to take the rind off. You eat it all, you know.'

The cheese was salty and dry, almost granular. Oil lay in a ribbon across its surface, then tarragon torn in rough handfuls and peppercorn chippings that were fruity, close to citrus, and stung my mouth, sending me back to my wine. I had chosen the bottle, a candied Albariño that narrowed into tartness at the end.

'No. We didn't mix much, either,' he said. 'Did we, Nancy?'

I remembered three older students, all men, who came and left according to the timetable and worked much harder than the rest of us. There had been a party at the close of the year in one of their homes. A hot day, a trampoline at the back. Turning sausages with a beer. A wife – two wives – and somebody's kids. A day of a certain kitsch appeal.

'Not really, no.'

He watched me remembering, but didn't help out.

I had gone with Nat. The whole class was invited and we ummed and ahhed and it was food, in the end, that swung it; we were living on chocolate fingers and Fray

Bentos pies by then and had begun to fantasise about what we might eat if we went. We took the bus with a bottle of better than usual wine and when it passed into the suburbs, we started to laugh and couldn't stop until we got to the front door and a woman opened it and we were suddenly, inexplicably, our best polite selves.

More dishes arrived. My favourite: little stubs of burnt chorizo in an inch of oily wine. Caper berries and padron peppers, blackened and collapsed. Some kind of deep tomatoey stew; I thought I saw a tentacle break the surface. Luke was greedy and slopped as he spooned.

'Do you remember in the summer?' I asked. 'That barbecue. Who was the guy?'

'Philip,' he said, way ahead of me.

'That's right. Do you see him still?' I asked.

'No.' A puff of amusement.

We had come ready to laugh; at the women's hair and jeans and their submission to small domestic lives. To show them what they missed and prove what we were not and still thought we never would be, but the wives were kind and interested and amused. They had jobs and attentive men. The food was as good, better, than we were used to. The salad was home-grown. For a while, we tried to please.

~

'Didn't we . . . ?' I asked him. 'Wasn't there a big game of hide-and-seek?'

That was later. We had started to show off. There were three cute kids and we competed to be named their favourite. Someone had insisted (was it me?) on making the cocktail we'd been drinking all that year and Nat and I ran to the off-licence for cider and the necessary alco-pop, rolling papers and more Silk Cut. It was a scorching day and my feet were slippery on the plastic of my flip-flops. I misjudged the kerb and stubbed a toe, yanking the thong right out of the sole. I hopped all the way back to the house, arms round Nat, pissing ourselves, my toenail jagged and my foot black with dust and blood. One of the adults found a plaster and suggested I clean up in a down-stairs loo. It was a tiny room and I couldn't get my foot up into the sink which made me laugh all the more.

'Are you all right in there?' somebody called from outside.

'Yeah yeah yeah,' I replied.

We made a messy jug of booze. When I got up to mix some more, one of the women pushed my glass in from the table's edge. Then we started the game and I ran for the end of the garden, zigzagging brainlessly trying to find a place to hide. I crouched in the damp dark circle beneath the trampoline, delighted with myself, my head low, legs pulled in, heart banging against my knees. The dead grass smelt bad and I tried to hold my breath though it made me dizzy, but nobody found me and I had to come out in the end when I heard them all on the terrace, calling for more drink.

'It started off hide-and-seek, then it was sardines, wasn't it?' Adam said. 'I'd never heard of that before.'

'Try these. They're good.' Luke edged the prawns towards me with his napkin. The flesh of my wrist seared briefly on the bowl.

'So it was,' I replied. 'I'd forgotten about that.'

It had begun to rain, and we dived for indoors. I remembered looking down stupidly at the trail of sloppy footprints I left on the tiles of her floor.

'Do you need a towel?' she asked kindly, so I dirtied that as well.

I told them how sardines worked and we scattered. We ransacked the house. We whooped and hollered. We made the children crazy. I went into her bedroom; I didn't see the affront in it. The curtains were thin and cheap and the smell, when I moved them, was of deepest sleep – warm bodies and old breath. When I heard the door, I peeped around the flimsy drop of fabric, and there was Adam.

'Quick,' I said. 'Come here. There's room.'

He looked at me strangely.

'Hurry up. Before somebody else arrives.'

I'd barely noticed him all day, but in the cool dark of the bedroom, I found I liked his looseness, the easy way he carried his height, the droop of his hair, the uneven roll of his sleeves. His face already showed experience. Mostly, though, I was aware of myself. The ten years between us, the distance into adulthood he had travelled, time he must – surely – want back. I had my cut-offs on, a month-old tan, it all still ahead of me. The booze rioted in my head. I took a step towards him. There was a sludge of compost on my thigh.

'Come in,' I said. 'With me.'

He held up both palms and took a big step back.

'I'm looking for my jacket, OK?'

He pointed. I saw a pile on the bed; my own, in smoke-wrecked denim, amongst them.

'It's over there.'

He leaned across for his coat, carefully, one eye on me, still, as though I might bite.

'Fine,' I said, 'do what you like.'

Back behind the curtain, I heard the door catch as he left and my throat was suddenly tight. By the time I went downstairs, he was gone.

'Nancy,' Ann called down the table, 'aren't you eating? You've got all the best bits up there, you know. Can you pass some of it along, please?'

He laughed at me from across the table, and I thought again of a wolf.

'How did you get home anyway? I've always wondered. What with that knackered flip-flop.'

'I've no idea,' I said. 'Christ.'

14

'Here,' he said. 'You'd better grab some of that food before she takes it all away.'

I let him fill my glass. I felt hollow with the shame of it.

'There's the last of the prawns,' Ann called out. 'Going, going, gone.'

But I couldn't eat. Instead I wished for home. My mortgaged terrace in its neat South London street, full of my things, gained steadily across two decades' worth of effort and sound sense. The known and the hard-earned. The warm rise of my children's chests beneath my palm, and my husband, Stef.

Two years, then, since Adam and I began.

2

There is a moment, sometimes, at my own front door, or just before, at the rough touch of the gate, when my children flood me. Part need, part panic – there's guilt in there, too – and I simply want to get in, feel their heat beneath my hand, wipe the smudges of the day from their faces and reassure myself that there is no problem in their competing lives that I can't make better.

Mid-week, then, late home from work, two litres of corner-shop milk moistening my leg through its plastic as I chased my key round and round my bag, and it was beginning to feel like the universe was against me. In, at last, and— Nothing.

I waited in the hall. I called a name. Just a heart-freezing silence. But they were not dead, of course, just plugged into their relevant screens. A couple of seconds and the littler ones were at me, mid-dispute over some slight they'd held in waiting until I got home. I subdued Jakey with a hug. 'Get off me, Mum, you weirdo,' he said, though it's all pretend. The middle child, twelve now, he receives my love more easily than the rest. He's a forgiver and a forgetter. There are no terms with Jake. Louisa peeled away.

'Where's Frieda?' I said. Fourteen; a sensible girl, but still fourteen.

'Where d'you think?' Jake replied.

'Free?' I called up the stairs. 'You all right?'

'Yeah, Mum,' she said and her voice was light and non-committal and the purest relief.

There are names for it all, in my profession. I catastrophise and suffer a generalised anxiety, albeit low-level. Maybe sixty per cent of my clients do, and a similar cut of the country, I'd estimate, though they may not name it as such, merely view it as a condition of living, as we all did, before the business of happiness began. The rest are angry; used to be men, but I find women are making gains. Something of the narcissist in there, too – that bit about the universe – but only a touch. Nothing I can't out-rationalise. I'd ask a client to note the trigger. Are there any physical sensations? The key is to breathe. Then breathe again. Are you dealing with fact or opinion? Is there another way of viewing the scene? Map an alternative thought. Have a read of the handout. And this was not new, any of it; I have always been this way.

Our house smelt of Stefan's lunch, Jake's trainers, Comfort, but mainly itself. They laugh at me for my nose but the smell is there, as it was when we first looked round. There was a time after we did the extension and the side return when it seemed to have cleared and the place felt new, though not necessarily ours, but the smell returned stealthily, an essence that wouldn't be extinguished. It is not unpleasant: a sourish mud and something more human; the past of the house floating round in molecular form.

Stef, whose religion is good taste, has a vision for our home, our family life, and is pained by the house's refusal to conform. Now there is a chip knocked out of the countertop where I dropped a pan and the surface is blighted by spilled coffee and wine and though we knew it would mark, agreed that we could live with the blemishes, he sighs each time he spots them. The back – all glass – is a nightmare to keep clean and the view, which we didn't consider before we started ripping out bricks, is forlorn; just two blunt tiers of hard-worked grass and at the end, Stef's shed. When I look out, I find my eye drawn to a window, halfway up the block of flats on the left side of our stretch, and the huge telly beyond that fills a wall and is always on. I can read the Sky Sports news feed along the bottom from where I stand, though I've never seen the person who watches it.

I went out and found Stefan in his office, designing something for a chain of dim sum bars on a large white screen.

'I thought you were finished,' I said.

'Hey,' he replied. He pushed his headphones off. 'How was your day?'

'Have the kids had tea?'

'As you're early I said we could all eat together tonight.'

He leaned his head into his knuckle and scraped back and forth; a little ritual that brought him out of his work. His hair is short and pelt-like, the skull showing faintly white beneath.

'I'm done,' he said. 'Let's go back through.'

He reached for me as I moved off, caught my shoulder and rubbed at the kink he knew just where to find.

There was a time, after Adam and I began, when my husband's touch felt wrong, an infidelity, in fact, but things resettle. You cannot sustain a state of constant internal conflict and survive.

'We need to do diaries,' said Stef. 'I'm getting busy again.'

'Ouch,' I said, as he pressed the nub of muscle harder.

Adam and I were to go to Cambridge next month. I had booked it on my usual travel site, an aspirational collection of boutique joints. The room I chose had clotted-cream walls, real furniture and rugs as threadbare as you might find at home. The inevitable roll-top bath. Once, I'd thought a decent room might soften it, pull the act into the orbit of my life, as if morality or risk could be moderated by a backdrop of acceptable soft-furnishings, as though it would have been the Travelodge that degraded us, had I chosen to sleep with him there. This too, has passed; it is simply nicer to wake up in a decent room.

Frieda leaned out of the bathroom window. 'Hey, you guys,' she called, her long ironed hair almost reachable.

'You want to come down now, honey?' Stefan said, and when we got into the kitchen she was there. 'I look like Daddy,' she used to cry, when she was younger, 'but I'm a girl.' Now she tried to paint it out with stick-on lashes and thick lines round her eyes and lips. All her friends look the same. I long for an indie chick, a girl who doesn't care, her guitar slung over her back – but that is another one of my secrets. I wonder, too, sometimes, if it would have been different had we sent her private. Would we have made that decision, swallowed up our principles, had we had the chance? But this is a thinking error – assuming life would be better if only it were different. I would have a client observe this feeling and rate it for intensity. And they're just as bad, those other girls. A bunch of them get on my bus. Just a different brand of sameness. Frieda is fine. We let her be.

'Hi, Daddy,' she said. She touched his arm lightly and circled away on her toes to see if he would follow her with his look. She practised her appeal on him, her happy face, her sad face and he submitted to it graciously with a lack of awkwardness I couldn't imagine in any other man. She came to me next. Her smell was vanilla, cherry and ink. I took one last long breath of her.

'Hey,' called Jake, suddenly, from the sitting room, 'Hi!'

I heard him scrabble to his feet, the clatter of a discarded remote. We three listened. The front door went. 'Uncle David!' cried Jake.

Frieda's face changed at the edges at my brother's name. I saw a hint of play. The reach of David's charm is wide. She turned from me, tucked into whatever scene she was now rehearsing, a finger tweaked in a caricature of poise or some early version of seduction. Too old now to run to him, she waited. Stefan looked at me.

'Seriously?' he said.

'I had no idea,' I replied, truthfully this time.

'I'll go get some wine,' he said.

I heard David speak, with some authority, about whatever Jake was playing on his screen. Then: 'Hello hello, anybody home?' and there he was, in the doorway, in old jeans, a shirt that hung off his shoulders, lace-up boots in the style he'd worn since college. A skinny lad, still. A boy of dips and hollows.

'Thought I'd pop in as I was passing,' he said. He is beautiful, always has been, if you can say this of your brother. We are nothing alike.

He hugged me, smelling warm and waxy and of my childhood. My first love, David, and the most enduring.

'How are you, Free?' he said, 'Come here!' and she did. 'Hello, lovely.' He rubbed her cheek with his knuckle and I watched her colour rise. 'What's new?'

'Drink?' I asked him and poured myself the last of the wine from a bottle pushed deep into the back of the fridge. It was astringent and so cold I thought I felt the density of frost. 'Stef's gone down for some red,' I said.

'I'll have a beer, if you've got one,' David replied, and knelt down to the cooler, glass-fronted, back-lit, and helped himself.

'How come you're passing?' I asked.

'Job round the corner. Did I not say? Have you got a fag?'

I found a pack in a drawer amongst birthday candles, playing cards and shoelaces. He stood at the back to smoke, the door open just enough. 'It's pissing down,' he said. The dog looped in and out, bringing the rain back inside with him in slashes, and when he stopped long enough, silty puddles collected around his paws.

'What's the job?' I asked. David drank from the bottle in long smooth swallows.

'Cabinets,' he said. 'Big house around the corner. Very nice.'

I spooned some olives into a bowl. The dog settled happily on my bag.

I have a sheet, somewhere, of David's sketches. Perfect 3D drawings, good enough to frame. He had described the different timbers that he used, their textures and grain. The problems of warp, twist and swell. The pros and cons of the dovetail joint versus the mortise and tenon. I remember the relief we all felt when he finally found his thing. He loved it, he told me; there is a special gratification in working with your hands. Not that I'd understand, he went on, living, as I do, in my head. I had agreed and felt a small dissatisfaction and wondered if this would be the year I finally started growing veg.

Stef returned and put a bottle on the counter.

'Hey, David,' he said and then, 'do you mind?' He raised the face of his mobile to us and pointed out into the wet. 'I've got to finish something.' He pressed a key on his phone and the light came on in his office at the garden's end.

'Wow,' said David. 'Cool.' Then: 'I'm not staying long.'

Lou next, skipping in in her outsized uniform. 'Mum, I'm starving. Hi, Uncle David. It's your birthday next week,' she said. Then: 'I saw it on the calendar.' She turned away to hide her flush.

'It is indeed. Forty years old,' he pulled her towards

him, onto his lap. 'What do you make of that?' He tickled her. 'Nearly as old as your Mum.'

'Nothing. I don't— I was just saying,' she cried in panic and scrambled away.

'Will you want to stay for dinner, David?' I asked. 'It's not a problem. I can always ring out.'

'Don't think so,' he said, looking down at his phone. 'In fact I need to be going. I only popped in to say hi. And I wanted to check what's left of mine in your cellar.'

'I thought it was all at Skyler's now,' I said.

'Not everything.'

He took a child down there with him and the dog, who loves the smells, and came back with a bag of old stuff.

'Taking more,' I said. 'Must be getting serious.'

'I'm off,' he replied. 'Thanks for the beer.'

'And we'll see you soon, will we?' I asked. 'Get together for your birthday? The three of us, perhaps?'

I was almost thirteen and David eleven when our sister was born. We would never truly be three.

David lowered his eyebrows. 'Call Madeline if you like,' he said. 'No fuss, though, please.'

He left with Frieda, who he was walking to a friend's to rehearse something for school.

'Bye, guys. Be safe,' I called after them. David raised his hand but didn't turn.

Louisa raced back through to me, squealing. 'Do you think he guessed? Oh, Mum, I didn't mean to make it weird.'

'Don't worry, Lou. He won't have noticed a thing,' I said.

'What about a cake?' she cried. 'Who's getting a cake?'

'Granny's doing it. Now go and get Dad. I need to order food.'

When she brought Stef through, she was still talking about the party.

'But would you like a surprise, Daddy, for your next birthday?' she asked.

'I'm not sure, but I'd be grateful, though; I know that much,' he said.

'Will we get to jump out?' she asked.

'You'd better ask your mum,' he replied. Stef turned to me. 'You've done a good job with this, Nance, you know.'

'We'll see. My parents in the same room. Skyler's friends, whoever they may be. It could be a nightmare.'

'Oh, Nancy,' Madeline had said, when I suggested the party a month back. We'd gone to hers for a change and she knelt behind Louisa, doing something off YouTube to her hair. 'Do you really think?' 'Yes I really do,' I said. 'If we don't do something, no one will.' However old we get, the age-gap between my sister and me never seems to shrink.

'Is this the final list?' asked Stef, walking around the island. The concrete had been his idea but when it was in, I found I loved it; the way it flowed in one long unbroken sweep. The drop into my sink is round and smooth as velvet.

'Yep,' I said. 'The ones in red are coming. The blue said no.'

'Who's this?' he asked.

'Alice? Just an old girlfriend,' I replied.

'Not just,' said Louisa, in a lascivious tone, 'Uncle David's first love.'

'What are you talking about?' I said.

'I heard Aunty Mads say,' and Lou had stayed of course, as Madeline and I talked. Flitting about. Pretending to read.

'Is that a good idea?' asked Stef.

'Mads doesn't know what she's taking about, she was barely at school at the time,' I said, but she was right. There had been a poetry to David and Alice, which started with their difference but became about their assimilation. He had borrowed some of her brightness when they were together, though she'd needed his edge just as much. They split when she left for university and she married young, a man I met once; handsome, bored and rich, who she had since divorced. I was curious to see what she had become.

'As long as it won't cause a problem with Skyler,' Stefan said.

'It shouldn't,' I replied. 'David keeps telling me she's a grown-up; I guess we'll find out.' I thought of her spiteful little face. 'I'm just trying to mix it up a bit. That's how good parties work. As long as everyone gets pissed at the start, we'll be fine.'

Stef gave a pinched look to indicate the ongoing presence of Louisa.

'Shall we do a cocktail, do you think?' I asked.

'Perhaps,' he replied, pulling out a bottle of something new. 'Top-up?'

'If you're opening it,' I said and we went through to the kids.

Jake lay on the sofa, fighting a friend on his screen.

'Just you two, right?' I said. He snorted at me without lifting his eyes. 'Shove up,' I told him, and sank into my slot.

Stef took our order for the takeaway, a tea towel over his shoulder to make us laugh. Lou's legs were heavy across my lap. The dog sat on my feet.

'How about a movie?' he said after he'd phoned it through, and we agreed on one we'd seen ten times before. He called for Frieda, who'd just got back. The wine began to do its work.

It is hard to see where Stefan has aged, he has the type of looks that hold: blunt bone-structure, thick cheek-bones, his nose just slightly flat. Light blue eyes and short hair since forever, cropped close to his well-shaped skull.

The movie began, so familiar that it bored me instantly.

Plus he has taste, which I can recognise, despite having little of my own, in his brushed plaid shirt and his stiff dark jeans and authentic work-boots imported from the USA.

'One minute,' I said. 'There's something I just need to check.'

'Shall we pause?' Jake asked.

'No, go ahead,' I said. 'I can easily catch up.'

I poured myself a drop more wine and went to the alcove that David had built, a knocked-out bookcase in what used to be the dining room; an awkward little adjunct that unbalanced the space. I felt a hope in my throat as I waited for my screen to wake, but we rarely email, and never text and there was nothing. It ruined me, briefly, nonetheless. Stef is a good man and a textbook father. A faithful partner. All of these things and more, but he is not Adam, at whose nearness all logic collapses.

They brought me through some takeaway, cool and separating on the plate and later, came in, one by one, for a tentative goodnight.

'Are you OK, Mummy?' Louisa said. I pulled her close. Always so dry, Lou, the skin tight and scaled under her nose, beside her mouth. Bleached to bone, she looked; pale eyes, white hair.

'I'm fine, sweet. Off you go.'

My mood had reached them, infused the house, but I refuse to lay that at Adam's door. I remember this – this restlessness, this inability to settle – from before. I am a working woman, my time with the kids is parcelled and discrete, and loaded because of it. It is impossible to wring satisfaction out of every occasion, on demand, and acknowledging this, making peace with it, saves a lot of unnecessary grief.

When Adam and I first began, my children's pleasure hurt me. It seemed too fragile, too tentative; I had the idea that it existed in reverse proportion to my own and in the darkest times, I thought we couldn't all survive. And then I came to see that our love – Adam's and mine – is beneficent. It shines its light on everything. It makes all of this easier. And yet, when, sometime after midnight, Free reappeared, owl-eyed at the edge of the room, I felt grateful for another chance.

'Sweetheart. Are you having a dream? I'm here.'

She came to me and leant her weight into my shoulder. Her closeness, and the wine I'd drunk, set off my heart. Her hair was rubbed to candy floss at the back and the trousers of her pyjamas pooled around her feet.

'Are you ill?' I said, reaching for her forehead and then mine.

'Maybe,' she said. 'I just woke up.'

'Take this off. Cool down.'

She let me slide off the thin dressing gown and I felt the skin on her arms pimple, and her exposure in her T-shirt. She sat on my lap then, and hunched her shoulders, her back a comma. I pulled her close and the heat left her body quickly, passing into mine.

'Do you want anything, darling?' I asked, into her neck. She had missed a smudge of foundation, which smelled of wet paint and powdered milk beneath the alcohol and cucumber of her wash. I rubbed it from her jaw. Her top gave off a delicious base-note of old sweat that had out-lived a hundred washes to be baked deep into the cotton by the dryer.

'A cup of tea?' she said, with hope.

'Not this time of night. How about warm milk?'

Then Stef was there.

'What's up?' he said.

'Daddy,' she called, and her bony bottom dug into my thigh as she pushed herself up. I watched their mirrored profiles, leant in close, and felt a strange intersection of jealousy and relief. I switched off the broadband, I let out the dog. Kicked the shoes into a heap near the front door and lifted the pile of clean clothes that needed taking up. I trawled the rooms for more discarded things and bent for the hem of Frieda's robe which had slipped off the back of my chair. As I lifted it, her phone slid out of a pocket and hit the floor with a rubberised clunk.

The knock woke it up, and I saw she had a text, 11.47 p.m. – too late, I thought, for a girl of fourteen. The drink turned a sour roll in my stomach and I felt a mother's vulnerability, my absolute dependence on my child. To make the right decisions, to be happy, to survive.

Stef stood in the doorway to the garden and whistled for the dog. It was Beatrice, her best friend.

Sounds intense. Can't W8 2 hEr mo xxx

Some girlish intrigue, no doubt, though I didn't like the tone, the ambiguity, the suggestion of risk. I heard the dog skid over the kitchen tiles in avoidance of his basket and felt sheer terror, a kind of slideshow in my mind, a Greatest Hits of chaos and disaster, but that moment always passes.

3

Two years, then, since I found Adam; since that first weighted meeting. But was it the start? To name it as such feels too fated, too certain. There was a time when it could have gone either way. I fell in love slowly, from a distance. In my imagination first. Old-fashioned, really; for a while it was all just dreams and deferral.

I caught the first flight back the morning after the conference, battered by a couple of hours' parched and restless sleep. There were a few people on the plane from the previous night, but we ignored each other comfortably. I ate everything that was offered, however it smelled, and tried to hide inside my book.

The evening had been long. More food was ordered, and wine. Adam told a couple of warm stories from back in the day and I recovered; alcohol will do that. His wife was an actor, I heard him say, and I imagined stage make-up and jazz hands. The management sent across a tray of drinks and a second, and from then, the night was broken by others' drunken mis-steps: the upended bottle, the inappropriate joke, Chloe's extended trip to the loo, where I'm pretty sure she threw up, all of which we shared, he and I, across the table, in an effortless telepathy. His hotel room was in a different wing to mine, so we avoided that tell-tale moment of goodnight.

On the plane, I thought of his face. There is something roguish in the set of it, long and bony, but the rest of him pokes fun at that. His hair is a collapse. He has a lolloping gait and is far too thin; he wears his trousers belted out of necessity. Colour and texture, angle and feel. The details began to assume a sort of meaning, as if he were complete and intended, like a painting or a book; beautiful and important.

A week later, there was contact; a group email from the conference's organiser asking for feedback. My address was the only one visible but I saw him at his desk, rating the experience 1 to 5. I answered the questions imagining myself him. On the final page I read, would we care to share our details with the group? I replied yes. Another week, and a message headed: *Intros!!* arrived.

Dear ex-delegates,
  See the inbox for your fellow attendees' addresses! Feel free to get in touch! Attached is a list of names and specialities also. I'll duck out now.
  Enjoy. See you next year!

His name was first and I wondered if he was quickest to respond and what that might mean. Emails came in across the day, vague and enthusiastic but Adam remained quiet; I watched for him from the fringes of the exchange, turning him over in my mind, and maybe that was harmless, a middle-aged woman's distraction, or else it breathed life into something frail and barely viable, one of trillions of maybes that would fall away if they failed to take root, and my attention was soil.

I found his wife online easily enough. His Facebook feed had looked unpromising, just birthday wishes and the odd professional approach but at the bottom of his timeline was one tagged photo, taken from behind, of him and a woman hand in hand at the top of an ancient sloped street in some bleached-out holiday town. The shot didn't tell me much, save placing them loosely in the urban middle classes with her rough straw hat and the corked backs of a pair of Birkenstocks. Adam's shoulders were holstered with the straps of a long-lens camera and a beat-up leather satchel. I watched the image for a while and came to see that his head was just inclined towards her, though she looked straight ahead. The post read: *Lazy Summer Days* and was dated the previous year. When I held my cursor above her, a name appeared: Tara Cole. Her account was private, though I found her elsewhere in no time. I pulled up a CV and a ludicrous head-shot and no evidence of work in the last ten years.

Summer came, and regular contact from the group. A pattern emerged. Ann sent details of her speaking engagements. That guy I'd sat next to at the meal kept trying to sell things; a week in a Dorset cottage, an unused exercise bike, his old car in the end. A woman I didn't remember pasted articles from *The Guardian* once a week and Chloe began each Monday morning with a joke related to the various therapeutic services.

Jake tore a ligament falling down a muddy bank and was on crutches for a month. I took my Aunty April for her first pedicure, which she hated and let me know by talking loudly and self-consciously for the full hour as we sat side by side, feet tepid in gently pulsing water, and Adam receded under the weight of all this dailyness, though I pulled out the thought of him, now and again, sitting amongst the family in a rare moment of stupefied rest, or more often when I was alone. He became my treat. I wrote a paper which was to be published in a journal and sent it, flinchingly, to the group. Their replies were kind and considered and I acknowledged my affection for our scrappy band.

Then one night Stef told me that he was ready to set up on his own; branding and design, still, but with an online twist. He had two clients ready to go, and how would I feel about giving him the shed and working from an office again? Delighted, I said and next evening, I emailed the group, subject: '*on the off-chance*,' asking if anybody cared to share as I was looking for space. Adam answered by reply, subject: 'Very weird' and wrote:

I do. I've just decided to get back into practice. Should we meet? Happy to help look for places, if you'll have me. Just let me know. Hope you're well etc.
Adam.

We met, the following week, on the last hot day of the year which smelt of traffic fumes and bitumen. He was late, and I leant into the warm brick of the building and waited, bouncing the estate agent's keys on their coiled plastic chain. I'd left my sunglasses at home and closed my eyes to slits, watching a thin white line of day between them. I wondered, loosely, what I was doing here, but six months had passed since I'd seen him and the whole thing seemed benign. I couldn't touch the danger of it. I almost dozed, and he surprised me when he pulled up in his cab, ten minutes on, full of apology. His fluster, the contortion of his limbs as he got out of the car, his fumble for change, all made me laugh. I guess the dregs of it were still there on my face, for when he turned to me, it was his smile in reply that was the hook. It was the most complete smile I'd ever seen, and I wondered how one man gained access, had the right, to so much pleasure. It pinned me to the wall, that smile.

'Good spot,' he said, in the end, and I felt myself come down. 'Café next door. I think I passed a pub back there.'

'Bit of a boozer,' I said.

'Best sort.'

'So it used to be a flat,' I said, when we got inside. 'The others are still residential.'

'Good for security though.'

The entrance hall was hushed and domestic; empty, save for a frill-edged table with a glass top and tapered legs pushed against the wall. Someone had arranged the post into four neat piles.

'Odd, do you think, for clients?' I asked.

'I don't know. Let's go up and see.'

I started up the stairs, but when I lifted my foot, the toe of my shoe had left a dark arrow point of dust on the carpet.

'Hold on,' I said and bent awkwardly to the mark,

forcing him back down the hall. From my vantage point, under one arm, I saw that he wore loose cotton trousers and the same belt as last time and I gave a sort of snigger; it was the nerves. We climbed, and the staircase moaned somewhere underneath us.

'Don't you feel like we should be whispering?' he said and his voice felt illicit at my neck.

'They're probably all at work,' I replied, but as we passed along the second floor, I heard a television start, the call of a furious studio audience.

It got hotter as we climbed and I wondered if he was watching the back of me.

'OK, so this is us,' I said.

The locks were new and the keys slid in flush. The owner must have knocked down walls, for the room we stepped into was large and had no equivalent in a home. It had been repainted in a blistering white, the smell of it still sharp. The front door shut behind us heavily, launching old dust into the air and I watched it rise, substantial as ash, reach its highest point and then start to fall back down slowly through blocks of silver daylight. As he walked into the room beyond, I saw a light layer come to rest in the weft of his clothes and on the contours of his hair. I had the idea of brushing him clean, the feel of his jacket and the bones of his shoulder.

'Let's open some windows,' he said. They had been painted shut and gave with a brief clean scream.

'That's better,' he said. I felt a breeze and heard traffic noise below and regretted the break in the seal of the place. 'What do you think?'

'I'm not sure,' I replied. 'It still feels like a house.'

'I know what you mean but this room would be a great office. You could put your desk here, facing that way. And the client there. There's plenty of space.'

He padded round in circles, the way the dog does before he comes to lie. His hands, by his sides, were long and curved as though he held a ball in each.

'Shall we look around the rest?' he said.

I passed through two more rooms which also failed to stick.

'Oh and there's a shower,' he called, out of sight.

I waited for him at the mouth of a brand-new galley kitchen.

'That's pretty handy. What's the matter?' he said. 'Don't you like it?'

He came towards me and I imagined us newlyweds, choosing our first place together. Discussing where to put baby. The best spot for our bed.

'I don't know,' I said. 'Do you?'

The skin under his eyes was shaded rain-cloud grey.

'I do,' he replied. 'I think it's perfect, Nancy.'

Downstairs, someone scraped a chair leg sharply.

'Maybe the walls aren't thick enough,' I said desperately. 'For clients. You know how distracting it is if you can hear next door.'

'Let's find out,' he replied. He went into the far room and pulled the door shut; a floorboard beneath it hopped. I waited, but nothing happened. I moved a little closer.

'Adam?' I said, with a warble in my voice, but he didn't reply.

'Adam. Do you want me to call out? Should I be the one calling?' I said but it came out feeble.

In the room beyond, I could hear him speak, his tone low and even. The sound was like an incantation or the repeated note of some bass instrument.

'Speak up,' I said, 'speak louder.' I laid my hands against the door. The finish was horrible, slippery and synthetic. His voice rumbled on and there was a rhythm in it, like poetry, or a story read to a child. I heard a lift, the *ee* sound, the last syllable of my name and pressed my ear to the clean poreless paint. Then the door went and I took one long lunging step inside. My palms met his chest, and I grabbed two fistfuls of his rough wool lapels to stop myself falling. My thumbs pressed into his shirt and I felt the slight give of his skin beneath it and the fragile slant of ribs. I loosened my grip and there was the faint crackle of hair. He was real now – this man – the flesh of him under my hands. I straightened and found the shallow dip at his neck. His Adam's apple bounced and his laugh, when it came, was huge and throaty. When he lowered his head, his teeth, at the back, were filled with wrinkled cushions of silver. His nose turned off to the left. I saw the shading of new whiskers at his chin and felt that I was watching the last seconds of his fine pale skin's resistance before the new beard pushed through.

'What on earth were you doing?' he said.

His eyes are hazel, like my son's, but yellower, in a shade of old bruise.

'What you told me to. Trying to hear.'

37

'And did you?' he asked.

'No. Well, just faintly.'

'But not what I said?'

'No.'

'Then we're good.'

He frisked himself for his phone.

'Do we know each other well enough?' I asked and blushed at the connotation.

He laughed again, fully, and I wanted to say: where do you hide your disappointment, your insecurity, your fear?

'I sat behind you for a year. Does that count?' he said. 'One row back, a seat to the left. You came in with that girl you used to hang out with, who always wore dungarees. You were late. Every week. And you smoked what I am pretty sure were Silk Cut and used to have one just before class because I'd given up and the smell of it nearly killed me. I leant forward, once, and sniffed your hair, but you must have felt it because you lifted your hand and nearly hit me in the face.' His eyes moved upwards. 'It was redder back then, I think?'

I remembered a Friday morning class. Dazed, most weeks; thick-headed from the night before.

'And a little bit longer,' he said. His gaze, like muddy pond, passed over me.

'Cerys,' I said. We had fallen out, late, drunk, over a boy she claimed she'd earmarked, in an awful tinted club with a revolving dance-floor, every surface sticky with booze and the bass a constant in your chest. She had pushed me, lightly, to emphasise her point, and my elbow knocked over an abandoned pint, which escalated things. I might have taken a step towards her but the boy moved between us, his palm at her shoulder. My win, and the closest I've been to a fight.

'They were the purples,' I said. 'Lower tar. I don't suppose you can get them any more.'

'Anyway, I'm in. It's perfect,' Adam said. 'But it's your choice, of course. Are you walking to the tube?'

4

My first appointment arrived early, waiting there as I shouldered my way in. Late February bitter with sharp sideways rain and my glasses all steamed up.

'Morning, Nancy,' said Lynn, our receptionist, a nice woman in her fifties, studying for an online degree in between answering our phone. She moved her eyes across significantly. Marie sat behind the door in her usual place; each client has one. Her arms were crossed but she released a hand to wave with her fingertips.

'Oh hi, Marie. Sorry. I didn't see you there. Won't be a moment,' I said.

'Can I help you with any of that?' Lynn asked.

'Yes, please.'

I straightened my arm which sent my handbag sliding. It landed in the crook of my elbow and bounced the coffee cup in my hand.

'Ouch,' said Lynn and passed me a handful of napkins.

'I just need to get myself sorted, Marie. Be five minutes, OK?'

The air in my office was dense and sour, the milk in last Friday's tea a top note. I shoved up the sash but outside was worse; wet rubbish and mildew. She could wait another moment or two. I sat in the client's chair to focus; a habit of mine.

I had tried hypnotherapy once, as a favour to a friend who was training and he had me lie on a water bed, my eyes masked, his voice, through earphones, very close. He asked me to imagine a safe place; a place where I felt secure and then to anchor it in my mind so I could return to it any time. I thought of a desert island, beach and waves, but it was just a holiday. My bed, as a child, and the moment when you lose your grip on the edges of the day, but that can feel like a tumble. The fork of a tree where David and I used to hide. I held up my hand for more time and heard my friend laugh and that brought him to mind; sitting apart, observing from his seat, looking for the meeting point of theory and my own peculiarities. I envied him in that moment. This is my safe space, other people's problems. The expanse that is my work.

The morning's client was in her twenties. Recently married. High-functioning. A sudden onset of anxiety centred around travel. No longer able to fly, though a recent promotion demanded it. I buzzed Lynn to send her through and stepped round from behind my desk. I like to shake hands.

'Hi, Marie,' I said.

She moved straight to her seat which was broad and upholstered with arms wide enough to rest a mug on, and sat, tugging her bag in close beside her. I took my place in its pair, as much space between us as the dimensions of the room would allow. She pulled out her book, black, hard-backed and identical to mine, though they are common enough. She likes to rest it on her lap and tilts it upwards when she writes, pressing the edge into the flesh of her stomach. 'I can push a table closer, if you like,' I'd offered, first time, but she told me she was fine. She wrote at oblique moments. I couldn't guess what, which I imagine was her intention.

'So how have things been?' I asked.

She was small in her seat, neatly set.

'OK, thanks. Fine,' she said, in an everyday voice.

'Great,' I replied, taking her lead, biding my time.

She gave a couple of quick nods which I mirrored; a tic that I've bent to use.

'Anything you've noticed, or thought about, particularly, this week?' I said.

'Not really.'

We play this game each time, committed to our polite exchange until I reference, always obliquely, the attacks which had left her kneeling on various platforms thinking she might die. She kept a hand on her bag, legs crossed. The slightest bounce in that raised toe.

'How has your sleeping been?'

'Not too bad. A little better, perhaps.'

'And getting to work?'

'I took the tube three times,' she said, shyly.

'That's brilliant. How was it?'

'It was OK, actually. Yeah,' she said.

'Can you take me through what happened?'

'I was fine going down, but when I got on it was a squash. My heart began to race, but I did what you said.

Observed my symptoms, went through the coping thoughts, and I got to my stop.'

'Well done. And the next day?'

'The same.'

'Any easier?'

'The same.'

'That's good, Marie. Do you see how much progress you've made?'

'Yes,' she said, though her face didn't show it.

'And have you been able to practise the breathing that we talked about?' I said.

'I've been a bit busy this week,' she replied, her eyes on me lightly. She wrung her hands, just once, but thoroughly, pulling hard along the top of each, right down to the tips of her fingers. She hadn't lied. I would have lied. A truth-teller, then. A scrupulous girl.

'I understand. But it's worth keeping going with it, if you can,' I said.

She nodded.

Behind me, my phone began to thrum.

'You can get that if you want,' Marie said, with an abrupt laugh. Her eyes, very blue, held mine.

'Sorry. I usually put it on silent. They'll go. You were saying.'

'I don't think I was. Was I?'

My mobile buzzed again. I heard it nudging along the desk.

'I'm so sorry. Let me just turn it off.'

I stood and laid my book on the arm of the chair, knocking off my glass. It fell, the sound of impact absorbed by carpet. Across the room, Marie plucked some tissues from the box.

'Please don't worry,' I called but she had started across the room.

'It's only water. It won't stain,' I said, but still she came. She knelt, her legs pressed together in an office skirt, the soles of her courts upturned, gashed and oddly indecent. She set to work, pressing thick wads deep into the pile.

'That's better,' she said. 'I've used them all up.' She put the sodden pile inside the empty box and handed them to me. This close, I saw she wore a thin gold chain tucked into her shirt. I dropped the lot into the bin and went back to my chair.

'So, I think it's time, soon, to start to think about next steps,' I said. 'As your symptoms are so much better, we could talk a little more about cause. Why this might be happening. Why now.'

She watched me, dead still.

'Anxiety doesn't simply appear. There's always something behind it,' I said. 'Your symptoms are sending us a message. We need to work out what that is.'

I saw her chest jump as though she'd taken a sudden unplanned inhale.

'As hard as it's been, these events can actually be an opportunity. To get at things that have been hidden up until now. Things that might have been holding us back.'

She gave a weak smile. This moment will excite some clients. For others, it can take more time.

'I hope that doesn't feel too daunting. We'll work together. I'm here every step,' I said.

I handed her a page. We were to start with something easy.

'This is a life events survey. It's a list of things that can happen that might cause stress, or trigger an emotional change of some sort. Some will be obvious. Others less so. Do you want to have a look and we can go through whatever seems interesting next session?'

'For me to keep?' she asked.

'Of course,' I replied. 'That's time, I think.' I have a large clock on the wall behind the client's head. 'We'll talk again in a week.'

There was a text when I turned to my phone, from Stef. *Free says she's ill? No temp. I've kept her off.*

Why does a mother feel so differently for each child? To talk of preference is to miss the point. Take fear, for example. Against this measure, Frieda tops the charts.

I wrote back: *OK. Slightly odd. Do you think something's up?* then scrolled through my phone to find the number of her school. I called it, and arranged a time to pop in for a chat.

In a while, I heard Adam arrive and went next door to him. We made love silently, by the bookcase, as we had before.

5

We moved into the office, Adam and I, a month after we had looked round, on a warm grey autumn Saturday of fat low clouds and incipient rain. My husband drove me with the back seat flat and the car full of boxes. I wore old jeans and Converse and an ancient plaid shirt and as we passed through town easily in the weekend traffic, no kids, he switched to Radio 2 and when Oasis came on, looked across and said I looked like the nineties. When we stopped for petrol, he bought me service station flowers, long and limp in dripping plastic.

We got everything upstairs in three trips and I offered him a cup of tea but he told me he had things to do. I thought I heard melancholy in the way he said goodbye and listened to his footsteps shrink as he passed down through the centre of the house. Quiet ballooned, and then I heard his voice, risen in welcome, the stress on the 'a' of his 'hallo' – never more Scandinavian than in greeting – and underneath it, Adam's low note.

I wondered how Adam's hand felt in my husband's. It is not beautiful, like Stef's. Veins rise along its top in a prominent Y. His nails are fitted too snugly to the flesh; curved, almost clubbed. The skin is dry, a little ashy. I thought, I would like to sit by Adam's bath and wash those hands, scrub them with the gritty perfumed wax I use all over, once a week, to slough off my own dead cells. Dip my fingers in the pot and draw out a handful, working it into the knuckles, at the roots, and the darkened patch between the first two fingers where the nicotine has stained. There are tiny beads suspended in the mix and in the heat, at the pressure of touch, they dissolve to release an oil and a deep clean ocean scent. When that happened, I would turn his wrist and work on the palm, the softer part. I would replenish him. Put life back into those hands.

I moved through to the hall, kicking a box into the doorway so I wouldn't get locked out, and leant over the bannister to better hear. Their introductions stretched into something else, but I couldn't make out a word. I leant a little further and the handrail creaked. Toast caught in the downstairs flat and the smoke alarm began and when it stopped, a few seconds on, I heard Adam's tread, rather close, and felt something like panic. I went inside and hid in the far corner of my office. My shirt smelled of too long in the back of a cupboard.

'Knock-knock,' he called, and I waited.

'Knock-knock,' he said again and I crossed the room and pushed open my door. There was his face, the smile that I have described. The same clothes as always. He stood on the threshold of the room, oddly framed. He looked like a portrait, with the raucous wallpaper of the hall behind him, the run of chestnut balustrade and his own general dishevelment set against the perfect blank of the walls. I saw he waited to be invited.

'Come on,' I said, 'come in. You don't have to ask. It's yours as well. Ours.' He stepped inside. I think I blushed.

'Where's your stuff?' I said. 'Is that it?'

He held a plastic bag.

'Coming in a van later on. But I bought us this.'

He reached inside and removed a large boxed coffee machine.

'Wow. You didn't have to.'

I acknowledged my disappointment. For a moment, I had hoped for chilled champagne.

'I didn't. We got two for our wedding. Shall I make us some?' he said and that feeling bent into an adolescent kind of hurt.

I heard him setting up the machine in the kitchen and an old-fashioned whistling as I emptied the contents of my boxes onto the floor.

'How do you like it?' he called.

'Long, please. Not too much milk.'

I sorted my books, mainly textbooks and a handful of novels I'd pulled out on a trawl around the house. *Anna Karenina* and *Middlemarch*, some Brontë and Hardy, thick grown-up books about life, love and mistakes; I had stuck to the classics in an effort to demonstrate learning rather than taste. I laid my painting against the wall under the spot I planned to hang it and opened my laptop to the end of the *Pick of the Pops* we'd been listening to in the car.

He brought me through a mug. 'Can I help with any of that?'

'Not really. Not till the delivery's been.'

He sat on the window ledge, back-lit, suddenly, by

48

a burst of bright wet light that singed the edges of his hair. His wedding ring was a loose rounded gold of the traditional type. Stef wore a platinum band, wider and flattened, with a planed square edge. Adam crossed his legs at the ankle, his feet reaching out into the room. His face was deeply furrowed, clefts running out from the sides of his nose. I knelt at a stack of case-notes.

'Rather gloomy choice, Nancy.'

'What? Why?' I said.

'This one's ending is grim, and she kills herself in that, if I remember.'

'Oh dear. I've got a load of Shakespeare somewhere. Perhaps I'll bring that in.'

'I'm going to go out for a cigarette,' he said, patting himself down.

'It's fine here, for now, I think. If you open the window,' I said.

'Do you want one?' he asked.

'Why not?' I said.

He pulled out a Zippo in old bronze. There was the clunk as he flipped the lid and the grate of the little flint wheel.

'That takes me back,' I said. Interchangeable nights of everyone over to someone's, the evening getting deeper and the boy next to you turning his lighter through his fingers in some weird demonstration of masculinity.

The flame was strong and white and arched towards me in a rush of breeze. The first pull crackled, a dry leafy compost cut with lighter fuel and I felt a chemical expansion behind my eyes, not altogether pleasant. I held my hand out to Adam and he placed the object in my palm, heavy and warm still from his pocket. I enjoyed the feeling of it there. It was worn and smooth and even the pits and dents were rounded and edgeless.

'Is it very old?' I said, turning it over in my hand.

'It was my father's,' he said.

'What's this?' I asked. There was a faint engraving on the lighter's spine.

'Ah,' he replied, 'what do you think?'

There were only traces, fine lines so shallow that I felt nothing of them under my thumb. A shape had been etched, rounded and bulb-like at the bottom, twisting and narrowing to a point above.

'I'm not sure,' I said. 'Did he do it himself?'

'No. My mother bought it for him. It's hand-done, though, to her design.'

'Is it a whirlwind?' I said.

He laughed. 'That's perfect.'

'What?'

'It's a new one, that's all. I've never heard that before.' He took it from me. 'But I see what you mean.'

'So what is it then?' I asked.

'Well, it's a thought. Or a wish or a dream, she used to say sometimes. He was away a lot and she gave it to him as a way of keeping her close, I suppose,' he said.

'That sounds like something out of a film,' I said.

He laughed again.

'It does, a bit.'

'Is that how they were together?' I asked.

'Sometimes. Not always. But they were a good pair.'

The sentiment of it hung between us.

'Anyway. He died, and she gave it to me. The best bit's refilling them though,' he said. 'Do you know how?'

'I remember,' I replied. 'You pull the bottom off, right?'

'Yeah. Do it.'

He gave it back to me. I pulled the casing away, revealing a slim tab of sponge underneath.

'Don't you pour the fluid into this hole?' I asked.

'You're actually supposed to lift that part out,' he said. 'Here, I'll show you.'

He reached into a box and took a biro. 'Hold still,' he said and brought the pen close. He eased the nib into the hole, his hand umbrella'd over mine. As he bent, I saw the place in his scalp where his hair began, like the aerial shot of a hurricane. In the lobe of one ear there was a nub of regrown flesh where he once would have worn an earring.

'Is my cigarette all right?' he asked.

I looked back to where it balanced on the window ledge.

'Fine,' I said, as a ridged column of ash tipped onto the floor.

He lifted the rectangle of wadded felt out on the tip of my pen.

'Once this is off, you pour the liquid in,' he said, close enough that I could hear the texture of his breath. It's hard to know for certain, but I think, had he tried to kiss me then, I would have let him. 'But I haven't got any, I'm afraid.'

There was the beep of reverse lights.

'That must be the van,' he said.

I'd paid for assembly and my office was arranged inside an hour; they even hung my art.

Tim arrived, later, an old colleague of mine who was taking the third office. He introduced himself to Adam heartily, and then asked did we mind if he put the radio on and listened to the game? It was the start of the rugby season, he told us. He wore the shirt to reflect his team. He kept the volume low and the mood was suddenly brisk and chatty as we worked out a layout for reception, dragging furniture back and forth, laughing about democracy and wondering how, long-term, this collaboration might play. Tim's mind was on the game though, and every now and then he gave a huge unexpected shout in response to it and Adam and I shared the briefest look that tightened the bolt of our connection. When his team won, Tim suggested a celebratory trip to the pub, but I had four missed calls from home by then, and left.

And so our weekday lives began. Adam brewed a strange floral coffee every morning – Tim couldn't stomach it and Lynn preferred tea – so he would make me a cup and bring it through, sitting a while in my client's chair as I drank. When I found myself moving my nine-thirties to ten, I felt a first weak acknowledgement of distance travelled. As I tell my clients, intimacy is a process.

I suggested a regular catch-up for the three of us to

talk through cases but Tim ducked out, saying he preferred not to discuss his work, it muddied things; he liked to keep his read clean. So Adam and I did it, alone, in a café across the park. We talked for hours, our clients a fine gauze between us. We learned everything about each other, told entirely through other people's lives. It was a perfect and lucid exchange; I left those sessions euphoric.

There were the lunches the last Friday of every month with anyone who was around and for a while Lynn came, looking between us avidly as we spoke until one day she said: 'My goodness. I can't keep up with you pair,' and never returned.

Tim had refused from the start. 'I don't drink during office hours,' he said.

'I never book clients on Friday afternoon,' I replied, 'and it's not compulsory to drink, but suit yourself.'

When I wasn't with him, I thought of Adam endlessly; he looped around my head like a track. On quiet afternoons he sat in reception – for a change of scene, to think, he said – and I watched him from my office, a pencil lodged above his ear like a waiter, his chin tilted to show his neck. I wondered if it was display; if it was, it worked. I watched him, and I craved him, like the mother in Rapunzel looking over the wall into the witch's garden, and wanting what she saw, whatever the cost. I forced myself into the habit of closing my door.

~

It happened in increments, with the occasional quantum leap.

A power cut just after lunch on a short cold winter day. Three clients in the book who I managed to catch and rearrange. Tim was away skiing and Lynn, who mothered us anyway with stuff she'd baked and hokey cold remedies, was skittish and girly.

'Christmas shopping!' she declared, at my door, already in her coat. 'Might as well make the most. Do you want to come?' she asked. Adam had someone next door, I could hear the low drone of the client's voice through the wall. I told her no and I waited.

'Still here?' he said, at last. My room was cooling steadily, its edges fading out.

'I was just leaving, actually,' I replied. 'I've got loads to do.'

'Like what?'

'Oh you know, home stuff,' I said.

'But you're not expected until six,' he replied.

'I know, but now I've got this time—' I said, briefly, weakly, hoping somewhere that he'd let me go.

'Exactly. A gift. Let's use it.' He reached his hand towards me and then changed his mind, sweeping it back behind him in a gesture of invitation.

'We can't go to the pub. I can't get home pissed,' I said, desperately, in a final cursory act of resistance.

'How about the cinema then?' he said. 'When did you last go to a matinee?'

'That's unbelievably decadent, Adam. It's worse than the pub somehow.'

'Do you think?' he said. 'How come?' but I was up and around my desk, grabbing for my things.

Perhaps it started then. Walking fast into the wind to keep up with him, his coat billowing back, grazing my hand. His face, in profile, dear to me already, and that mouth, curved upwards in a lupine smile. We took the bus to the Ritzy and now and again, around a bend, over a bump, I felt the press of his leg and poured my intent into those points at which we met. There was a moment when one whole side of us was briefly connected and I thought I saw him acknowledge it with a slight sideways smile.

The film starred George Clooney, a slow tale of middle age and loss of hope that seemed too obviously to be sending me a message. A couple of rows back, a young couple kissed wetly, and more, which made me anxious, though Adam laughed at their noisier adjustments. The romantic convention, his hand dropped off the armrest, his fingers tiptoeing along the back of my chair, didn't happen. We had a gin and tonic after at the bar. I had to ask.

'What did you think of me, Adam, back at college? When you first knew me?'

He rubbed his throat. His earlobes are rather long and flat. 'Let me think.' His chuckle was like the beginnings of a growl. 'Perpetually in motion, that's what I remember. Even in class.'

'Neurotic, you mean,' I said.

'No. Not at all. Just kind of buzzing. As if you couldn't keep it all in.'

'Why weren't we friends?'

'Friends?' he said. 'I couldn't have got anywhere near you, Nancy.' His smile showed teeth.

'Why? What do you mean?'

'You were constantly surrounded. And forever on the move.'

He lifted his face up off his hand, his cheek briefly corrugated.

'You're a trier, you know. Always striving. And you haven't changed one bit.'

We sat on short stools and his legs were crossed high and tight before him. He dropped his hands onto his knees.

'It sounds exhausting,' I said.

'You tell me,' he replied.

I raised my eyebrows, stirred my drink.

'And we're friends now, aren't we?' he said. 'I took my time. I found my moment.'

We said goodbye, went home to our spouses, but our love took flesh that day. Tried a first wobbly step and found itself sound.

6

On the way to school Stef and I went through the sayables: stress or boys, maybe even something low level online. He'd thought there was no need when I told him we were to go in, so I shared a couple of approximate tales from my own case-load and he decided, where's the harm? When we got to reception, I half-expected to find Frieda waiting, her little face beneath that morning's hair, backcombed and sprayed and established off to one side; the cloth bag with the shoes in that I knew full well she changed into on the bus, in a puddle at her feet. But I had asked Miss Millar, a new teacher, to keep the meeting between us. I had the sudden wish to be in her office, out of sight.

'No need to worry,' Miss Millar said, when she came out, younger than me by a decade, dressed in practical jeans and canvas pumps. 'She's in class right now. You won't bump into her. Can I get you some tea?'

'So how can I help?' she said, when we'd all sat down, looking between us cheerfully.

'Well, things don't seem quite right lately with Frieda,' I said.

'I see,' she replied, with an exaggerated look of concern. 'I'm sorry to hear that. Can you tell me more?'

'It's hard to put a finger on it exactly. It's a general sense really,' I told her. 'I mean, I'm aware that with boys you tend to see explosions. I'm a therapist, you know,' I said. Miss Millar acknowledged this with a thin little smile and I felt my own ridiculousness. 'With girls, I find it can be subtler. More of a slide. I'm worried Frieda's sliding,' I said.

'Any specific examples?' she asked.

'I think she's got some sleeping issues,' I replied, though Stef looked at me sideways for it. 'And she's been possibly faking, or rather exaggerating, illness to get out of school. So I was wondering if something had happened. Some problem here, perhaps?'

A kind of siren sounded, long and throbbing, and then another noise began, a rolling mass of sound. The accumulation of a thousand children's feet and voices, oddly inhuman, just the occasional discernible word breaking free. It felt impossible to survive out there, in that.

'None of that's ringing any bells to be honest, Mrs Jansen, but let's have a look,' Miss Millar said. She woke up her screen.

'So her grades are slightly down in these last tests,' she told us. 'No observations though. Nothing's been red flagged.'

'She's spending a lot of time on her drama,' Stef said. 'Perhaps—'

'Can I see that?' I asked.

Miss Millar looked at me across the top of her computer. 'There's confidential stuff on here, I'm afraid.

We're tasked with safeguarding your daughter's privacy as I'm sure you know.' She flipped the screen back down.

'What I certainly can do, though,' she said, 'is log your concern. And I'll ping a mail over to all of her teachers to bring them up to speed. And I'll need to ask you, now, if there's anything else? Any changes in the home environment that we might usefully become aware of?' she said, and then she watched us.

'Oh. Wow. OK. Well, home. Things are fine, largely, I'd say,' said Stef. 'I mean we're like any other couple in the sense—'

'No, Stef. It's big stuff she means. Health. Or issues with the other kids or something.'

'Well actually, Mrs Jansen, I'm interested in anything which might give us some insight,' she replied. She looked back to Stef but he was silent now.

'There's nothing,' I said. 'Perhaps it's just her age?' and thought, I would pity that from a client.

'Entirely possible,' Miss Millar replied, 'either way, I'm glad that you came in. We do like to be thorough. We've had a couple of missed opportunities,' she went on. 'We're all doing our best.'

We had received the letter about the suicide attempt and I'd seen a couple of eating disorders in the corridors before. She took us through next steps. There is a system. Frieda could be talked to, gently; peer mentors assigned. 'But the request for that action will have to come from you, Mr and Mrs Jansen. As you instigated the concern. As I said, there are no markers our end.'

On her wall were framed intentions. BE THE CHANGE

A photo of a group of girls playing an aggressive game of football. All that hope.

'Oh no,' said Stef. 'That won't be necessary. Thank you for your time.'

I drove, racing Frieda's bus, though I didn't say so. Stef was silent beside me, wedging the heel of his hand against the dashboard in response to one sudden turn. I made no comment, and he dropped his arm and drummed his thumbs. We got home with minutes to spare and Stef passed straight through the house and out to his office, calling back to me that he needed to catch up with work. Meantime I stage-set the house to happy families. I lit each lamp. I advanced the heating. I cooked the chicken I had planned for the weekend and then the children arrived, together, the smaller ones shouldering their way in, pin-balling down the hall towards me. Lou, already indignant, Jake hunched low over his Muttley laugh.

'What's all this?' Lou said, at the kitchen door, smelling my effort. 'Is Dad's light on out there? Why are you both at home?'

'Why not?' I said, chopping veg under task lighting.

'What are you doing?' she said. 'Why are we having a roast today?'

'It's your favourite, isn't it? Get on with your home-work. We're eating at six.'

Lou let herself be appeased and settled at the island.

'Will you help me, Mum? It's History. Sources,' she said. She spread open a huge exercise book before her.

'That's your dad. Call me when it's French.'

Jake went to the fridge, shouting down at his friend on FaceTime and Frieda moved through the kitchen noiselessly with her earphones in and an abstract look. She took a glass of water and, by the sink, I approached and touched her shoulder. She blinked me into focus and gave a little wave and I saw a thick oval scab on her thumb, nail width, that I wondered if I should worry about. Then she left the room, her face cast down, a huge bag on her back. Her hair had sagged across the day, it lay over one shoulder sadly, like an animal's hide. Stef came back through, clearing up the mess as I made it and I asked him to pour me a drink. The wine was from the fridge door and could have been colder, although it tasted better this way, peach and slate, a little oiliness. I stirred a splash into the meat juices, enjoyed the chemistry, and worked at the burnt bits with a wooden spoon. The heat of the hob, a six-ring range, steamed the windows, Radio 4 bubbled gently, low enough to obscure bad news, our kids – good kids – were all home and accounted for. There was a villa booked for summer, we had a tutor to help with exams. There was a dog, for God's sake; his snout resting on Louisa's foot as she worked, walked every day by a woman I paid to do it as none of the rest of us had the time, but it guaranteed nothing. None of it made us safe.

We sat to eat at six, ridiculously early, a little heap of amnestied devices winking at me from a shelf over Frieda's shoulder. When I asked: 'How was everybody's day?' Jake lay down his fork and said:

'Lou's right for once. This is actually very weird,' and then despite Stef's look, actively counselling me to stop, and in full knowledge that later, in bed, he'd tell me that I should try to ease up, be light, I said:

'Guys, I just wanted to take this moment, now we're all together, to say something important.'

I had their attention now, and the weight of it prickled at the back of my neck.

'Look there's nothing to worry about,' I said, but my laugh was unconvincing and nobody joined me. The kids were still and alert. I saw my strangeness in their faces, the idea of my mutability begin. I thought I felt them pull away. A little crack start in the land between us.

'No. Guys. It's not something bad—' I said, and then Louisa began to cry, quite suddenly, her face instantly wet.

'Lou, what you are doing?' I said 'What on earth's the matter?' but still she cried, her head bowed, tears dripping straight down into her food.

'I know what it is,' she said. 'You and Daddy are getting divorced.'

'Oh don't be ridiculous,' I said. 'It's nothing like that.' I thought, again, how like Madeline she is, how very much third child. 'I just wanted to check in, you know, a quick family audit, as we're all here.'

Her father went to her. 'Your mum didn't mean to frighten you, Lou. It's OK, honey,' but she wouldn't submit to him, her shoulders were set rigid.

'More of that crap she does at work,' Jake said, just loud enough.

'What was that?' I asked but didn't press it. He looked down at his plate, his forehead compressed in fury.

'Lou, I'm sorry,' I said. 'Please. Come on.'

'Just shut up, Lou,' Jake said, shoving his chair back from the table.

'Hey, Jacob,' said Stef, still kneeling, 'you know that we don't use those words.'

'Why are you crying? Do you even know what you're crying about?' Jake said and Lou's sobs escalated. She shook her head, like the dog, flinging snot and tears around her.

'That is so gross,' Jake cried, his mood flipping instantly. He snapped his thumb and middle finger together, making an impressive click.

'Jake. What are you doing? Sit down,' I said.

'What's the matter with her? She's mad! You're mad,' he yelled at his sister, in glee, in sudden delight, and then Lou had pushed her plate away, gravy breaching its side and she was gone and Jake was calling: 'I didn't — She's just— It's not fair,' in various rotations and I was shouting too: 'Why do you always have to—' but I wasn't sure what, or at whom. Stef left, Jake tried for the door, and I let him. The dog bolted for bed.

Only Frieda remained. She held her place at the table, her hair tied back behind her, now, in a loose high bun, working her way through her dinner steadily. I took myself to the sink and drained my glass, long and deep. She reached behind her and pulled her iPhone from the pile.

'Free, as it's just you and me, could we talk, for a minute?' I began.

'I don't think so, Mum,' she said, sensibly. 'It's not the best time right now. Wouldn't you say?'

I heard Stefan, upstairs, knocking gently on Louisa's door. Frieda eased an earbud in with her thumb, moving her head against it in adjustment. I found my face in the window's wet reflection and then the screen of my neighbour's TV beyond. Stef was back, cool and sober.

'Give it up for tonight, Nancy, eh?' he said, as he passed, and I smelled his scent, cool and green, and his sweet clean flesh underneath it. The weight of our nineteen years pinned me back down into my life.

7

Six months until I touched him. Six months, living in proximity, Adam and I; a clear run towards that moment.

Friday lunchtime, then, the top of a tall office building, our meeting done. We waited for the lift, he wore that same fibrous jacket, his hair a mess above it, angling off this way and that. The lift arrived, the door opened to a pack of bodies and I stepped in, Adam at my back. We turned and began to go down. The drop to each floor was fast, landing with a deep voluptuous bounce that I felt low in my stomach. In the crush, it seemed OK to close my eyes. I let myself lean into my toes and my nose skimmed his coat. It got hotter and a bag nudged the hinge of my knees, nearly knocking out my legs. We hit street level and the lift emptied until just he, I and one other remained. What I should have done then, was take a big step back into all this fresh space, but instead I touched him, definitively. I laid my palm against his back, hard enough to feel the angle of his shoulder blade. He made no response, but kept his place until the lift's last mineral grind and we reached the lowest floor, where I had parked the car. Then he reached his hand over his shoulder and laid it flat upon mine.

'Bye, then,' the other man said. Adam's touch was a gentle pressure across my knuckles. 'Guess I might see you guys there.'

Neither Adam or I flinched.

'Yes. Goodbye,' Adam said. 'Perhaps you will.'

I was driving. The car was cold and we still wore our coats. I turned the heating up and a column of parched heat moved my hair and began to warm my neck. The outside of our little fingers grazed behind the gearstick.

'Will you go?' he said, eventually. 'Shall we go?'

I nodded, my eyes on the road.

'I think so. Don't you?'

'I do.'

I dropped him off and went home.

Stef had fixed a net across the width of the kitchen table and was playing ping-pong there, with Jake.

'How was it, babe?' he said.

'Good, interesting.'

'What do you think, then? Worth a try?'

'Well it's a popular therapy. It should bring in a few new clients. Or as a supplementary thing, perhaps. But it'll take an initial outlay.'

'How much?'

'Dad, can you concentrate?' Jake said.

'Maybe eight hundred pounds?'

'Go for it,' he said. 'Why not?'

The dog butted my leg until I scratched behind his ear.

'Mum,' called Lou. 'I need you to look at this.'

'It'll mean a night away from home, though,' I said, although it made me sweat beneath my coat to voice it.

'You should do it. Expand your skill set. We'll manage,' he said. 'Won't we, Jakey?'

'Yeah,' Jake said. 'I'm thrashing you, Dad. Can you at least try?'

Lou came through with a painting limp in her hand.

'When are you going, Mum? I don't like it when you go away.'

'You'll be fine, sweet. It's not for long.'

'Who will you talk to?'

'Oh I don't know. I'll meet people. Is Frieda here? What do you want to eat?' I said.

Lou turned back down the hall, all mismatched proportions like a game of Picture Consequences, with the bunch of her hood and her sweatshirt as broad as it was long, then the drop of her leggings, thin as string, into the great wide mouth of her Uggs.

'Come here, Lou,' I called and she turned back to me in delight. She shinned up my front like a monkey and I held her there for as long as I could stand, her legs wrapped round my waist, breathing in her unwashed hair. There is something dissociative about the ecstatic state.

8

There was ground to be made with Marie. I got to the office for five past eight.

'You're early,' Lynn said, when she arrived. 'Can I make you a drink?'

I had a coffee before me and a nonchalant air when she showed Marie through.

'Morning, Marie,' I said, as she settled. 'Is there anything you'd like to start with today?'

She made a play of thinking, and told me no.

'So, how was your week?' I asked.

'Oh. Good, thanks.'

The sun was low and bleached, halving the room.

'And the travelling?' I asked.

'I caught the tube every day,' she said.

'Brilliant. How did you find it?'

'The same as before.' Then: 'I remember those.' She pointed at my shelf. Shakespeare's complete works, leather-bound.

'You collected them month by month, didn't you? Out of the back of a magazine,' she said.

'That's right,' I replied.

'They're from when we were children. We had them, too.'

She reached across and bumped her finger along the books, spine by spine. She paused on one and tilted it towards her with difficulty, breaking the line. I waited for her to take it, but she pushed it back flush. With another client I might have made something of her choice.

'We never looked at them once,' she said. 'Did you?'

'No,' I replied.

'Well, you've found a use for them now,' she said and we smiled together at that.

'So shall we have a look at the homework from last week?' I said.

'Sure,' she replied and pulled the sheet out from inside her book.

'What struck you?' I asked.

She tracked the list with the nib of her pen and came to a stop.

'Well there's the job thing, obviously,' she said.

'Could you read that statement to me, please?'

'It says: *Change in responsibilities at work.*'

'And why did you choose that?'

'I got a new job. Remember?'

I heard Tim greet a client in reception, booming and absolute.

'Of course. Anything else?'

'Not that I can see.'

'What about: *Outstanding personal achievement*?' I said.

'Oh, I wouldn't go as far as all that,' she replied, with an unsuitable giggle.

'Well your new job amounts to a huge promotion, as I understand it?'

She coloured a little and I took my chance.

'You've come a long way in your life, Marie. You know, that can bring issues.'

She dropped her chin.

'One idea I wanted to share with you. There is a theory that the sort of anxiety that you've been experiencing – this sense of some external danger – can be a stand-in for a more internalised threat. A difficult emotion that you may be trying to suppress.'

I paused, waiting for the tweak, the wrinkle of disdain that Marie shows at the rim of her nose. It didn't come.

'For example, for some, success can be tough. You might feel guilty, or unworthy, or that your achievement can't be sustained. Your anxiety could be seen as a form of self-sabotage.'

'Oh no,' she said. 'I don't think any of that,' and I believed her. Marie is proud.

'OK,' I said. 'We'll keep thinking. Perhaps next time we'll go a little further back.'

I am ambitious for Marie. I want to help get her where she is headed.

'Take this home,' I said. 'These are some questions about your family background. Mark what resonates and we'll see where it leads us. Patterns of thinking and behaviour can start very early in life.'

She tucked the new page into her handbag and the old one slid down her lap. I saw, before she grabbed it, that she had highlighted four or five statements and little scribbles of notes all over. Her look, as she pulled it back towards her, dared me to ask.

'See you next time,' I said, breezily. 'You have a great week.'

As she left, I heard Adam arrive, late today. I listened to his good-mornings and went to him.

'How are you?' he said, looking tattered and lop-sided, his glasses on a string around his neck. At her desk, Lynn turned, raised the phone and began to talk decisively. I closed the door so we could kiss. When I pulled away, he rubbed his thumb across my eyebrow and I tucked my head into his neck and felt my hair snag on his chin and the press of his ribs. I wondered if he'd lost weight.

'Come and sit with me,' he said. 'I need to get ready.'

He had cycled to work and wore an old jumper. He set up his ironing board, shook out the shirt from his ruck-sack and began.

'My client's tricky,' I said.

'Marie? It's still early days.'

'I know but I can't seem to reach her.'

'You want to tell me about it?'

'Not really. Not yet.'

'Take it slowly. You'll get there.'

The iron gave a puff of steam as it travelled around the collar's curve. I smelt hot metal and singed cotton.

'Did your mother teach you that?' I asked, from his ancient client's chair.

'She did. You do the yoke next. This part here, across the shoulders, see?'

'Cambridge soon,' I said and levered off my shoes. 'Can we punt?'

'If weather allows. Have you been there before?'

'Once. For a wedding,' I said. Horrible, a contrived and competitive affair.

The intercom buzzed. Adam looked up. 'Is that you?' he asked.

'Don't think so,' I said. 'No one until ten.'

'Same here. Unless he's early.'

Adam laid down his iron and we had both turned our heads to the door when Lynn began a hectic banging.

'Nancy,' she called in panic. 'Come out. Please. It's your husband. And your children too.'

'All right,' I said, and opened the door to her stricken face.

'They're here,' she said, taking my elbows in her grip. 'They're coming up,' and I would have liked to slap her but instead said, calmly: 'It's absolutely fine, Lynn. Now, please—' She dropped her hands. 'Sit down,' I said, 'Don't worry. I'll get the door.'

'Hello,' I called down into the chasm of the stairwell.

'Mummy,' Louisa said, barrelling into me, arms round my waist, forcing me back into the room.

'What are you doing here? What happened to school?' She pushed her face deeper into my front. Behind me, I felt her fingers working on the ball of the Blu-Tack she carried everywhere.

'So this one's ill now,' said Stef. 'What do you make of that?'

My husband stood in the doorway like an advert for a supplement, all vigour, good health and equilibrium. Handsome in a suit for a pitch later that day, which seemed to emphasise his outdoorsiness instead of bringing him into any sort of corporate line.

'What's the matter, Lou?' I said, looking down at the top of her head.

'She felt sick,' he replied for her.

'You were fine when I left this morning.'

'It started in the car,' he said. Patient, amused.

'Were you reading, Lou? Or looking down at the phone. You know that's not a good idea,' I said. She shook her head, setting her ponytail swinging, thin and off-centre.

'There's a vomiting bug,' she said, into my shirt. 'Everybody's got it.'

'Anyway, Lorene can watch her, but we were on our way back home and thought we'd call in and say hi, eh Lou?'

Stef made no move towards us; we all seemed oddly fixed in place, like characters in a bad play. Lynn upstage, her hand still at her throat and Adam's door gaping in the wings, full of portent.

'Can I look inside your office, Mum?' Lou said. 'It's ages since I've been here.'

'Of course,' I replied, and then:

'Hi. Sorry.' It was Adam. 'Hello, everybody. Sorry, I just need to shut the door. To get changed, you see,' he said, which worked as an invitation to look at him, slope-shouldered, the fresh shirt draped over an arm, his trousers tucked into his socks, still, from the bike ride in. 'I've got a client due any moment.'

'Hey, Adam,' called Stef and crossed the room in a few

long strides. 'How are you doing?' He took my lover's hand and then the top of his arm as well. 'It's been a long time.'

'It has,' Adam said. 'I'm well, thanks. How are you?'

Stef's grin was broad, enthusiastic, robust. Adam, a head taller without shoes, looked crabbed and underfed. I could see his discomfort but he didn't cringe. He held his spot, and that reached me as devotion. I felt a truth, in that moment, about my feelings for him, and a sudden tip of vertigo, but then Lou had reached for my cheek and turned my face down to her, she needed water, a tissue, a biscuit, a hug.

'All good. Yeah, we're good,' Stefan was saying. He cast around for conversation. 'Starting to think about the summer, now. You know, holidays, and such. And you're well? You and—' but he got there in time. 'Tara?'

Behind me, Lynn rubbed her hands together, I could hear the sound of papery abrasion.

'We are, thank you. Yes, fine.'

'Lou,' Stef said, 'do you want to say hi to Adam? Mummy's colleague?' Louisa turned her head towards the men, her ear still pressed to my heart and gave a soft hello. Adam smiled and raised a hand.

'Louisa,' Stefan said. 'Stand up straight, please, honey, when someone's—'

'It's OK. Really,' Adam said. 'I should probably get back. Well, it's been nice to see you.'

'Yeah, you too, man,' said Stef. 'We should get together. A dinner perhaps. Your wife's an actress, right? Our oldest, Frieda, would love to meet her. She's getting very, very into her drama.'

'Yes,' Adam said, 'I'll mention that to Tara.'

'That would be amazing. I know meeting her would make Free's day. Or hey, what about the party, Nance?'

'The party?'

'We're throwing a party for David, Nancy's brother, this Saturday. It should be fun. We've invited everyone. Why don't you guys come too?'

The door buzzed. 'I'd better go,' said Adam, 'that'll be for me.'

Lynn, at the intercom, said: 'It's for Tim, actually.'

'Is he here?' I said.

'Oh yes,' Lynn replied. She slipped into his office and then out again, quickly.

'I'm so sorry everyone, but could you please—? Tim says . . . That it's not terribly professional, this great big crowd.'

'Of course,' I said. 'Louisa, Stef, would you come into my office? Just while this client arrives?'

Then Tim was in the room. Stefan knew him better. 'Tim,' Stef said. 'We'll be out of your hair just now, but we were talking about the weekend. We're having a party. Adam's going to try to make it. Would you be great if you could too. More the merrier, right?' Tim looked between us all in a kind of bafflement.

'Stef, please come here,' I said. 'The client will be up. It's simply not appropriate,' and at that, Tim raised his hand to his mouth and coughed, like a kid hawking a swearword into his fist.

The woman arrived and Louisa listened behind my door.

'Do you know her, Mum?' she whispered. 'What's the matter with her?'

Then she and Stefan left, creeping through reception, but in the hall I heard his voice, loud and full-bodied, swollen by the acoustics of the space.

'Ill?' I heard him say. 'You're in the best of health, my girl,' and then I think he must have tickled her, for ribbons of her laughter reached back to me. I raced out to the hall.

'Be safe,' I called down. 'Lulu, be safe.'

'We will,' Stef shouted back. 'Have a great day.'

9

'Did you see him? He looked terrified!' Madeline said, after, at the bar.

'He's OK,' I told her.

'You sure? I thought we'd fucked up there for a moment.'

'Look, he's enjoying himself already.' We watched our brother across the room. 'Come on, I said. 'Let's get him a drink.'

He had arrived on time as we waited in the dark. I heard the door bang at the bottom of the stairs and then David, his voice like water boiling in a pan. The room reacted with a surge of murmurs. His footsteps, getting louder up each step, made me giggle. I counted down from 10, but had only got to 4 when I heard the catch of the handle. The flick of the master switch (my job), a whump of power and the scene was revealed. His face a snapshot of surprise. He gave three exaggerated blinks.

'Happy birthday!' we chanted, in the usual way, keeping decent time, the final beat drawn out. Seventy-six of us, if everyone who had said yes, turned up, and brought no extras. A few loose cheers and sporadic claps and at last, David smiled. There was a tiny collapse across his shoulders and then he gave a sudden harsh laugh, a kind of aftershock. I felt something difficult in it, but the rest heard invitation and he was swamped. Madeline and I, the sisters, stayed where we were.

'I'm not convinced, Nance,' Mads said. 'He looks a bit freaked out.'

David was moving, acknowledging people blindly as he came.

'Quick,' I said. 'We'll catch him at the bar. There's prosecco till it runs out.'

'This could only be your work, Nancy,' said David, when he got to us.

'Well, I couldn't have let your special day go unmarked,' I replied. He laughed again, broader now, somewhere up over my head. When he was finished, I kissed him, a hard meeting of cheekbone.

'Here,' I said. 'Have some fizz.'

'I'd prefer a vodka tonic,' he replied.

I leant a long way over the bar to attract the barmaid's attention.

'You know you have to pay for that,' she said. 'No spirits on the tab.'

'It's fine, Nancy,' David interrupted. 'I can get my own.'

He gouged the lemon a few times with the end of his straw and drank halfway down the glass.

'So what do you think?' said Madeline, with her prettiness and bounce and her hair that smelt of the tropics.

'I'll tell you when this begins to work,' he replied, setting the ice tumbling and then drinking again.

'Oh look,' said Mads, 'here's Skyler.'

Her hair was freshly black with a brutal fringe cut into it. She wore a kaleidoscopic dress over thick tights and a pair of stompy boots. I thought I spotted a couple of new piercings. She held her arms out towards him as she came, in a camp impersonation of bashfulness.

'You were in on this too, I suppose?' said David but his voice was rounded and teasing now.

'Of course,' said Skyler. 'We've been planning it for months.'

'Really?' she'd said, when I told her the idea. 'You won't have to do anything. Just turn up,' I replied. 'Fair enough,' she said. She'd invited their crew, as she put it, and brought a huge bowl of hummus, though I'd told her I'd got the caterers in. It sat at the end of the bar beneath a thickening khaki crust.

'Look, I did the ceiling!' Skyler told David. 'At nursery. All the kids helped. We used the recycling, see?'

She walked him across and Madeline and I went, too.

We were upstairs in a pub; a big square room of dark paintwork and junk-shop portraits with stencilled windows and a horseshoe-shaped bar that halved the space. One side had been cleared for dancing and she had fixed her paper chains here. They curved out in shallow loops

from a hired mirror-ball; snippings of newspaper, colour-
ing and old test sheets. There were stickers and handprints.
Crayons, paint and glitter. When I craned my neck I could
read neat columns of numbers curling off inside a link. He
reached up to touch one and tiny coloured flakes dropped
down, turning slowly through the air.

'Like confetti,' she said and watched him. I saw three
little chips of cerulean settle on his cheek, the kind of blue
I might have chosen for a wall. It looked beautiful, I had
to admit. Our mother, Kath, had arrived earlier with a
bag of hand-stitched bunting and taken it straight back
out to her car.

'So that's what you've been doing, is it? I was beginning
to wonder,' he said, which was a lie and we all knew it.
Skyler leant in close and hummed up into his neck.

'It's gorgeous, Skyler. All this effort you went to,' he
said and she rolled her eyes towards me then, in a lazy
kind of a challenge, her mouth still behind his ear.

'Expecting someone, Nance?' David said, when my
head snapped around again at the sound of the door.

'Pretty much everyone we ever knew,' I replied.

'I'll come, Nancy,' Adam had told me the previous week.
'If you want me to. If it'll help.'

'No way,' I said, 'I'll deal with it,' but Louisa had raced
home to Free and told her about Adam's wife – this actress
– and she'd looked her up online and fallen in love and
begged: 'Please, Mum, you've got to make this happen
for me,' and I told her, 'I can't force the man,' and Stefan

said: 'Come on, Nance. If he can't make the party we can always try for another date.' Now, despite the risk and the difficulty, I found that I wanted him here.

I had dressed carefully, first in a shirt that Adam had bought in some queasy signal of allegiance. It was a deep marine silk which seemed to move by itself, its colour shifting and shading. Louisa had stroked it with her fingertips and then her cheek. 'It's so soft,' she said. 'Looking at it makes me dizzy,' but its trick relied on contrast, the regulation of a suit or the ease of old jeans. So I bought something new; a dress, overpriced and exquisite. A sheet of weighted crepe the complicated shade of frozen dusk, a cold hard purply blue that sucked up all the light. Overpriced and exquisite. The sleeves were long and pulled in at the wrist to a slim fold of cuff. The neck was a low shallow V. The skirt fell from the waist in deep loose pleats and I bought the boots, too, that the model on the website had worn. It was a subtle outfit of inference and suggestion and when I saw myself in it, I felt a kind of triumph. When Louisa appeared in the mirror by my side, she said: 'You look amazing, Mum, but not one bit like yourself,' perhaps the only thing that could have made me love it more. It struck me, later, that I was dressing as the inverse of my idea of his wife.

'Is that Alice, just arrived?' I said. The party was getting noisier. 'My goodness, she hasn't aged one bit.'

'Her?' asked Madeline. 'Wow. She looks kind of expensive.'

'Oh, she is,' I replied.

Considered and adult, her handbag strapped across her chest, she helped her dad out of his coat. Still that kernel of beauty; as distinct now, divorced, two kids down, as at nine years old when she joined my brother's class and, honestly, he fell in love. Something about the proportions of her face. Whatever it was, it had held.

David watched over Skyler's head until she felt his lack of attention and reached up to his cheek, like a child.

'Come on, babe,' she said. 'Let me show you the set-list for the band.'

He found an easy smile and scratched at the roots of her hair. I felt a little taste of it myself; I seem to access others' pleasure, these days, or the ghost of it, as though I'm tapped into this huge network of gratification. The thought of Adam made me shake, my teeth rattle in my head.

'In fact, we really should have a wander,' I said to David. 'Go greet your guests.'

'That, dear sister, is why I never got married,' he said. 'Well, one of the reasons. You do it. You invited them.' Spoken with his own one-sided smile, but he wasn't joking.

'I guess I'll do a circuit,' I said. 'You'll help me, Mads, won't you? At least say hello.' She followed me wordlessly, still looking down at her phone.

We went to Dad first, who wore a blue cotton shirt bearing the memory of the hanger in two little humps halfway along each shoulder. I saw the wide dish of his breast and remembered the feel of it under my cheek, the peace it brought down on me, and the way I used to wonder whose innards I could hear, his or mine, compared with Mum's embrace, all ribs and adjustment. Large, my Dad, but strong, and of a type they don't seem to make any more; firm and fixed and London with a seam of vulnerability. I found it in the hold across his shoulders, in his face, turned away from the screen on a Saturday afternoon, caught on a thought when he should have been watching the game. It is a funny thing. I went to him, and took his hand in mine. He had polished his shoes. I refuse to abandon him to his unsuitable wife.

'It's a brilliant place, Nance. Good job!' he said. He stood with his sister, April, and her husband Pete, all in a row, looking out across the room in an arrangement that made them look geriatric.

'Will there be food, love?' said April. 'I'm sure you said there was food.'

I could see splinters of plucked hair below the main sweep of her eyebrows and the sparse growth above her lip which had been dyed a weird Hollywood blonde. It was Aunty Ape who gave me my first intimation of the upkeep being a woman demanded, even one as unequivocal as her.

'There is. Plenty. People will bring it to you. Are you going to say hello to Mum, Dad?'

'Course I will. Where's Justine though? I haven't seen her for a while.'

'There she is,' said April, as Justine shoved the weighted door out from the loo. Pete crossed himself at the sight of her, a decades old joke.

'Better be off,' I said. 'I'm doing the rounds.'

'Send the birthday boy over, when you find him,

will you, love?' said Aunty Ape. She loved David best, but I didn't take it personally; she would always have chosen the boy and he is handsome and unpredictable, like something out of one of her romances, which turn on jeopardy, but always end well. She dragged a lipstick across her face for David, more than she did for me, or Uncle Peter, her treasure, who fetched and carried for her, bought her chocolates, rubbed her feet and didn't warrant a mention.

'Birthday boy?' I heard Dad say to her as we left. 'He's a grown man, April, not ten years old.'

I'd found four of David's old football team online who came without their wives. They drank their pints genially, stood in a circle in matching polo shirts and I flirted with them en masse, as was expected. 'Still playing?' I asked, though they all looked overfed and age-blown. One of them mentioned Ape, who hadn't missed a match and always carried sweets. I brought her over and left her to do her thing. She was cawing loudly by the time I left.

And there was Alice. I paid for a gin, served badly in a long narrow glass, and went over to her. She smelt of the salon when I kissed her, scorched air and product. Her hair was shorter than I remembered; the cut traced the line of her jaw and the skin of her neck, newly revealed, was whiter than the rest. Her blonde remained ridiculous; a flat effortless silver and when she bent down to her handbag and the hair fell forward, I saw that the back, at her nape, had been shaped into a sharp V, the perfect counterpoint of toughness. When she straightened and it was hidden again, I felt like I'd been told one of her secrets. It was genius, that cut; I could have written a paper on her hair.

She asked me how my kids were: 'Fourteen, twelve and ten, right?' and I said what I always say, about boys being like dogs and the trouble with teens, and that Lou was a typical third; none of it quite true, none of it bringing my children into any focus, but she smiled and said:

'Easier for you, though, in your profession.'

'I wish,' I replied, though really, I thought it probably was.

'Are you working?' I asked.

'A couple of non-execs, to keep my hand in,' she replied. I'd always admired her for her brains. She'd done so much better than the rest of us. Then I saw her gear up, and she said: 'I just wanted to tell you, Nancy, how kind it was of you to invite me. We used to be good friends.'

'We did,' I said, smiling her comment away. 'Have you had the chance to say hello to him?'

'Not yet,' she replied. David stood where it was loud, shouting over the music at his girlfriend's friends and rocking back on his heels as he laughed. He saw us and waved.

'You guys going to come dance?' he called across comfortably.

'In a bit,' I replied. Beside me, Alice turned away, pretending with her phone.

'And thanks, sis,' David said. He held his hands wide, palms up, and looked skyward, as though he were praising something. I couldn't help but warm under his blessing.

'Maybe later then,' I said to Alice when she'd finished with her screen.

'Perhaps,' she replied. We watched a little while longer as Skyler stomped and whooped, dancing alone in shards of light to a guitar-heavy tune.

I paid little attention to the kids. Lou, pretending to be chased, grabbed my dress with a filthy hand, my thigh her pivot. Jake kicked a balloon in a corner, toe, toe, heel, then settled on a bench with his screen. I looked for Frieda, but couldn't find her. There was the familiar drop. I took the door down to the street, slopping my wine in the rush, and found her sitting on a picnic bench next to the road, squeezing the bud of her huge top-knot. She dropped her hand to someone over the table but it was only Stef, who had made her laugh. He rubbed the peach of her cheek with his knuckle.

'Join us,' Stef said.

Frieda pushed her forearms across the table towards him, giggling still, giddy and weak with it.

'I need you both,' I said. 'I've been looking for you everywhere. Granny's ready with the cake,' I said, though I'd planned it for half an hour's time. Frieda stood, the back of her cheap cotton skirt hopelessly lined and I smacked the creases out of it for her.

We didn't bother with the lights this time. Mum appeared from the kitchen, we all sang, and I watched the teardrops of flame bend and quiver as she got closer to David.

'What shall I do with it?' Mum asked the room weakly, as she reached him. Sensible shoes, the grey stark in her hair; my mother, who had once taken up space in the world. Raised three kids, packed lunches, arbitrated our fights, which David started and I finished. The fact of her as once my father's wife was astonishing. David took the cake and I heard her quietly say:

'There's carrot cake at the bottom, do you see? Then chocolate fudge and Victoria sponge, jam no cream, just as you like,' then something else, too low for me to catch.

He blew the candles out and kissed the top of her head, I saw her press her nails into her palms with the pleasure of it, and the moment came when David should have spoken – just a few words, to satisfy the room – and I knew that he would hate that, and so would not. Instead, he stood there, making no effort at diversion. Our mother's eyes roamed, the crowd's unease churned around him but David simply held his calm, waiting it out, a slight lift to his mouth. My father once made him sit at his tea for a full two hours. When he still wouldn't eat, Dad scooped up the plate and swore in the kitchen, which was unusual. It cracked when he banged it down; I found two pieces later in the bin and cut my hand with a tiny nick.

'Nancy. Where's Nancy?' Mum said, vaguely, a couple of times and I could have helped at that point – I usually did – but instead, I played a little game. I was at the end of the bar on a low wooden chair and edged myself back into the space under the open hatch. I will, I told myself, just a little while longer, and I could see them searching for me, openly, now, my sister and husband bent forward out of the line, astonished that I hadn't declared myself. David wouldn't ask – that would be to concede – but I knew that he waited; curious at the delay but confident that I'd come through. And I was going to; I stood and took a big breath in, and then Mum began. Just one syllable at first; aborted. An audible swallow and then a little mouse's call for three cheers. The room responded with respect and relief, the sounds swelling with each refrain and when it was done, the need for him to speak had passed and there were handshakes and hugs that took him up off his feet. I saw him find Mum across the room and thank her with his look. She turned away and moved through the guests oblivious to them, alight with her son's approval. I sat back down in my seat.

Then through the pack, there was Adam, a head above the rest. I waved and he smiled and it seemed as obvious a declaration as a plane dragging its banner across the sky, but his attention dropped and I saw Tara, his wife, for the first time, or rather little clippings of her. Thick dark hair, pulled up in one decisive twist. A tiny stud at the helix of an ear, which I would have loved for myself, had I had the nerve. A face of strong contours, of the type that suggests certainty and holds through time and never takes a bad photograph, and I knew that were she here in any other capacity than my lover's wife, she was the woman I would most want to talk to in the room.

She led him to me, threading through the guests, her arm twisted behind her as they came. She dropped his hand to take mine; warm, still. We shook and a cluster of bangles in the thinnest gold fell this way and that.

'Nancy,' she said, 'at long last.' Her voice was soft and slow; she made you bend to catch the words. Her clothes, all sorts of folds and drapes, were not my style but perfect, nonetheless.

'Hello,' I said, 'thanks for coming.'

'Thanks for inviting us,' Tara replied. 'How was the surprise?'

'Sorry?'

'For your brother. It was a surprise, I think?'

'Oh yes. Very good. He liked it. Hello, Adam.'

He stepped around his wife and kissed me dryly on each cheek which was new, and a little sad. Still, the smell of his detergent and his cheek's rough scratch launched a loose roll of longing in my stomach.

'What a wonderful cake! Your mother's so talented,' Tara said and then her scent reached me too, bergamot and something baser and I realised I'd smelt traces of it before on Adam. Her wedding band was plain, identical to his. She wore no engagement ring. Her nails were neat and filed and left unpainted.

'Mum?' came a voice from behind me.

'Yes, Frieda,' I said, and turned to her, fully, happy to break the lock of the conversation.

'I just— Um—' She looked squarely at Adam's wife.

'Hello,' she said, 'I'm Frieda. Pleased to meet you.' She held out her hand.

'Delighted,' said Tara. 'My husband tells me you're an actor.' I saw Frieda gulp.

'Well, yes,' Frieda said.

'I was just going to get a drink,' said Tara. 'Will you

come with me? I'd love to hear what you're working on now,' and with a light touch at my daughter's arm, they left.

'She's very kind,' I said.

'Yes. She is.'

A girl came by with a tray of quail scotch eggs and a hollandaise dip. I was hungry somewhere under the booze, and took one, but it was too big for a mouthful and reluctant to submit to a bite. We looked out across the room.

'Is this OK?' he said. 'Me being here?'

'Better than you not,' I replied.

'I was watching you from the back—' he began, and then 'Well, hello,' said David, suddenly, hot and loud from the dance-floor. He put his hand on my shoulder to steady himself and turned to Adam, pivoting on his heels. 'Someone else I don't quite recognise. Though I imagine we've met, haven't we?'

'I'm Adam, Nancy's colleague,' he said.

'Ah, of course,' he said. 'Adam. That's right. Nancy talks about you. I'm David. The brother.'

'Good to meet you. And happy birthday,' Adam said.

David looked between us, quickly. 'Oh sorry. Were you talking shop or something?'

'No, not at all,' Adam said. 'Just chatting.'

David laughed, slightly wildly.

'God, really? Do you do small talk, Adam? Nancy's useless. I thought it was a therapist thing. Or maybe it's just her brains. She's the smart one, as I'm sure you know,' David said and clutched me weirdly, his arm around my back.

'Making you what, the beauty?' I asked.

'I was thinking more brawn.'

'You build things though, if I'm right?' Adam said.

David turned his head towards me slowly.

'Something like that. Nancy is a great one for blowing my trumpet.'

I could see Frieda, across the room, looking up at Tara and talking with great animation, her fingers stretching out into star bursts when she made a point.

'Don't worry, Nance. If you've got places to be. I'll take care of your friend,' David said, with a closed little smile. 'We can talk about you.'

'It's OK,' said Adam. 'I'll leave you both to it.'

'Well, he seems nice,' said David, as he left. 'Where's the other guy? Aren't there three of you?'

'Busy tonight,' I said, though I hadn't mentioned the party again to Tim.

'Oh, the pair of you gang up on him, do you? You exclude the poor thing,' David said.

'Don't be ridiculous,' I replied. 'David, you'd better not be high.'

He laughed and rubbed his hand back and forth across his brow.

'What are you, my—? Oh but my actual mother wouldn't nag me about this on my fortieth birthday, would she, Nance?'

'I have a fourteen-year-old daughter around here somewhere.'

'Which has nothing to do with it.'

'But you hardly set an example, do you? She loves you. She looks up to you.'

'Righto,' he said.

'Don't be so glib.'

'You don't be so smug,' he said. 'Nice view from up there, is it, Nance? On the high ground. Your favourite spot.'

'Oh fuck off, David.'

'Cos I can see pretty clearly from down here too,' he replied and gave a wink, unfocused and lewd, launching a little dart of fear. He leant to my ear.

'Look at you, blooming in your new frock. The benevolent hostess. Enjoying yourself?'

'It's not my party. It's yours.'

'You can't bullshit me,' he said. 'I know you far too well.'

'I've no idea what you're talking about.'

'Oh lighten up,' he said. 'Come on. Come with me. Have a line. Just a little one. Like old times.'

'Don't be stupid.'

'Your husband never need know. It can be one of our secrets.' He tapped his nose. This close his breath smelt oddly sweet.

'David,' I said and but I wanted to appease him now. See that dangerous look drop off his face. 'Don't let's fight. It's your birthday. Don't you like the party? Aren't you enjoying yourself?'

But he wasn't listening any more. Adam had joined Tara under the light of a faux Victorian sconce. She acknowledged him with a brief, warm look.

'Ah,' said David. 'Interesting. Is that the wife?'

Later and the party eased. Most were drunk. The band played 'Nine to Five' and everybody danced. Jake skidded about, enjoying the crush. Aunty April and Pete moved carefully, looking down at their feet and visibly counting. They went, the two of them, every Wednesday, to a class in Dorking. They'd made a lot of new friends. Then the next song began and Stef, who been twisting at the fringes with Lou, tapped Pete's shoulder, who stepped aside, and took April in his arms in a show of gallantry. He swung her around easily, her hair lifting and her face raised with a look like a child on fairground ride. I stepped back to avoid them. The football team were in amongst it somewhere and even Mum swayed gamely on the edges of the floor. David and Alice were catching up, at last, and I watched them for a while. They had slipped back into their old opposition, her a little too together, him smiling and avoidant. At last, Adam came to me. He was pissed, I could see that; the booze subtly altering the contours of his face.

'I've been trying to get to you for hours,' he said. 'Come over here. Where it's quieter.'

'OK,' I replied.

'Follow me,' he said. 'We can stand next to the bar.'

This side of the room felt like later, scuffed and askew. A barmaid texted and ignored a rash of empties. We stood side by side, facing back out into the room. I love him best in profile; though he is not at his most handsome, he seems at his most true. I like to see the workings of him, the hop in his throat that gives away too much. The little hairless square under his chin.

'I'm warm,' said Adam. He shrugged off his jacket and laid it in the crook of an elbow, folding his other arm beneath.

'That's a beautiful dress,' he said.

'Thank you,' I replied.

'A little closer, Nancy, please,' he said. 'Just a step.' He was near enough, now, that the nap of his jacket caught on the sheen of my sleeve.

I first felt the brush of his nails against my arm. A light stroke, back and forth; its effect was narcotic, out of all proportion. My perception shrank to that narrow little panel of flesh. I shifted, and he adjusted his touch. He caught the edge of my breast and there was the gentle press, through silk, of his knuckles, one by one.

'Laugh, Nancy,' he said. 'Pretend I've just told you the funniest thing you ever heard,' and I did, I threw back my head and laughed, too high, too long, as though I'd never stop.

Then, with the heat from all the dancing, Skyler's streamers began to drop, one by one with a slow motion beauty, and then in a sudden flurry, like blossom. People aahed and where a few hung together, the little ones took the ends and danced the maypole in high skips. Skyler reached up and took my brother's face in her hands and the feeling of it passed through me like a shudder and I thought, if he turned to me, if Adam dipped his face to mine and kissed me, it would be worth everything that followed. Tara was coming, now, with a mellow smile, and he didn't stop, nor did I move. I simply waited for her to reach us, stupefied by her husband's touch.

'Hi guys,' she said. 'Nancy, I want to tell you, your daughter is an amazing girl.'

I nodded and she went on to tell me why. Her talent, her commitment, her good sense, didn't I find? I told her that I did.

'And I've just had a chat with your mother, too. What a lady.'

'Do you think?'

'Of course. She was telling me about her work. So inspiring. Such energy!' and I could have asked: What work? The art she makes in her upstairs room? Or the stuff at the women's refuge she does every now and again, although she talks about it more? But I said nothing, dazed at Adam's hand. And then Madeline was there, with a careful look and her teacher's tone.

'She's fine, OK, Nancy. I don't want you to panic, but Frieda's in the toilets chucking up. She's just a bit pissed. That's all.'

'Oh no,' said Tara, in distress, in astonishment. 'Are you sure? She seemed so— Oh dear.'

Frieda was finished when I got there, limp but coherent.

'I'm all right, Mum,' she said, pale and glistening. 'I just need to sleep.'

'I'll take you home,' I said, and sent Mads for Stefan and the kids. The band was doing 'Do You Love Me?' but little could be heard of it over the bawl of the crowd.

'Can you tell Mum and Dad we're going?' I asked her, when she was back.

'Yeah I will,' she said and then grabbed my shoulder and whispered boozily: 'What about the bill though, Nance? I was just behind the bar, and the tab ran out hours ago.'

'It's fine,' I said. 'Get them to put it all through on my card.'

The cab journey was quiet. Frieda sat between us, eyes closed, a victim to every kink in the road. Lou and Jake, opposite, were alert and fearful, their gazes on their sister.

'Is she ill?' one of them asked.

'She's fine,' I replied.

'Is she in trouble?'

'No she's not.'

I slept on her floor with a bucket, on the mattress in a bag she used for sleepovers. Unrolled, it bore the traces of her most recent midnight feast: shards of softened Walkers and a Haribo packet with a cola bottle glued to the side. The sheet hadn't been washed and it smelled of girl; some other girl than mine. There were no posters on her wall but logos of bands instead, names I'd heard of but couldn't place. From my vantage point I saw a lighter under a drawer and prayed it was just for the candles she so loved, fragranced in Paris, hand set in blasted glass, costing weeks' worth of chores. I thought of Adam, raising his dented Zippo, illuminating his face. My mattress lay close to her window and I listened. London outside sounded like threat, brakes pressed too late, wild animals, unaccompanied girls. I fell asleep full of the dangers of the world.

10

Marie had a new haircut, razored short into the sides. It surprised me.

'Wow. Your hair looks great,' I said as she came in.

'Thanks,' she replied with a slow full smile. She sat. I let her organise her things.

'How was your week, Marie?' I asked, when she was ready.

'It was fine,' she said.

'That's good. Is there anything you'd like to begin with this morning?' I asked. 'Anything that you've been thinking about, or noticed perhaps?'

'Not really,' she said. 'No.' Her knees gave a brief skitter.

'Then shall we talk about the homework? Did you get the chance to take a look?'

Frieda had been fine the previous day, not even ill. Stef cuffed her gently as she ate a large breakfast.

'One of those things,' he said but she dipped her face, not ready to laugh.

'Mummy, was Frieda drunk last night?' Lou asked.

'Well, she is nearly fifteen,' Jake said.

'Don't be so silly, you two.'

'What will Grandpa think?' said Frieda.

'I doubt he even noticed. Or I can tell him you had a bug,' I said. 'No harm done. Forget it.'

I missed Dad's call that morning and my brother's too. When I saw David's number again, Stef said: 'We're eating. Can't it wait?' and I let it ring out.

'I made a copy for you this time,' Marie said, and passed me the sheet. I was feeling worse than the day before. Too much food and sleep.

'How did you find the exercise?' I said. I looked at the page. I know the shapes. It was to be resistance then.

She touched her new hair lightly. 'Fine. I mean, I've done it, but I'm not sure it's going to be very helpful.'

'Why's that?' I said.

'Well, my answers are all noes. Except for when a no is wanted. Then it's yes.'

I nodded and then corrected her.

'I can see why it might seem that way, but there are no right or wrong answers here,' I said. 'Your responses are completely valid, whatever they are.'

She glanced down at her notes and back. Marie hates to lose eye-contact.

'It's just there's not a whole lot to talk about. My parents didn't do these things, or make me feel like any of this,' she said.

She dropped a finger to her page.

'And the other stuff I can't remember. What they said if I got angry. When I cried. It was all too long ago.'

'So there were no difficulties, at all, growing up, that you recall?'

'We were normal,' she said.

'And what's that?' I replied, with a tiny smile.

'Just normal.'

'You're lucky, then. And in the minority.'

I took a pause, but I had found what I needed.

'One observation,' I said. 'There seems to be very little emotion here.'

I held up the sheet. She moved her hand across to her bag.

'What do you mean?' she said.

'No anger or conflict. That's quite unusual. Especially during the teenage years.'

'That's how I remember it.'

'Yes, I'm sure. You can find that in some families certain feelings are disallowed.'

'I don't recognise that.'

'You might well not. Where emotion is discouraged, we can bury it very deep.'

She recrossed her legs and her shoe dropped away from the sole of her foot, though she snapped it back quickly.

'But these things have a tendency to resurface, Marie. Sometimes many years later and in very different forms.'

'Don't try and fit me in that box,' she said.

'I wouldn't,' I replied. 'I'm not. Can I put something to you?'

'If you like,' she said.

'You strike me as a classic good girl. Hard worker, loyal friend and so on. Does that sound about right?'

'Are you telling me that's bad?'

'Not at all. It's just that such a role can be confining. It's much harder to throw off approval than ambivalence, or criticism,' I said.

'Why would I want to throw it off?' she replied.

To live, I thought. To find out who you are.

'Perhaps you wouldn't,' I said lightly; 'it's simply about understanding the roles we find ourselves in. And knowing there are ways to break free of them, if we so choose.'

She shut her book with a crack.

'I don't recognise any of that,' she said again.

'That's fine,' I replied. 'Let's move on.'

A family is nothing but a collective idea, sustained by belief. If conviction fails, the family becomes fragile. It can unravel fast.

When the new baby comes we will be complete. So spoke my mother – a common enough phrase – but with that sentence, the planet listed and I realised that we were makeshift, partial. I grabbed for David. I told him how it was and he listened seriously and suggested we make a chart to count our sister down. Now a parent myself, I take care with the words I choose.

A day or two shy of spring, Mads was born and we breathed out, but it didn't make us whole; we loosened instead. She cried, with croup, it must have been, for several hours each day, and David and I would tear through the rooms, roaring till her sound seemed distant and tiny, delirious with the abandon of it. When we were done, we lay star-shaped on the floor, listening to our children's hearts bang; me, at least, too old for it at nearly thirteen. One time, Mum came after us, the baby bucking in her arms and yelled:

'Stop this now or I swear to God I will completely lose my mind.'

We spent half an hour straightening things and pulled her away from the radio, where she sat, very close, to show her what we'd done, but her face was jammed and she said: 'Yes, but who do you think does this every other time you make that mess?'

David ran and cried in the bottom of the airing cupboard; a favourite spot. 'Leave that door ajar, David. You'll kill yourself in there, one of these days,' she called.

Space opened up in the family which felt, for a while, like freedom. We took money from her purse and she didn't notice. We tried to learn to smoke. And all the time Mum was changing, though David claimed he couldn't see it. She began to take less care. Her accent narrowed and refined. Dad crept into the house each afternoon, looking room to room as though he was frightened of what he might find, something totally changed, like the scientist who turned into a fly. There were no rows, just a thickening silence and a terrible change in habits. Routine moors us; the first Sunday lunch without Dad was irregular, the next, catastrophic. David and I gave ourselves secret names and tried to build something separate. Dad lasted until Christmas.

Marie's idea of her past was holding, but there will be a chink; she wouldn't be here if there wasn't. I ran my hand over her life to feel for it; it is my job and the therapeutic hour that she pays for leaves ten minutes at the end for just this. I will find the trail that keeps taking her back and send out my birds to eat those breadcrumbs up. Adam slipped a note under my door: *Four days XXX*, it read, but I couldn't wait and I went to him.

11

I had cried, first time, with Adam, and he let me, his nose deep in my hair. I'd expected it, or similar. It was not the shock of a clichéd act in an ugly room, our empty clothes a rebuke to us; nothing like that, though some of the details suggested that scene. My things, yes, they were scattered; we were not so old and polite as to have folded them. From where I lay, I could see my bra hanging oddly from the arm of a French grey valet stand, still curved at the bust as though it held somebody else's breasts. My trousers, on the floor, were hinged at the knee, like the chalk outline of a corpse after a long fast drop. The side of my face was soaked and my cheek slipped off my arm onto the hotel linen, thinned to reveal the pillowy diamonds of the mattress protector beneath.

'Are you OK?' he asked.

'We have no concierge,' the receptionist had told us proudly, as we bumped our cases up the warped stairs behind her. I wondered what she saw; our two separate bags for one night, mismatched, clearly hailing from different homes. She unlocked the door with a key on a huge silk-tasselled fob. 'What do you think?' she asked, with confidence. She didn't come in; there was nothing inside that needed demonstrating.

We circled the room separately to ease those first moments alone. The original window stuck briefly as I shoved it and left a splinter deep in my thumb but it didn't seem the moment to make a fuss. Behind me, he shut and opened cupboards, then exclaimed.

'Nancy, come and look at these.'

The top drawer had been lined with thick tracing paper and on it were pencil sketches. I saw woodland creatures, pictured from above, perfectly anatomically correct. A fox, a rabbit, a hedgehog and a vole. I pulled the sheet out carefully – the drawings were faint – and held it up to the light.

'And here,' Adam said.

The next page showed wigs, or faceless hairdos, in every conceivable style. I found the one closest to mine, and his, and we laughed at them. I saw each of my children's too, and Stefan's, but none of that made any difference. On the last sheet was a range of kitchen cupboard staples, packs of spaghetti, tins and trays of eggs, stylised and retro.

'These are my favourites,' he said, and I felt his proximity.

I smoothed the sheets back inside the drawers. They had each been trimmed to size and fitted the wonky lines of each space perfectly. I pushed my finger into the corners to work them flush, taking my time.

When I straightened, Adam was beside me, leaning back against the dressing table, his weight in the heel of his hands and his feet crossed in those shoes I love, his scuffed brogues with the tubed leather laces. He looked at me sideways, across his beautiful worn profile.

'Do you suppose we should unpack?' he said.

'I don't think so.'

'We can talk, Nancy, you know. There are things that I can tell you. About this. Or how I feel,' he said.

'You've prepared a speech?' I asked.

'Well no,' he said and his smile cut a deep gully down from the side of his mouth, pulling his skin tighter across the bones of his cheeks. I thought how that ridge might feel, under my thumb, that moment so close now.

'Then let's have a drink,' I said.

'Good idea,' he replied and came over and kissed me.

'Do you need a tissue?' he asked, later. There were flowers on the bedside table; five or six stems arranged in a shrunken milk-bottle and a little heap of dropped stamens next to it. The air felt thick with pollen and I gave a deep phlegmy sneeze. His body as he crossed the room showed its age. His chest had a scoop out of its centre. His arse puckered at the point that it met his legs. He was hairy everywhere, to varying degrees and in many shades.

'Are you OK?' he asked again, when he came back, and slotted his fingers between mine.

'I am,' I told him. The pattern of his eyes, this close, was complex and perfect, like the twist of a child's kaleidoscope.

'Don't cry any more,' he said.

'I won't.'

It wasn't regret, or sadness, or shame. The feeling bore some relation to those hours after I had given birth. I had the idea that I'd crossed a great space, everything changed on this, the far side. There would only be before and after, now. I felt humble and tiny and thankful. He made us tea.

When we left, I asked about the drawings at reception and she said it was the work of the owners' daughter.

'Did you get a dirty one?' she asked with a snigger. I told her no. 'Oh right,' she said. 'They can sometimes be a bit rude.'

I wondered, did the artist sell them? 'It's just a hobby,' the woman replied. 'She's only something like twelve.' I thought then, that I had seen the child, if it was she who whipped a croissant at breakfast without pausing to sit down.

When I unpacked, at home, melancholy but focused, I found that Adam had folded one of the pages in the bottom of my bag. I used it to line my own drawer; Louisa sniffed it out within the week. And so began what passes for tradition in a love like ours. The exchange of unlikely gifts, innocuous-seeming tokens we can keep close, carry in plain sight. The blouse. A poem that he found after I told him I'd never read one that felt real. Dishonest little items that I let my children exclaim upon, turn over in their hot greedy hands. I take a pleasure in their enjoyment. I deny the risk and bask in the lie that these trinkets tell, that I – we – are still whole.

12

I got home to the dog waiting anxiously at the door and a woman's voice in the kitchen. Skyler, out of control, was disconcerting. She hadn't lined her eyes with their usual charcoal sweep and through an unplanned parting at the back of her head I saw tight twists of hair in odd, neat rows. She sat with Stef at the long table.

'Where's David?' I said, a little parcel of anxiety unwrapping in my mind.

'He's gone,' she replied.

'Gone where?'

'Fucked off.'

'Ah.' I bent down to hug her, though she didn't respond. She smelled of stress sweat and old booze.

'Have you got a tea?' I asked, though they both had full cups. 'I'll get myself a tea,' I said.

Across the kitchen, I heard her voice start up but it was obscured by the blast of the hot water tap. When I came back, she looked down into her mug and swam the bag around by its string.

'What happened?' I asked.

'Nothing,' she replied, like the kids, after a breakage. There was a hole in the thigh of her leggings.

'When did he leave?' I said.

'Sometime while I was asleep. I got up and he was gone.'

She dug a nail into a groove in the table.

'So yesterday?' I said.

'Yes, yesterday. I woke about eleven and he wasn't there. I called him but it went to voicemail.'

'Shit,' I said and felt for my phone. She muttered something but her head was low and I couldn't make it out. Stef put a hand on her arm and gave me his signature look, counselling caution, time and tact.

'Did you speak to him, Nancy?' she asked.

'No. I missed the calls.'

Skyler looked up. She had tiny features, the sharp appeal of a fox. I had felt her dislike and the edge of competition in the way she puffed out her lip if I touched him, the sentences she began with: 'You know, the thing is about David—' I allowed it. Still, I felt she could be cruel.

'I'm sorry, Skyler, I really am, but you should know, this is not the first time.'

David is a master of retreat. You can see on his face when he has had enough; of the game, the conversation, the night. His eyes slide, his knee begins to jangle.

'What do you mean?' she asked.

'Well, he leaves. It's what does. He goes for weeks, or sometimes months, and when he's had enough of wherever he's been, he comes back.'

He fixed a lock on his bedroom when he was twelve. 'Talk to me, David, please,' I'd shout, through the door. 'Just tell me what I've done,' but he was immune to my need.

'Leave him alone, Nancy,' Mum said. 'Give him his privacy, for heaven's sake. We're not all like you.'

I watched Skyler processing this news; the scud of various emotions pass over her face.

'Why didn't anyone tell me?' she said in the end.

'Well, it's not as if we are all exactly—' but Stef touched my arm and I stopped.

'He hasn't done it for years, Skyler,' he said. 'Not since I've known him, at least. I guess everybody hoped that the last time was— That, really. The last time.'

She nodded, her chin on her fists, her elbows splayed.

'Look, he may very well be back,' Stef said. 'It's only been a day. Do you think—? Was there anything at the party?'

'He was pretty out of it,' I said. 'If that's what you're asking.'

'Oh hardly,' Skyler said, with a short, dry laugh. 'That was not a big night, believe me.' She tipped her head and looked at me curiously. 'He's not the boy you see, you know, Nancy.'

On her thumb I saw a ring that I had given him. He didn't like to travel and for years I bought him something from each trip. This was Rhodes, early nineties. On Skyler's tiny finger, the dolphin's nose and tail were hopelessly overlapped. She saw me looking and tucked her hand into the other palm with a locked smile.

'What, the one who got his stomach pumped at age fourteen? He did rehab a long time before it was considered an interesting choice, Skyler.'

I saw a brief shading of doubt and tried not to take gladness from it.

'Look. This isn't helping,' said Stef. 'I guess— You know, forty can be a big thing. The party, perhaps—'

'The party?' I said. 'You can't seriously be suggesting—'

'I'm not suggesting anything, Nancy. I'm simply trying to understand.'

'The party,' Skyler scoffed, 'Oh yes. Your stupid party.'

'Hold on,' I said. 'He took a bag.'

'What?' said Skyler.

'When he came here last week. From the cellar. He took an old bag.'

'I wouldn't read too much into that . . .' Stef said, but Skyler dropped a shoulder and began to weep and I, too, felt the beginnings of a familiar hurt. She pressed her forehead gently to the table and Stefan left his chair to crouch down by her.

'Do you think there's someone else?' he asked me, later, in bed. I was reading a textbook for next day in a ghastly Americanised prose.

'No. Why would there be? He would just dump her if there was. It's not as if they've got all this.' I drew a few loose circles in the air to indicate our connectedness. Implicated and dependent.

'Could he be depressed?' Stef said.

'It was discounted years ago.'

He turned onto his side and pushed up on an elbow, his cheek resting in the palm of his hand.

'Don't worry, Nance,' he said.

'Look, I'm fine,' I replied. 'If you need to sleep.'

He ran his hand up my arm, his nails flat like tiny spades.

'It's OK,' I said. 'I have to read.'

Stef pulled on his eye mask and was instantly quiet, but for the odd little trill and shudder. I looked over the top of my book and thought of David. That time, when we were teenagers, that he almost got us killed.

He had come to Nottingham at the end of my first year, arriving in someone's mum's old Volvo and re-contextualising me instantly with his subtle London edge and the assurance of a wage, a fold of notes he'd earned on a building site packing out a back pocket of his jeans. The sight of him, an anomaly in the student bar, made me laugh out loud and I wondered why I'd kept him away for so long.

We were up late in the kitchen of my halls, my flatmates talking while he watched and smiled, when a boy I'd never seen before came to the door and said someone across town had mushrooms, did anybody have a car?

David grinned like the Joker and waited, testing me out; daring me to forbid him, to expose myself as lame. The other girls were silent, shoulders up, hands clamped between their knees.

'Well?' the boy said. 'Anyone?'

'I don't,' Vicky replied, at last.

'All right. Just asking,' he said, confused by the atmosphere, and had turned to go when David called:

'I can drive, mate.'

That the boy was midway through a long night was clear. He looked fluey; his hair clumped and crunchy where he had sweated and then let it dry.

'Look, I don't know how much he's got,' he said, earnestly, 'but we can split it, if you like?'

'Don't worry. I'll take you,' David said. 'Anyone else?'

Vicky, who I still talk to, said no, which left Anna and Kate. Anna was tough and cool, with a stud in her nose and ugly clothes; Kate, all gloss and a crazy streak. He had the pick of them – the tone of the evening had made that clear – but preferred to leave it to chance. He is a believer, David, in all sorts of things. Mulder to my Scully.

'I'll come,' I said.

David smiled up at the ceiling.

'Come on then, sis.'

He swung the keys around his finger.

'Should we wait up?' Kate asked.

'Why not?' he said.

The car was huge and smelt of dog and David's homemade bong. In the footwell I found a swimming bag with a name embroidered on it. Charlie Holmes.

'Travel sweet?' he said.

'I'm Daz, by the way,' called the boy from the back.

'Where to, Daz?' he said.

'Right at the main road. Five minutes, mate. Tops.'

I usually took the bus to college, travelling slow along the ordained lane. That night, waiting to pull across the road, in a car, more stoned than pissed, I saw that the traffic was fast. I tried to process the scene; get a feel for speed and distance, but the lights had tails like comets and space had become elastic. Our own car gave a tinny little shiver every time something big passed by.

'You hear that? The way the noise of each car gets higher as it comes close? That's the Doppler Effect,' Daz said. 'By day I'm a physics—'

'Shh,' said David. He turned the music down.

'We could just turn left, you know, and go round the roundabout,' I said.

'It's fine,' he replied. 'Hold on.'

David pressed his foot down on the pedal, I saw his leg brace. The engine rose, but time seemed to lag. When we moved, though, we moved fast, with a shriek and a kick out at the back.

'Whoa,' said Daz, catching a handful of my hair as he grabbed for the headrest.

There was no chance of stopping in the space between the lanes, though when David turned right, hard, there was a second inside all the movement that felt like stasis. Then we were off up the road, the two boys whooping.

'Christ,' said Daz, 'I'm flying!'

David laughed and laughed until Daz was impelled to say: 'Share the joke, mate.'

I held the sides of my seat. My heart banged and clamoured.

'David,' I said. 'I think the man in the car next door is trying to tell us something. He's wound his window down.'

'I need to drive,' he said.

'Pull forward, I'll see what he wants,' said Daz. He gave a thumbs up to the driver, still buzzing. 'Open the window, will you? It's child-locked.'

Air boomed around the car. My ears popped.

'It was an accident, mate,' I heard Daz shout. 'No harm done.'

I looked across. The man, with his arm stretched out in the space between us, wanked the air slowly and pulled a little nearer.

He followed us for twenty minutes or so, sometimes behind but when space allowed, alongside; close. He caught the wing mirror at one point and all three of us screamed. I saw the driver laugh then, mouth wide, before he finally took his turning home.

When we arrived at the address of the guy with the mushrooms, we were too late. Back at mine, David and Anna shagged noisily in the bedroom next door. He had gone when I got up; left a note, this time. *Thanks for an ace weekend, sis. Need to get the car home. Love you. xxx.* He never visited again.

I have shared this tale many times across the years.

'You should not have been driving in that state,' Mads said, when I first told her.

'Oh well. We lived,' I replied.

David raised an eyebrow at one of us.

I've held it up time and again, in demonstration of us, a snapshot of personality, a shorthand for our relationship, of the way we two intersect. It always gets a laugh, though I think sometimes I hear a high note of shock as well. I imagine people taking it home, chewing it over in dark bedrooms before they sleep and thinking they find things in it that I didn't intend. It is exposing, yes, and not without kink. Neither one of us comes out particularly well.

Yet I approve this version, in all its love and spite. Is it honest? Events unfurled exactly as I describe.

13

I took to watching Frieda. I trailed her, like a lovelorn boy or the world's worst spy. She noted it; she would raise those thatches of clotted lash and pitch them in my direction but when they reached me, I didn't know what to say, and she saw this, and swivelled them back.

I formed the impression that she was sad; something in the bow of her shoulder, the dip of her head – she looked like a girl who bore a weight – and then I lifted her bag and found she did. The laptop and a tablet and any number of borrowed books. Delighted by a problem I could solve (a second bag, on the other arm, to even the load), I went to her.

She stood against her bedroom window in a reflective skater skirt and a tight sheen top, an outfit whose proportions made no sense to me. The skirt sat way above her waist and the vest – or perhaps it was a leotard, it ran so smoothly under her waistband – had a high neck that met her chin, and deep-cut armholes exposing an odd view of side-rib. She wore jelly shoes of the sort we would have used on pebbly beaches, updated with a chunk of neon heel. Her legs looked cast from a mould; smooth, blemish-free and hairless since the day she turned eleven and begged me to show her how to shave. Next, the tang of Immac in her room and the tangle of furred wax strips stuck to the bottom of her bin. Now, she runs her hands up and down her calves in absent moments, feeling out any prickle of missed hair. 'Oh hi,' she said and raised her phone at arm's length with a face we've all seen before in a thousand magazines.

She clicked, and checked her screen, pressed a sequence of keys and said: 'What?' No grudge in it.

'Nothing,' I said. 'Oh yes, your bag's too heavy. Come sit with me. We'll buy you another off the internet.'

She took off her clothes. Her skin glittered and smelled of bubblegum from the body cream she liked, but I could still see traces of her baby self. The abrupt cut of her forehead into her hairline. Something in the angles of her when she bent forward to step out of her skirt. I wondered if these were essentials or whether I'd look across one time and they'd be gone. Her pants sagged and said the wrong day of the week; they were old childhood to the pristine white of her bra which she briefly admired, looking down at herself. She slipped a thumb under one strap and adjusted it needlessly.

'Or some underwear?' I said. 'You could do with an update.'

She laughed at me, quite fondly, and pulled her onesie up and over each shoulder; her favourite one, the one with the ears. Her phone pinged on the bed and what she read there made her shout out a laugh and I saw that whatever was happening in the space beyond her handset was real to Free, not this thing that I tried to bring back to life each night after a long day's work, this notion of family with its meals around the table, gobbled up before I'd had the chance to sit, and the chalk-board cupboard-fronts, one for each child, lagging with out-of-date appointments. Christmas cards signed *Love the Jansens XXX* as if we were a collective noun.

'I'm busy, Mum,' she said. 'And I don't need another bag. Thanks.'

Her plume of fringe had been knocked askew when she pulled off her top. She saw me notice and raised her hands to it and adjusted the clips behind the swell of hair. When she dropped her arms, it stayed put, meshed and lacquered, looking for the life of her like some Southern debutante's drunk mother. Then she watched me patiently until her look drove me out of her room. 'Shut the door, Mum,' she called, and when I went back to do it, she had turned away too, to get on with – what?

'Don't you think that she seems secretive?' I asked Stefan, later. We had eaten moussaka which she asked for, now, instead of spaghetti bolognese, which I saw was to do with carbs but indulged, nonetheless. She ate with too much care. I saw her ease her aubergine out of its custardy cast with the tip of her knife and the way she moved the mince up the rim of the plate to drain the meat's fat. I had cooked Jake penne so he could, to some degree, recreate the old dish. Lou ate what she was given and barely seemed to notice.

'It's not that, Nance,' he said. 'She just lives in her phone. That's how they are,' which was true; it was always there, before her on the table, or if she sensed my mood, on her lap, heating up a little strip on her thigh. It rarely made it to her pocket; when she walked, it rested in the claw of her grip.

On Wednesday, when David still wasn't back, I called the family.

'You what, love?' Dad said, as though he hadn't heard; a new habit. The world was becoming confusing to him, speeding up, spinning off, while he slowed and narrowed. He was coping, for now. He had his strategies. We gave him space.

I said it again.

'Can't the girlfriend help? Whatshername. Have you asked? There must have been a row,' he said, cleaving to his view of things.

'Well.' He blew out hard when he understood.

'I'm putting the phone down now, Dad,' I said.

'Will I be seeing you next week, love?' he asked.

I texted Justine later to get him to tell Aunty April.

Madeline cried, straight away. Kitten, we used to call her when she was born. Her sounds were weak and tiny and made us cruel.

'Mads,' I said, her sobbing low but persistent. 'Come on. I need to get off the phone and call Mum.'

'Do you think he'll come back?' she asked.

'How would I know?' I said. 'He usually does.'

~

Mum took a long time to answer and I felt angry as I waited, as though she were deliberately evading me. When I heard her voice, though, I told myself to go easy. She sounded paper thin.

'Hello, dear, how are things?' she asked.

I could see her, standing at the window of her cottage, paint down her front, an undertow of turps and the paraffin cream she used to stop her hands from cracking.

'David's gone. He's left again.'

She was quiet on the line. My impatience rose.

'Are you still there, Mum?' I said.

'I am. Yes. Well. I hope he's keeping himself safe,' she said, at last.

'Is that all you've got to say?'

'I imagine he needs some space,' she said.

'And that's OK?'

'I don't know what you mean, Nancy.'

'What about the rest of us?'

'Well if you mean Skyler, I suppose it must be hard. But to be honest I'm not sure—'

'Not Skyler. Us. The family.'

'Well, I don't see what anyone can do other than wait.'

I left him messages. *David. She tells me you've gone. What the fuck?* I think the first one ran. He may have laughed at that, if he listened to it; at its sweet familiarity, our relationship encoded in my tone. 'I'm Nancy-proof,' he started to say, at about thirteen and it was true, from then he simply shrugged me off. I tried his number again when I got off the phone from Mum, sitting out on the sofa in reception after everyone else had left, a radiator ticking evenly. But this time it didn't even ring and I imagined him stepping out along a sunny pavement, chucking his mobile behind him in a careless loop that somehow found the bin. He is like a cat, my brother, always falling on his feet. I saw him at night, slinking, stealing the best bits out of bins and bathing in the moon. His cold nose on a suburban patio door as he peeped into over-lit rooms and then he was off, up and over the wall. I was jealous of him then.

That evening, I snatched Free's phone. My arm moved suddenly, before I'd acknowledged any sort of decision. Her screen clattered against my rings, the handset was wider and thinner than mine and my grip was slippery – I was sweating, already, in response to my act – I nearly launched the thing straight back at her. It came to life in the struggle, lit up in my palm, but I didn't dare look down. Instead I held it, weakly, in the space between us and watched her watching me, like the dog will if another comes for its stick, waiting for the opponent's move.

'I think we should limit screen time, that's all,' I said and handed it to her in a pathetic reversal. She took it wordlessly and turned away. I should have said sorry but my frustration and the fact that I have to feel all of her pain, real and imagined, forever, and in technicolour, when I'd learnt, years ago, how to swallow my own, had contorted into rage.

I logged on to the school website to check her grades, plotted on a graph with their new software. There was the dip they'd talked about, and a steady climb back from that point. Weekly data from various tests and observations. So much work these poor kids have to do. I called the teacher again who had nothing to add. And so I watched her, and she bore it, though it added to her load.

The others saw. There was Louisa at my elbow, with a question or a story she had written, something or other that she wanted me to see. A scruffy effort, when I turned to it, knocked up with no other aim than to distract me. I knew to set my face to interested, a lesson learnt in the earlier parenting years, but my youngest was too shrewd and she heard my deceit. I nearly asked her: 'What is it you want? What can I give to you that will ever be enough?' but hid the thought inside a brief stiff hug which she succumbed to, eyes closed.

On Thursday Stefan spoke to me. I found him at the sink rinsing mud from Jake's trainers, turning the soles carefully in a thin coil of water.

'Hi,' he said. 'I'm glad you're here. I wanted to have a word.'

He propped the shoes up against a windowsill. A blast of bleak sudden sunlight forced me to move.

'How are you?' he asked.

'Fine thanks,' I replied. 'How are you?'

'Look I know this isn't easy,' he said. 'This business with David.'

I saw him think to come closer and change his mind. I felt for the island behind me.

'I'm OK,' I replied.

'I realise it's complicated,' he went on. 'I'm trying my best to understand.'

My husband's family are a neat and forthright four who live two hours away by plane. 'Thank you for this,' his father said, that first Christmas they visited, when he opened my gift. 'It's beautiful but I can't wear it. Long fibres, see?' He gave a large moist sneeze and handed it back. 'I'll have it,' said his sister and took it from my outstretched hand. 'Yeah. This will look good on me,' she said, holding it against her chest. She wore it for the rest of the week. 'Hey,' she said, on the last night, 'is your dress meant to look like that, or has it got rucked up?' 'That is the design,' I replied. 'Oh right. I see. Nice,' she said. 'I like it.'

'I'm fine, Stefan,' I said. 'He does this. It's happened before.'

Upstairs, a child knocked tentatively on another's door. 'What?' Free yelled. 'Let me in and I'll tell you,' came Louisa's cool reply. I heard the lock go.

'Are you though?' Stefan asked.

I turned back to the kitchen. Cleared a surface. Stacked a mug.

'You seem stressed.' he said. 'And if it isn't David, then—?'

He watched me, his legs folded neatly at the ankle. He wore the slippers I had bought him, a lovely pair of sheepskin scuffs.

'Oh Stefan, where's the problem?' I said. I tried to accelerate it. I wanted it done. 'I'm busy. I'm tired. That's all.'

'Maybe I can help,' he said. 'If you talk to me.' His look was long and narrow. 'But I can't if you won't.'

I felt a little squall of panic.

'Well I do miss David,' I said, in a rush. 'I mean, inevitably. And there's Frieda—'

'Are you guys fighting?' said Lou, from the doorway, in the funny sing-song voice she used to hide behind.

'We're just talking, sweetheart,' I said.

'Well, can you stop it, please, it upsets the dog.'

She dragged him in as evidence, doleful and splay-legged.

'Let him go, Louisa,' I said. 'I don't think he's enjoying that.'

She looked between us, trying to read the scene. Gauge the nature and scale of the problem. I had done the same, as a child. I thought of telling her that what we were doing was normal; that conflict is not wrong. Anger is a valid emotion.

'What's for dinner?' she said, in the end. Conforming to the easiest version.

'What do you fancy, honey? I could do a curry, if you like,' he said.

I listened for frustration; a thread of resentment or irritation, but I couldn't find it. She went to him.

'You can chop, if you like,' he said. 'How about that?'

She barged him, rubbed her head against his jumper till it fuzzed and he wrapped her in an arm, scratched her shoulder roughly where he reached it. This is what they do for comfort. I left them to it and the kitchen door swung shut behind me, save for one thin drop of light.

I paused in the hall and their natter picked up; Lou chirruping at her father, Stefan's grumble of reply. It was dim out there. I gripped the radiator, its thick bands of cast iron cold against my skin. Ahead, the TV blasted and Jake railed briefly against some injustice on his screen. Frieda, upstairs, was silent, though perhaps she crossed her room; I heard the low complaint of a floorboard.

I would have liked, at that point, to simply go. No drama; no need for flounce. Just pick up my bag from its place and go to Adam, feel the steady heat of his touch. Close my eyes against him for an hour or two. Instead I thought of a summer, years ago.

It was our final holiday as family, that last seaside afternoon. The tide out, a line of choppy glint at the edge of the horizon. Mum sleeping with Mads, newborn, beached on her front. Dad fighting the windbreak and David and I walking and walking until they were tiny behind us.

'Let's stop here,' he said, next to an inland shallow, scum-rimmed, full of low-nappied toddlers. 'It's just the right wetness. You start the castle. I'll dig a moat.'

I gave him a spade. He worked fast, and I worried for my fingers as he carved a square of ditch, trapping me in. I turned out my first bucket but the sand flopped like wet cement. David scooped it up and lobbed it into the pool of paddlers with a deep swallowed plash.

'Do you think they'll get divorced?' he said.

I pressed down into the sand and water rose in tiny bubbles around my fingers.

'I should think so,' I replied.

'What about us?'

'What about us?' I said.

The weather felt busy and malicious; the sun, just now, a thick column of heat. Everything slowed.

'What if they split us up?' he said.

'They can't,' I replied. He burrowed, still, intent.

'They can. They can do whatever they like.'

We filled two buckets, packed down hard, their handles strained and threatening to pop their sockets. Two perfect castles this time, and so we went for shells to stick along the walls; limpets, mussels, cockles, and a perfect auger, spiralled like a unicorn's horn. Then my favourite bit; everyone's favourite. David filled the bucket and sluiced water into our moat. It raced around to meet itself, thick and muscled, and just for a second the channel was filled, until the sand began to drink it up. We watched, crouching easily. He peeled a rind of grimy sand from beneath each nail.

'We could always run away,' he said.

The frame of his ribs was clear under his skin; a child, still, to my adolescent. I hated that distance. I wanted to yank him across that space.

'We could do it now,' he said.

I tried to find our parents. It was our things that placed them; the skew of the brolly, the buggy's wonky stance. David waited, flinching at the swoop of a fearless gull.

'No that's silly,' I said. A cloud crossed the sun and then

the sand came to life, shadows racing like speeded-up film. 'Let's wait and see.' I pushed up to my feet, but his face showed worry and I knew I had planted it there.

'It'll be OK,' I said. 'We've got each other. Always and forever.'

I don't know where I got it from but it sounded like poetry for that second. I snatched for his hand, slick and grainy.

'That is the gayest thing I ever heard,' he said and we laughed, then, until we tipped over onto the sand.

At bedtime, Frieda came to me. I heard her stop outside my room, her pause lifting my eyes up from my book.

'Mum,' she said in the doorway. 'There is one thing—'

'What's that, love?' I said, making a silent prayer that I could grant it.

She settled at the end of my bed. Her face, when she looked at me, was pure want.

'I've been meaning to ask—' she said.

'Fire away.'

'You know Tara?'

'You mean Adam's wife?'

'Yes. I was wondering. Can I see her, do you think? I mean, she said I could. When we met at the party. And I've spoken to her since—'

'You've spoken to her?' I said.

'She gave me her number. I wanted advice on a piece. But I do really need to show her.'

She brought her hands down onto my legs, gripping them tightly through the duvet.

'Please, Mum,' she said. 'I thought I'd better ask.' Her pen must have leaked for she left three smudged prints on the cotton.

'Yep, you're right, you really should be asking about going round to a strange adult's house.'

'But it's Adam—' she said.

'I'm aware of that, Frieda—'

'Nance,' said Stefan. He shut his laptop, pulled out an earbud, dropped onto his back. 'It's a good idea,' he said, up towards the ceiling. 'What is the possible harm?' His movement made me aware of the heat of the bed. I lifted the duvet and dropped a foot to the floor.

'Well, it's a bit of an imposition,' I said. 'That's the thing. I mean, they don't have kids of their own, so—'

'It's not. I know it's not,' Frieda said. 'She told me it's fine.' Her eyes were wide and glassy. 'She wants to help. She says that I'm talented—' and then she stopped, leaving that statement in the air, and it was clear that to object any further would be construed as a challenge to that analysis.

'You can go, all right?' said Stef. 'Done. It's fine.'

'Yeah, great, thanks,' said Free, and she was off.

'Stefan—' I said.

'Give her a break, Nancy.'

'OK, but you and I could perhaps have—'

'And give me a break, too,' he said. 'Leave it. And by the way, she told me earlier she wants a party for her birthday which I've said she can have. Here at home. We could do family first, I suppose, if that's what you want.'

'Good idea,' I said. 'Yes, let's do that. We can put faces to a few names,' but he had turned onto his side and resumed his viewing. Next door, her white noise machine began and above it I heard the lovely cadence of her voice as she rehearsed alone.

I had asked Adam near the beginning why they hadn't had children.

'It just didn't happen,' he said, and though it was crass, I went on: 'So you tried?'

'We did,' he said, his body cool and pale. He watched me seriously. 'But we never got pregnant.'

'Did you consider adoption, or any of the other routes?' I said. 'I mean, if it's OK for me to ask. Unless it's private.'

'Private?' he said. 'We're in bed. I love you,' and I wanted to allow that logic, but all the time we slept each night with someone else, there would be these huge unknowns between us. 'No. We just accepted it,' he said.

'Tara too?'

'Yes, of course,' he said.

'I see.' I don't know how I would have felt if he'd said it was his decision. That she had cried and begged but he wouldn't hear a word.

'We never saw a doctor or had any sort of intervention. We just got on,' he said. 'Is that hard for you to understand?' There is a scar, a line like a snip of white cotton, under his eye where as a boy he'd been bitten by a dog.

'No. Of course not,' I said, and that was a difficult moment, a hard knowledge to swallow. It was their kindness to each other, their serenity, the lack of blame – what a team – but most of all, the confidence they must have shared in believing that the two of them, alone, would be self-sustaining across these long mid-life years.

I tried to hold my face steady. He gave me his smile, mainlined to my heart. And I reminded myself that their optimism had been misplaced. That he was here, after all, with me.

14

Sitting up late in the corner of a Cambridge basement bar, feeling beautiful and tragic, a melancholic barman mixing cocktails and talking gin botanicals to a soundtrack of elevator jazz, I loved my lover, that night, for very many things. His curiosity and kindness as the sour boy talked, the way his Adam's apple jumped in that long ill-shaven neck, the cross of his legs on a high stool that pulled the same old trousers tight across the thin arc of his thigh. I spotted various signs of age and ill-attention, the hang-nail that he bothered as he talked, the spider nevus burst beneath one eye and the lone blue thread that trailed from a shirt sleeve which I had to pinch out after pulling it made things worse, and they moved me, every one. When I noticed where he'd tried, matched his shirt to his socks and the slick of creme in his hair that made it greasy, nothing more, I couldn't help but reach across and kiss him. I drank it up – all of this – that's how I knew I loved him, and it presented in me as this seismic desire. We could have gone to bed then; it was late and the promise of it passed between us in the grip of our fingers under the bar. I'd had enough to drink, a smear of elderflower at the back of my throat outliving the booze, but instead we ordered another. I'm not sure if it was his idea or mine.

'When can we do this again?' I said, feeling feverish and desperate.

'Whenever,' he replied. 'Name the day. And we've got all of tomorrow.'

'I know.'

'I have a slightly odd request,' he said. Two shallow dimples like arrow tips appeared at the side of his mouth. 'I don't know what you're going to think.'

'Go on,' I said, wanting him to ask something of me.

'How would you feel about meeting my mother?'

'You told your mother?' I said.

'I did. A while ago, actually.'

'Why?' I asked.

'Because I'm happy, and I knew it would make her happy, too.'

'And did it?'

'I think so,' he said.

'Were you unhappy before, then?' I asked.

'Of course I was,' he replied. 'Weren't you?' and I told him yes, though I wasn't sure this was true. There had been that time when we watched a film, the whole family crammed onto the sofa – uncomfortable, but no one willing to concede – and the love scene arrived and the hero took the woman's face in his hands and they kissed, the camera locked in close, the music swelling and I felt my eyes spring tears and I thought: 'That will never again be me. I will never again abandon myself to a kiss like that,' and I felt a grief, I don't deny it, but unhappy? No.

'You didn't strike me as unhappy,' I said, 'when we met. Met again, I mean. I never saw that.'

'Because I wasn't, when I was with you,' he said, and like a girl, his compliment thrilled me.

We were the only ones left. The barman ran a twist of tea towel around the inside of a glass. He switched the music to his choice.

'So,' Adam said. 'My mother.'

'Yes, of course,' I said, 'I will,' and I was excited, despite myself, at our progress through the protocols of courtship; in the abstract, at least. 'Won't that be difficult, though. Or odd?'

'I don't think so,' he said. 'And— I've got you something.'

'A present?'

'Well, yes.'

He handed me a box. Inside was a thin gold chain hung with a tiny oval pendant. I raised it on my fingertip and saw that it was engraved with the markings from his lighter, though the strokes were simpler. I thought of a teardrop this time.

'It's for when we're not together,' he said.

'It's beautiful,' I replied and I kissed him, but then there was a sound at the top of the stairs, the high calls and ragged step of the very drunk and we stopped, for, fact remained, we were doing something we shouldn't have been, and didn't want to get caught at it.

The staircase was made of steep, uneven stone. The white point of a shoe appeared, then a great ripple of opalescent satin and a bride stepped into the room.

134

Around her came two bridesmaids in draped lilac, eager for the bar, and finally the men.

'Watch out,' she said, as one of them stepped on the edge of her gown.

'Champagne, shall we? Or shots?' said the first girl and the barman adjusted his demeanour for her, a potentially single woman of a suitable age. He gave a little tug at the bottom of his waistcoat, took up a shaker for no reason.

'Hel, d'you want a shot?' the bridesmaid called, again.

'Fizz for me,' the bride replied. Her husband wore a blown rose buttonhole and a tie in the bridesmaids' shade. He took her round the waist and held her there while he thumbed the keyboard of his phone with his free hand. She waited, looking around her with an air of benevolent privilege.

'Can you turn the music up?' the second bridesmaid asked. Her hair was a mass of connected braids. 'We want to dance!' but the barman was more interested in the friend, so she span off into the middle of the room, calling out little phrases of the song when she knew them. A man with a full beard and a rubber ring of fat around his middle turned a long low twist in front of her, up and down he went, moving his hands to his thighs, after a while, with the strain of it. The girl whooped and the bride watched on, while her husband texted.

'Is anyone going to help me with these drinks,' the woman at the bar called out. The last man in the group came over. He nodded at Adam.

'How was the day?' Adam asked.

'Decent, all in all,' the man replied. He gave the matter

more thought. 'Yeah. Good turnout. I'm the best man,' he said. 'And the brother.'

The cork popped and everyone turned to the noise. The barman smiled down at the bottle, aslant in its tea towel.

'Can we offer you a drink?' the bride called across to us suddenly. 'I can see we're interrupting,' she said, with a kittenish look.

'That would be lovely,' Adam replied – I don't know why – good manners, perhaps. The barman reached for two more glasses and kept his next pour short.

'In fact, let us,' Adam said. 'Another bottle, please. Congratulations to you both.'

We raised our glasses and the bride approached. She pulled her dress to the side and sat on a stool, her legs lost in the wedge of ruched material.

'Cheers,' she said. 'Thanks for that.' She bent a little towards us, and said, in a whisper: 'So, does it change things then?'

I looked at her stupidly.

'Being married,' she said. She nodded at my hand which lay on his thigh. I wore a Tiffany engagement ring that Stefan had chosen, and a platinum band. I felt a little thrill at her mistake.

'I know I feel different,' she told us, 'already. At least I think I do.' Her stare was fixed but lazy and I'd seen that look on David and wondered if she was high.

'Oh, I'm not sure. What would you say, darling?' I said, in a playful voice. I dropped my cheek onto his shoulder and rubbed my face there, in the gap beneath his jaw. I smelt warm skin, tobacco, day-old hair. Somewhere under the booze, it seemed funny, a game, at the least; perhaps more.

'Go on,' she said, leaning closer. Her chest and arms twinkled with some reflective cream or powder. Her teeth were scrubbed and even, as pearly as her gown. 'Tell us your secret.' She lifted her shoulders to relieve a pinch somewhere in the boning of the dress and a ledge of bust emerged above it.

Beside me Adam was unreadable and I found I didn't know how to reply. Her group had reassembled at the bar and the dancer mopped his beard with a napkin after the exertion of it and watched us. He whispered to the best man next to him.

'You're getting something right. I can see that much,' she said, and gave a sloppy wink and then a long, low, rather accomplished whistle. 'Share the wealth.'

'People either work or they don't,' Adam said flatly, in the end.

The bride looked disappointed.

'Oh right.'

'Helly,' one of the women called.

'What?' she said wildly, looking back over her shoulder, as far as the constraints of her dress would allow. When she turned to us, her expression was wiped clear. 'I probably better go.'

'Congratulations, anyway,' Adam said again.

'Yeah, thanks,' she replied, and slid off her stool.

'Let's drink up,' he said.

'What's the matter? We've got another half-bottle.'

'I want to leave,' he said.

'OK. Let me just go to the loo.'

As I passed, the one with the beard got up and something in his swagger and the way the others watched – covertly, so they thought, though they were far too pissed for that – made me hurry. When I got back, he stood with his arm around Adam, calling across to his friends with a wide-mouthed laugh. He yanked Adam closer, the sides of their bodies bumping, and I saw Adam resist.

'No need to take offence, mate!' the man called, 'I was only asking. Oh, watch out. Here she is.' I felt a deep hot flush.

'Let's go,' Adam said, when I got to him.

'Oh, don't leave,' called the man. 'Don't be silly. I was only messing.'

'Sorry about him,' the bride said. 'Come back here, Dave.'

Dave left us in comic dismay.

'What did he say?' I asked.

'Nothing,' Adam said.

'What?'

'Forget it, Nancy, he's an arsehole.'

'Seriously. I want to know.'

'He said that we couldn't possibly be married. That we were obviously just fucking,' Adam said.

'And what did you say?'

'Nothing, of course.'

The barman pushed the bill towards us and Adam reached for his wallet.

'Cash,' Dave cried from across the room, 'what did I tell you?' He held his hand up to be slapped though no one did it. 'Shut up, you silly bastard,' I heard the best man say.

'Come on,' Adam said.

'Why should we? I don't care what he thinks.'

'Well, I do.'

'But why?' I asked.

'Because it demeans us, Nancy, that's why.'

'I'm really sorry,' the bride said, with an exaggerated grimace, as we left. 'I hope we didn't muck up your evening. And thanks for the drink, yeah?'

'Night night, sleep tight,' called Dave in a sing-song voice and at that, the whole party collapsed.

'Adam,' I said. 'They were idiots and completely shit-faced.' In the lift I held his hand, damp with the stress of it. 'And did you see that dress?' but something had curdled, nonetheless.

At home, next day, I found that I'd been missed. My family had stalled; they made that plain with their hugs and homemade cards. I was surprised, Stef knows the routine backwards, but it seems there are things only a mother can provide. The fact of the children, in front of me, under my hands, felt, for that second, like bliss. I took my place in the machine of the family and it started up again.

Later, overnight bag emptied and clothes churning in the wash, I went through to the kitchen, ostensibly to write up notes. My hangover jangled and I was less tired than I should have been, but it was dark and hard-edged out there, with the underfloor heating off and just the cupboard spots dropping narrow light onto the work-top. I pressed my hands down into the concrete and slid them out until my arms lay flat, the cold reaching my brain paradoxically as heat. Lou crept up on me. The first thing that I knew of her was her soft voice, close by.

'Did you find anyone to talk to, Mummy?' she said. She stood a socked foot on mine.

'I did,' I replied.

'What was her name?' she asked.

'Her name was Helen,' I said.

'What was she like?' she asked.

'Horrible,' I said and Louisa laughed. 'Come here. Shall we go through to the others?'

'In a bit,' said Lou.

'How about I make you a hot chocolate first?'

I let her toast marshmallows for her drink, one white, one pink, over the flame of the gas hob on a skewer.

'Watch out,' I said, 'don't let them drip.' She sat up before me on the counter and I held her bony knees and enjoyed her total commitment to the task. Her hair was greasy at the roots and a clip had worked its way around the curve of her head and hung uselessly from low down one lank curl.

'That's enough,' I said, as they puckered and burnt. 'Don't touch the end.'

I lifted the mug and she eased the marshmallows off with a fork. She took the drink, I saw her eyes refocus above it, and she asked, 'What's that?'

'What's what?' I replied. She was looking at the base of

my throat and I thought for a terrible moment there was a mark there; a bruise, a thumbprint.

'This thing,' she said, and took my pendant, lifting it as far as the chain would allow.

'Oh,' I replied. 'Haven't you seen it before?'

'No,' she said. She turned it over, flipped it back.

'Probably not. It's fairly new.' She nodded. She squeezed it between her fingers and it dulled at her touch.

'What do you think?' I said.

'Pretty,' she replied. 'Did Dad get it for you?'

'I got it for myself. Do you want to have a look?'

'Yes please,' she said.

'You can take it off.'

I turned my back to her and pulled my hair aside. She had some trouble with the catch and I worried for her brittle nails, then she had lifted the necklace away from my chest and up and over my head. She laid the necklace out neatly on the counter.

'What is that?' she said. She traced the pattern a couple of times with the tip of her nail.

'Have a guess,' I replied.

'Fire,' she said decisively. 'In a forest, or something. It's a flame.' Then: 'I like it. Can I wear it? For tonight?'

'Of course,' I said, 'it will look beautiful on you,' and I pulled her to me hungrily, gobbling up her warm stale smell.

15

Marie brought her own coffee now, in a tall, black insulated beaker which leaked water from between its walls, leaving a puddle on the arm of my chair that we both ignored. I wanted to tell her that it was the dishwasher, that mine had done the same. She needed to bin it, and start again. Today's lipstick, though, I liked.

'So this morning, I wanted to broaden things out, Marie, if you don't mind. Could we talk a little about your relationship?'

'Sure,' she said. 'If you want.'

'Would you like to start?' I said.

'Oh no,' she replied. 'You go. Just ask away.'

A riff on reluctance, a play on the reticent child.

'Mark, I think you said? How does he feel about your new job?'

She looked down at her lap where her skirt pleated evenly.

'My job? He thinks it's good. Yes. He's pleased.'

'And does he work in a similar field?' I asked.

'He's in construction,' she said. She held herself neutral and alert.

'And do you place a similar emphasis on career, would you say? As a couple?'

She looked at the art over my shoulder, a huge scabbed oil by a local artist of sky, sea and landmass all bled into one.

'Probably. About the same.'

She liked to make me work, but it takes someone rare to sit out a decent-sized pause. Sure enough, in a bit:

'I mean, I do work longer hours now and there's the travel. He doesn't like that. Or I should say he doesn't exactly love it.'

I let my face go serious.

'Though it's great to have more money coming in,' she said.

'So the extra income has made a difference?'

On my pad I drew a little row of £ signs till they no longer looked like themselves, all warped and stunted.

'Yes. We do more. We eat out. We've booked a holiday.'

Marie is taking them places.

'And how does he get on with your family?' I asked.

'He goes to football every weekend with my dad. They've done it for years,' she said, and I looked and I listened, but there was nothing; she has a knack for blankness and I wondered if she was throwing me a line. Marie is not stupid. 'It's nice,' she finished.

'It is,' I answered, and thought, who is that lipstick for? And those nice new courts and your Karen Millen suit? It is for her, for now, and some of it for me, and for the audience she imagines she will find, when the future she deserves finally begins. Because it's not for them, for dear old Dad and Mark at Selhurst Park every Saturday since day dot, enjoying the crowd, looking forward to their pint; oh no, the hop of her toe tells me that, a little too quick, and the smile that gets stuck halfway up one cheek. Still, I let her talk.

'And what about children?' I said.

Frieda had visited Tara that weekend. I knew things now I didn't want to know. About the tea they drank together from a fine bone china set that lives high up on a shelf. The way each piece lies snug in dusky velvet until Tara eases it out with a special tool designed for the task and hands it to Frieda to polish with a thin lint cloth. A gift from the wardrobe master at one of her best shows, Free tells me, a wonderful old queer, and her eyes shone at her own infraction but I knew it was a challenge and I let it go. The tea itself is something smoked and floral to be drunk as it is, no milk, very hot. Frieda wasn't sure at first, but had a taste for it by the end of her second cup, and wants me to buy some for home, if only she can remember the name.

'Children?' Marie replied. 'What about them?'

'I wondered what you thought— Whether you and—' my eyes dropped to my pad, 'Mark had discussed it, at all?'

'No,' she replied with a high glib tone and a whiff of insolence.

'You've never considered whether you might like to start a family at some point?' I asked.

'I'm not even twenty-eight,' she said, with a chilly look

and I wondered if that question had become inappropriate now, even within the therapeutic context.

'Of course,' I replied and made a note, but I remembered how it was to be that age, its ruthless singularity.

'So tell me about your interests, Marie,' I asked.

She started to reply.

'What did you do?' I had asked Frieda, 'over there?'

'Well we looked at photos and worked through old scripts,' she replied. 'She was so beautiful, Mum, when she was young,' Frieda said, with a kind of yearning. I heard about Adam's wife in Shakespeare, in *Cat on a Hot Tin Roof*.

'Well, I've never heard of her,' I said.

'Why would you? You know nothing about the stage,' she replied.

'And where's Adam, while all this is going on?' I asked.

'Adam?' she said, as though it were the first time that she'd heard his name.

'Yes, Adam.'

'Oh I dunno. Somewhere.' She watched her finger, held in front of her face, as she looped it through a lock of hair.

Marie was talking about a friend and a singing group they might join.

'Sounds great,' I said.

~

Then Frieda had given a private kind of laugh.

'What?' I said.

'He's actually quite sweet.'

'Who?'

'Adam,' she replied.

'Sweet?' I said.

'Well, he came in, in the end,' she said. She had already described the room in which they worked – a kind of sitting room for Tara alone, wallpapered in an old-fashioned style, lined with her books and framed artefacts. Ticket stubs and invites. Messages scribbled on bar napkins. All manner of relic and memento. Proof of her experience and depth.

'He dragged in the old trunk,' she said, as if I knew of it. 'And we all got changed into real-life costumes from the stage!'

'What, all of you?' I said. 'I can't imagine Adam in a dress.'

'He wore a hat,' she cried, close to delight, her finger wedged in a tight coil of hair. 'He played the dowager. We were reading Oscar Wilde. He did this brilliant voice,' and I had to turn from her, from that scene, in case some of what I felt showed on my face.

'Well you mustn't bother them too much,' I said.

'It wasn't bother,' Frieda replied. 'Tara said she had a great time and I should definitely come again.'

And to Marie, I said, yes, that all sounds good, it is important to have new experiences, to continue to evolve and then I took her back to Mark and what he likes to do, and she told me the gym, certain shows on TV, the pub, and we stalled. She started to pinch, just lightly, at one elbow's inside crease. Connections are being made.

'I suppose it's very quiet over there?' I asked Frieda.

I imagined Adam's home marked by lack. My daughter, a gift, touching colour into everything.

'Not really, no,' Frieda replied.

'How do you mean?'

'I mean it's not quiet at all,' she said.

'How come, though? With just the two of them?'

'I don't know,' she said. 'That's just not how it feels.'

'I don't— So what is it like then, would you say?' I asked, but I was losing her now. She gave me one quick derisive look and checked her phone, tapping fast with her thumb.

'Fun? I dunno. Whatever, Mum.'

'Well it's a big ask, Saturday afternoons, that's all,' I said. 'We need to be mindful. They're probably busy,' but Frieda didn't bite.

'They weren't busy at all,' she said, airily, but she had turned from me now. 'They weren't going out for hours.'

'Did they go out?' I said. 'At night, you mean.'

'Uhh, yeah. I just said so.'

I followed her down the hall.

'Where did they go?'

'Mum,' she said, over her shoulder, my grip on her attention thinning all the time. 'Don't be a creep.'

'I'm not. I'm just interested. In what other people do.'

With a huff, she turned to me on the stairs. 'Some restaurant or other. Their favourite place since always. Maybe you and Dad should try something like that for a change.'

And: 'It's interesting,' I said to Marie, 'because there is a view that anxiety can arise from a sense of being stuck. We all need to feel that we are inhabiting our lives. Making progress through them.'

'I see,' she said.

'One of the things this process can offer is the chance to understand our deeper wants and needs,' I said. 'We can discover what really sustains us, or makes us tick. It can be about much more than just getting rid of the unpleasant symptoms you've been experiencing. We can find out how to make your life richer. That's the ambition here.'

I gave it time to percolate. She wrote it all down.

'So, this week's homework.' She dropped her pen in her haste to take the page, which slipped down the side of the cushion to join the cache of coins and the odd forgotten tissue. 'Same as usual. I'd like you to read through this sheet. Tick everything that feels appropriate.'

'Yes. I will,' she said. 'Looking forward to it,' and her look was strange; a kind of jumpy fragile hope.

'We'll get there, Marie,' I said.

She tucked her book between the teeth of the zip of her high-street handbag, and left.

~

I met Tim outside, next to the kettle.

'Long time no see,' he said. 'How's tricks?'

'Very good,' I replied.

'How was the conference, by the way?'

I chanced a look at him but he was watching his hand bounce a teabag lightly in a mug of milky water.

'Fine. Great, actually,' I said.

'What was it about, again?' he asked.

'Oh, lots of speakers. Psychodynamics. That was one,' I replied.

'Didn't know that was Adam's kind of thing,' he said. 'Sounds interesting.'

'It was.'

I went to reach across him but he held his space and I straightened again.

'Could you pass me that, please?' I said, pointing along the countertop.

'What?' he replied.

'The sugar. There. In that pot.'

'Oh right,' he said and pushed it towards me. 'Catch you later, then, I guess,' he said, and I breathed out, but then he was back, filling the space at the end of the little galley kitchen.

'Meant to ask,' he said. 'Any notes?'

'What?'

'Or handouts? Anything worth sharing? I don't want to get left behind. It's not convenient for me, you see. The travelling. What with the family.' He gave a little laugh. 'Young family, I mean. I know you have family, too.'

'I'll see what there is,' I said. 'I'll email you something.'

'Not a biggy,' he replied. 'I can always try Adam.'

'You know they don't have children, Mum,' Frieda had said, hours later, her feet up on my lap. I didn't go through the charade of asking who.

'I do,' I said.

'Why is that, do you think?'

'I don't know,' I said. 'What makes you ask?'

'Oh nothing,' she replied and then, after a bit, 'I might not bother, myself.'

'Bother with what?'

'The whole kid thing,' she said, with a roll of her eyes. 'I might just give it a miss.' She swung her legs down and off she went, humming something, absurdly elegant in her old grey school socks.

16

I headed across town to meet Adam's mother. Waiting in a panelled tea room, I was expecting a little bird, sharp hair and waist, a postwar suit – I hadn't ruled out a hat. Genteel and English, anyway; I think it was the fact of the tea. Something in the orthodoxy of it charmed me and I felt girlish and bashful in line with the scene. 'She doesn't drink any more, that's why,' Adam said, when I told him this, which was new and possibly important, but then she had arrived and she was just like him at the door, angular and mobile. She had a grey crop and a small bag on a narrow strap that emphasised her height and I thought she might be elegant but then she saw him and started towards us and, closer, I saw that her clothes were old and her haircut merely practical. She knocked a coffee cup as she came, filling its saucer, but her eyes were on her boy and for a moment I shared her emotion, either for Adam, or as a mother, met with the face of the man your child has become. When she raised her arms and I saw the sag at the back of her trousers, the cinch of her belt, it could have been him. I felt like thanking her for loving him so well. Then she kissed me too, crisply, on each cheek.

'This is Nancy,' Adam said. 'Nancy, my mum, Vivien.'

'I'm here for no other reason than to meet you,' she said. 'I just want to know you a bit.' Her eyes were not the same though, a cool light blue. A screech of steam from the coffee machine broke the moment.

'I appreciate it,' I said. 'I'd like to know you too.'

'I'll get you a coffee, Mum,' he said. 'Do you want another, Nancy?'

'Let me,' Vivien said, 'while I'm up.'

'You're so alike,' I said, as we waited for her.

He laughed. 'You should have seen my father. Short and fat.' She seemed entirely unselfconscious in the queue. Her bone structure alone, the way her face was pinned between the bridge of her nose and her cheekbones gave her a kind of command. I couldn't find a single cue of femininity on her.

'So you know each other from college, I think?' she said, when she was settled at the table. My legs bent neatly under it, but the long bones of their thighs were pushed up high. I felt small and badly designed next to the two of them. 'But you practise different methods, if I'm right?'

Adam was eating, a plait of custardy pastry, so I replied.

'Yes we do. There's an element of analysis in my approach,' I said. 'I look at the history. Adam focuses on the problem the client presents with, so he's all about the here and now.'

She looked across for his response.

'Basically, Nancy's the purist,' said Adam.

'Really?' I said. 'I've never seen it that way.'

'Nancy needs to know why. She unpacks everything and then puts it back together again in perfect working order,' he said.

'If only,' I replied, and off we set and Vivien indulged us, watching on as we twisted everything into flirtation.

'So what does that make you, then, Adam?' she said, after a while. 'If Nancy's the purist?'

'Me?' he replied. 'Hmm. Let me think.'

I felt her wish to speak and then her deference to me, her son's lover, but I remained silent and sipped my coffee instead, which was already cold and had a smattering of grounds circling its surface.

'A pragmatist, perhaps?' he said. Then: 'You don't like the sound of it, Mum.'

'I wouldn't say that.' She considered him seriously. 'But no one wishes compromise on their child.' She turned to me. 'I understand you have children, Nancy.'

They shared the same slouch across their shoulders, a function of their height, which brought her head in close as we spoke. Her attention cast a sort of spell on me.

'I do,' I said and I began to tell her. I spoke of Frieda's gift for the stage, then Jake and his rugby – an exaggeration, verging on a lie – and all the time, she maintained that same warm steady interest and I thought, you must be hiding it away, some envy, some pain; you, the mother of one childless son, who will never come close to all of this again.

'Such a pleasure, children,' Vivien said, with her implacable good will. 'Despite all the difficulty along the way.'

Adam sat between us with that loose blithe smile and I wondered, what would it take to hurt or shame these people? In a fresh betrayal, I let myself imagine my children under her love. A Christmas, perhaps, in Adam's childhood home, the big house in Ealing he had told me about. No screens, a piano, old-fashioned carols. The kids scrubbed and candle-lit, everything forgiven and forgotten. My own best self at the middle of it, happy, tranquil, satisfied; all lessons learnt.

'I mean— It would be lovely for you to meet them. I would love that, Vivien,' I said, suddenly, rashly.

'They sound absolutely wonderful,' she replied and sat back into her chair, 'but I don't suppose that will be possible,' and I wondered, briefly, could it be that they don't want what I have got?

'I'll get us another, shall I?' said Adam. 'If everybody's got time?' and I told him no, that I had to leave. Vivien asked for a sandwich and a tea. I reached for my bag but she stopped me with a touch.

'Is it difficult?' she said, when he had gone. 'Sharing, I mean?'

'Of course,' I replied.

She nodded.

'I'll admit to you, when he told me, I was surprised.'

'About me and him?'

'Yes,' she said. 'Have you met Tara?'

'I have. Very briefly.'

'What did you think?' she said.

'I don't know how to answer that honestly,' I replied.

'Yes, of course, it must be impossible for you to see her

154

clearly while you are doing what you're doing, but come
on, Nancy, you must have formed some kind of impression.
And please don't mistake me. It's not that I judge. But I am
interested to know.'

I thought of Tara at David's party, her bracelets travelling up and down her arms as she spoke, their tinkling
accompaniment. Her low steady voice.

'I felt she had a kind of composure. A grace, even. She
struck me as very much her own person,' I said.

'All true,' Vivien replied. 'I find her rather self-absorbed
myself, but also very self-sufficient. I think, in a woman,
these qualities are rather rare. I found them very appealing
and I thought they would help her keep a man. She isn't
needy. I cannot see her becoming familiar. As I said, I was
surprised.'

'And do you like her?' I asked.

'Oh yes,' Vivien said. 'I like her very much. Yet she has
failed to keep Adam. There is something between you
two that seems to have trumped whatever they had. And
I accept it.'

'Thank you,' I said and had to fight to keep the elation
off my face.

'I can see that you love him, Nancy, and I know that
he loves you. So I am interested to see what will happen
next.' She began to arrange sachets of sugar, some wide
and flat, some long and thin, in a small white china bowl,
as she waited for me to reply.

'Next? We don't really . . . consider our relationship in
those terms,' I said.

'How so?'

'Well, it's not as if I am free. You know my situation,' I said, 'I have no choice.'

'No choice?' Vivien gave a chuckle. 'Life is nothing but choice, Nancy.'

'I don't agree,' I said. 'Sometimes things happen and we have to find a way to live with them.'

'Indeed they do. When Adam was a boy, his father died suddenly. I'm sure he told you. But it's what you do next, isn't it? When you find yourself in a new situation.'

'I am a parent,' I said.

'Quite.' She touched the back of my hand again, lightly, across the table. It was colder than his and under-stuffed. 'And I'm a parent too. I am here to meet you, today, because I welcome what will make my son happy. But it strikes me that as things are, you're asking an awful lot of him.'

'I see the opposite,' I said. 'Being with Adam, I risk hurting my children every day.'

She considered this; I assumed she had conceded the point.

'You do, you're right,' she said, 'and yet you continue to do it.'

From the counter, Adam called across: did I not want a drink to take away?

'You have everything and he has nothing,' she said. Her tone was steady.

'I don't understand what you're saying, Vivien. What do you want?'

'Me? Nancy, who cares what I want? What does Adam want? I wonder, have you ever even asked him that question?' And I hadn't, of course, I'd merely presented my conditions, which he had accepted. There had been a conversation very early on when I said: 'You will never force me to choose, will you? Can you promise that? There are my children. You must understand,' but he had only laughed. 'I will never force you to do anything, Nancy,' he said, and so we continued. I wondered what Vivien knew.

She sighed. 'I do remember love, Nancy. The way it feels. But you must see that as things are you are limiting his life. You are shrinking it to tiny. Just to you, in fact. I hope you can carry that. And you, with so much already on your plate.' Then: 'I'm sorry. I didn't mean to upset you.'

'You haven't,' I said. 'I'm not.'

'It's just my son is a generous man. You don't seem the sort of person to take advantage.'

'OK?' Adam said, over the top of his tray. Her cup of tea slid around it dangerously.

'Bye-bye then, Nancy,' Vivien said. 'I'm so glad we had the chance to chat.'

At home my husband cooked squid.

'Hey,' he said, when I found him in the kitchen. 'Something good for tonight. I got it from the fishmonger's.'

He lifted a white plastic bag and the thing inside rolled and settled wetly.

'Your favourite.'

'It is,' I replied. On holiday I always chose squid. It had become a joke, about my fixedness, but my fidelity too.

'Come,' he said. 'Let me show you.'

He tipped the bag and the animal turned over itself heavily onto the board. It smelt of nothing much; brine, maybe ozone, a trace of cucumber.

'It's an arrow squid, see?' he said.

He unpeeled two flaps tucked tight around the body.

'So you start here.'

He pulled off the head. It came away clean, with just the slightest viscousy click, trailing stringy innards.

'We need this bit,' he said, holding the perfect little flower of tentacles before me, like a gift. 'But not all this.'

The guts shimmied gently. He made a swift cut with a sharp knife just above the flat black eyes.

'You remove the beak,' he said and eased his thumb into the bud of tentacles. He found something there, and reached another finger in after.

'Got it,' he said, but whatever he held was tiny, and had gone into the bag with the rest of the ruins before I could make it out.

'Will you fetch me a bowl?' he asked, and I brought him the metal one. What he tossed in sluiced a half-circle up the side. He smoothed the squid's casing flat with both palms.

'This is the mantle. It's beautiful, no?' he said, and it was, an opaque ivory speckled with bronze in spots and circles. Freckled and ancient-looking. More sun-blasted than sea. His nails began to work at its rim. I noticed the deep bend of his thumb and it pleased me, as always. He took grip of a sliver of frayed edge and peeled a little, then ripped the membrane from the flesh in one perfect piece, limp and translucent.

'You chuck that, and then you need to pull out the quill.'

It came out from the sheath of the squid like a smooth shard of plastic, just as you see them washed up on the beach. He scraped the tube of flesh with the back of a knife, sliced it into rings and the squid was food.

'I was thinking chilli and garlic. And rice, if you like?' he said.

He pushed the board away and leant back against the counter to look at me. He wore jeans and a sweatshirt in navy marl. A neat crop of beard.

'Delicious. Thank you, Stef. I do appreciate that, you know.'

'You don't have to thank me. It makes me happy to prepare dinner for my wife.'

I stepped towards him.

He held his unwashed palms before him.

'Hey. Be careful.'

I moved between them and laid my whole length against him. He smelt as he always did, of lime and forest and deep cold water. His childhood, I imagined, the place of his birth, though I'd never been. I let him take my weight.

'How are you feeling?' he said.

'Oh, not so bad.'

'Everything passes, Nancy. It won't be like this forever.'

'I know.'

17

'There's somebody else,' she said.

'Who is this?'

'Skyler,' she replied. 'Who do you think?'

'Sorry. I didn't recognise the number.'

'I found a note. I went through his things.'

'What does it say?' I asked. I pictured my father, the little nod of confirmation he gave when things went as he expected.

'It was a tiny scrap. Some bullshit.'

'What?'

'*Always and forever,*' she said. 'I mean—'

'That's me,' I said.

'You what?'

'It must have been from years ago. It's a thing we used to say. When Mum and Dad split up.'

'Well I'm sorry, but that is all kinds of fucked-up,' she replied.

'Not really. We were children—'

She must have dropped her hand from her mouth; her laugh sounded miles away.

'Shall I come round?' I called.

~

I went to their home the next day. It wasn't a bad place, a second-floor flat in a squat block off Wells Park Road. The ground floor was all garages, painted green, next to an area that had been turfed in a fake-looking grass, prickly and bright, like the stuff they lay the meat on at the butcher's. Satellite dishes ran around the block in three tiers, each fixed at an identical tilt which made me think of sunflowers raising their faces to the light. I stood outside and counted up and along until I found David's home. Theirs was one of the smaller flats, so didn't warrant a balcony. There was the same wisp of curtain as always.

We'd been here once before, Stef and I, and eaten Mexican, taco and enchilada sitting on cushions round a low table. Tequila with the worm still in, which someone had given them, and mariachi music that David had burned onto a disk. Next-door joined us, late; a white man with dreadlocks and flared jeans, and his spacey girlfriend, and I squeezed Stef's hand at the sight of them but he wouldn't acknowledge it. On the way home, when pushed, he just said: 'Live and let live, hey, babe.'

Skyler buzzed me up wordlessly and I took the stairs, a slippery wood laminate peppered with heel marks. She had opened the door before I got there, in slippers and one of his old jumpers.

'Hi,' she said. 'Are you early?'

She gestured at me with her bowl, a fork upright in noodles. 'There's probably more. If you want it,' she said.

'I'm fine,' I replied. 'I'll eat when I get home.'

She turned into the hall. Overhead someone crossed the floor heavily.

'Do you want a tea? Or I might have some wine, I suppose,' she said.

'A tea's good, thanks.'

'Go through. I'll put the kettle on.'

I sat on the sofa, old pilled wool you could feel the springs through. The room was square and white and unadorned. It showed its function everywhere, in the wires that had worked free of their tacking and the pull for the blinds split out into a fuzz of grubby fibres. There was damp in the wall shared with the bathroom that I smelt before I saw, bubbling under the paintwork in one corner. A beanbag was the only thing recognisably his, a gift from Mads that had somehow survived. I noticed two framed posters from movies I'd never seen, and a laptop on a desk next to a messy pile of papers.

'I added milk,' she said. 'We don't have sugar.'

She put the tea by my foot and sat cross-legged at their table to eat.

'Skyler,' I said, finally. 'I just wanted to check you were OK.'

'Why?' she said.

'Well, on the phone, I thought you sounded a bit— Overwrought.'

'Overwrought? Your brother fucking abandoned me.' She went back to eating steadily.

'I know.'

There was a pinboard on the desk, leant against the wall,

part hidden by the swamp of filing. Postcards and cuttings. Beach, jungle and city. Meals and views and water. I'd put together similar – a collation of my adventures – to take with me to university. David had watched as I assembled it, a dry run on the floor to see what should go where.

'Tell me about. This place,' he would say and point.

If I couldn't think of anything, I made it up.

'Planning a trip?' I asked Skyler.

'We were,' she said. 'Did he not say?'

He had got bored, after a while, flicking through my clippings.

'Why are you taking all this stuff, anyway?' he asked.

'To remind me,' I replied.

'Then why not an album?'

'Why not this?' I said, my colour rising.

'Because it's not for you,' he said, 'is it? It's for other people. To make you seem more interesting than you are. Do you think it'll work?'

I wanted him to rip it up then, to save me the job, but David, when he chooses, has magnificent restraint. So I did it myself, scrunched the whole lot into my bin. He laughed.

'Shall we burn it?' he said.

'We'll burn the whole house down.'

He went off for lighter fuel. The flame was sudden and columned and heated my necklace so instantly that it burnt my chest. The bin seemed to thrum and I thought it would tip – surely – then it was gone; the fire sucked back into itself like magic.

~

'No, he didn't actually,' I told Skyler.

'Oh right,' she said. 'He felt that was your thing, travelling. That's probably why.' She stretched her leg and turned an ankle. Under the table, I saw one of David's boots. A sock hung from the collar.

'Well, it was,' I said.

'Did you never wonder why he didn't go, though? When you were growing up?' she asked, and I realised that I hadn't.

'I guess he just didn't fancy it,' I said.

She puffed a breath out of her nose. 'Well he fancies it now,' she replied, but any fight had dropped out of me and I just felt sad for my brother and the things he hadn't done. She took her bowl through to the kitchen. The high-pile rug had left her leggings lightly furred.

'Look I'm just here to help, if I can.'

'But why?' she said, and turned to me, her movements sudden and complete, like a cat's. 'You don't even like me.'

I felt bloated in my suit and thought, at home they're out of milk, and Lou has lost her French, and Stef needed reminding to take Jake's snack. As for Frieda, I don't care if it's normal, I feel her distance from me like a thumb twisted in a wound.

'I need to leave,' I said, and switched my laptop bag to the shoulder that ached a little less.

'Fine,' she called after me. 'And don't come back. I don't want your help.'

She was in the hall now, shouting after me down into the stairwell.

'I refuse to be one of your good works, Saint Nancy. His words,' I heard her shout above the rat-a-tat of my shoes, 'not mine.'

But I didn't go home, I took a bus instead, heading the opposite way. The lower deck was quiet and I sat by the window behind the driver, listening to the engine's build and drop and the percussion of the gears which I could feel beneath me as well as hear. The repetition made me sleepy. In the seat behind, a schoolboy crushed a bag of crisps into dust before he ate them.

We moved into a part of South London I didn't know. The place looked poor yet felt suburban and the tempo was changed, there was less hurry out here. I felt the neighbour-hood's boredom and it slowed me down again. I allowed myself a daydream. I imagined Adam and I running away to this place. They wouldn't follow me here. There was nothing in these streets for Stefan or the kids. He wouldn't find his coffee, or a work hub or discover something awe-some that was local, artisan or niche. There were no tutors or green spaces. It's not that Stef would condescend, if he found himself passing through; God no. He wouldn't speed up as the roads got grimmer, or flip the locks. Just move our big car steadily on, telling the kids: 'Don't worry, team, we'll get where we're going soon enough,' and somebody would want a wee, or a treat, or to change the song, or take their turn in the front but he'd smooth all that away and they'd keep rolling through, until: 'Here we are,' and they were out the other side. Perhaps they would come upon a van selling hand-thrown pizza, or find that the road had opened out into a square of better housing and pull up outside a newsagent on the corner, each child leaning down to choose an out-of-season ice-cream from the chest that took them back to holidays. And they would forget about me, who had watched them go by from behind a scrap of something I'd nailed up to keep out the light.

I could live here, in this place. I had forgotten that I was adaptable, the surprise legacy from the collision that had been Mum and Dad and which I'd once considered my greatest gift. But they are not. It has been my life's work to root my children deep. Their selves have been my project, winkled out then smoothed and polished till they are shiny and certain and impermeable. They are fixed now, and a transplant would be brutal, maybe even fatal. I, though, could still imagine invisibility; the lovely freedom of it. I could live here with Adam, pulled out from under the weight of my own expectations. Everything I needed within arm's reach.

The boy behind me got up, a little shower of crisps tumbling from his lap as he passed. I pressed the bell for the next stop.

In the street, on a whim, I googled David's work. I dialled the number and someone answered in a gasp on the final ring. I heard a big echoey space behind him.

More work than time, David had said, from my sofa, drinking wine at 5 p.m., and all sorts – you name it – kitchens, wardrobes; in fact, sis, he said, and he bent across his lap at this, an odd set to his face, just recently, a headboard shaped like a sleigh, for a girl, just like you always wanted. Remember? It was beautiful. He wished I could have seen it.

'David?' said the man, 'Hold on.'

He told a long tale at a new Japanese, about a set he was building, for the stage, he declared, how cool is that? He described a field of trees; oak, ash and beech, accurate to each leaf, painted by a mate.

I remarked upon the cost, high for regional theatre, perhaps.

He said some local guy picked up the bill.

I said how about we all of us go and watch?

He told me it was while we were away.

Then a new voice came on the line. 'You after David?' it said.

'Yes please. He gave me this number.'

'Haven't seen him for months,' the man replied. 'Tell him to ring me, though, if you find him,' he went on. There's a ton of work, turns out, in flooring and roofs – David's thing. For a skinny lad, he said, he really can lift. And a lot of people doing up, these days. Cheaper than moving. Then something sounded in my voice and the man put the phone down fast.

Every lie has an intent. Perhaps David hoped to make us proud. Mum loved it, of course, to have at least one creative child, though Dad didn't understand; he thought it a step backwards in our family's passage. Unless David wanted my envy. To see my own life shrivel a bit, next to his. I caught the next bus home.

18

I went with my mother to look at art. She had been waiting for this show for months, on life-drawing, her passion, if such a word could be applied, and had bought a ticket for David too, who liked this kind of thing. In his absence, she offered it to Madeline, but Mads had phoned me earlier in an anxious state, struck with a vicious cold and convinced that Mum should not be forced to visit a gallery alone.

'She does everything alone, Madeline,' I said.

'I know. That's what I mean,' she cried.

The office felt loaded and unstable. Adam had asked me if anything was wrong and I told him no, but couldn't meet his eye. I had no clients after lunch and so agreed to go, with a view to making an effort.

I met Mum off the first cheap train. She wore the satchel she used for London strapped across her chest and a pair of comfortable shoes. We walked the distance to the gallery.

The exhibition was in the basement, dark and quiet and temperature-controlled. It was empty and our feet made echoey taps and our voices bounced around.

I enjoyed the flirtatious letters between the artists and models, but struggled to extract meaning from the art, which just looked like pictures to me. In the third room, Mum slowed down.

'Look at this, Nancy,' she said. 'Lovely, don't you think?'

The drawing was a seated nude. Chalk on paper; bronze strokes on a page of light ochre as though it had been singed. The woman was viewed from behind and her head, in profile, was shaded out.

'Where's her face?' I asked, but my mother ignored me. The figure was drawn simply, in rough even strokes. She was muscled and strong, in the bulge of her calf, across her shoulders and through the curve of her hip which cut a deep cleft into her waist. She looked power-ful, a woman who might simply get up and put herself to work. My mother did not. She stood close to the art, her programme pressed to her front. Her face was still and she had slowed her eyes and passed them quietly across the canvas, left to right, blank and thorough; she stayed that way for minutes, entirely passive, waiting to receive the message of the work. Her undyed hair tapered into fine points resting across each clavicle. Her tunic and trousers, in natural shades of taupe and mustard, were unfilled. She looked like a nun on a day out in home clothes. I took a seat on the bench behind her, my head in my phone, reloading and refreshing though there was no connection down there. In the end, I got up and nudged her, more roughly than I'd intended.

'Come on, Mum,' I said. 'I haven't got all day.'

She swayed a little as she absorbed the blow, but her feet remained steady.

'I'll meet you in the café, Nancy,' she replied.

'What do you want?' I said.

'A latte, please, when I get there,' she said, her eyes still on the art.

She didn't rush. I had finished my coffee by the time she arrived, and chosen lunch. She pulled the bottom of her tunic aside and sat.

'We need to order, Mum,' I said.

'I'll have the soup.'

'You don't even know what it is.'

'It'll be fine, thank you, and oatcakes, please, instead of bread, if they've got them.'

She took a small bottle of water from her bag and drank a sip. I found a waitress, and ordered for us both.

'And how are the children?' Mum said.

'OK. I think,' I replied.

She'd swapped to her other glasses and I had her full attention now. Her skin was perfect, sealed and poreless, white and fine like muslin. The bridge of her nose, knobbed as a knucklebone, wore a skein of fine red scratches.

'There's been something with Frieda,' I said. 'She seems quiet.'

I hadn't planned to tell her, but her eyes on me, light and constant, made it happen.

'She is quiet. You were quiet,' she said.

'Me?'

'Yes, Nancy. You. Some of the time. When you let yourself be.'

I remembered action, effort, making a production of it, to winkle David out, or get a smile from Dad. He came to watch me play netball on a Saturday afternoon and would stand at the chain link fence, in the sunglasses he wore with less self-consciousness than the other dads, ankles crossed, one toe tipped into the ground. He was smarter, too, in his weekend things, and the parting in his hair and the press of his collar showed his difference far more than his accent. Knowing he was there made me ruthless; I looked him out when I got done for contact, ready to collect my wink. I found an extra inch at the sound of his holler, though it made me wince as well. 'You're a force of nature,' Dad used to say. I heard it, I liked it, stuck my flag in it. David had to choose from what was left. Childhood as land grab.

'I always think of David as the quiet one, growing up,' I said.

'Yes, I know you do,' she said and there it was, the pinch at the end of her caress. It was a reflex, and I saw her almost instant regret. I was filling the space made by Dad leaving, I almost said, but it would be hard to come back from that.

'So are you worried about Frieda?' she asked, in a step towards me.

'Honestly? I've no idea.'

'What does Stefan say?' she asked. For a woman so many years alone she still set store by the opinion of a man.

'He thinks she's fine.'

She nodded and reset the cutlery, straightening her soup spoon and knife and refolding the white paper napkin. She moved the flower that sat between us – a single light-deprived stem in a test-tube – to the table next door, and said:

'That's better. I can see you now.'

Her soup came, a thin grim broth. She stirred it, setting vegetables bobbing, and waited, her spoon planted deep, for mine to arrive. The same girl brought it over; a vast ham and Gruyère toastie beside a heaped ramekin of tomato chilli chutney. Mum frowned at the sandwich, its size, or else the dribble of cheese establishing itself on the plate in its moat of grease. She brought her spoon up and across to her mouth neatly.

'Would you like a taste?' I offered, and shoved the sandwich towards her. It sagged around my grip, threatening to leak.

'No, thanks,' she replied, with a hint of recoil.

'Oh whoops,' I said, as a teardrop of cheese hit her napkin. She folded it and tucked it under the rim of her plate.

'Did you talk to David at the party?' I asked.

'Not so much, dear, no. But I felt that he seemed OK.'

'I met Skyler the other day. She was no help,' I said.

'Ah well. Have you thought of Alice? That pair had a chat.'

'I saw. Not for long, though. I'm not doing it, this time, Mum. Phoning around.'

'Fair enough,' she replied.

'Don't you feel hurt by him leaving again?'

She laid down her spoon and pushed her half-drunk

soup away. 'I don't see his decision in those terms, Nancy,' she said.

'What terms?'

'In terms of how they affect me.'

'So you're saying I'm being selfish?' I said.

Louisa shares my mother's face, wan and pious. It pained me, now, to look at hers, so similar to my child's, and feel that stab of dislike.

'Not selfish, Nancy, no.'

'What then?'

'You have the tendency to put yourself at the centre of things, dear,' she said.

'I find myself there,' I replied.

'No, you assign yourself that position. There's a difference. I'm merely asking, can you not let him be? This family's not so easy.'

'You're telling me,' I said.

'I was talking about David.'

She had always tipped us out of sync, into competition, though he claimed he couldn't see it. I searched her face now for tone or emotion; I, who can find offence in the set of her mouth, the hook of a brow, but she was perfectly still. I used to love that poise in the old photos. She had been a tiny blonde with a face like architecture when she first met Dad; beautiful, though something closed in the cast of it. There was no display about Kath, April told me once; it was hard to find a place to park your eyes on her. And Dad by her side, stiff suit and bearing. One hand resting lightly on his lapel. The story of their courtship was pure fiction; Mum's sixties swinging in the usual way when Dad walked into her bar. She moved in with him in a matter of months. A cultural tourist who stayed for twenty years then packed up and left, going back to her middle-class beginnings.

'What family are you referring to anyway, Mum?' I said and at last, there was something. A long tired sigh, a feint of exhaustion.

'Oh this,' she said. 'I was with your father until you were thirteen, Nancy. And it was he who upped and left as I remember.'

Dad had come to me to try to explain: 'I know it's hard to hear, Nance, but there it is. We all deserve to be—' and I knew he wanted to say loved, but he couldn't, kneeling by the side of his eldest child. 'We all deserve a bit of respect,' he said in the end, and I understood, his needs were simple and she could be cold.

She broke an oatcake into smaller pieces, and ate them dry, one by one.

'And I know it hurt you when I moved back home but you were grown by then. A mother, yourself,' she said. She put our house on the market the week after Mads got her college place and was gone before the summer was out, to a village outside Market Harborough, ten miles from where she was born.

'I don't begrudge you that at all,' I said and it was true. Her leaving had been a sheer relief. She had thinned, by then, to the point that we could almost see through her; the cost of her sacrifice to us everywhere. When I visited her in her cottage with its garden and a studio, she had taken flesh again. This new Mum, with mud on her boots, a bicycle and a cat, was in fact the old one. I saw that her time with us – the city, motherhood, my entire growing up – had been the anomaly. She had slipped back into an earlier skin and found a perfect fit. She was blissful and that look on her face cast me out.

'You seem rather cross, dear,' she said.

She'd always borne the brunt of my moodiness, and taken it. Guilt, I put it down to. A clever kind of masochism. She submitted to my punishment yet retained the high ground, sitting quietly as I stamped about, a futile domestic tyrant, diminished by my own meanness.

'I'm fine,' I said.

'I don't owe you an apology, Nancy, you know. We each have a responsibility to live the best life we can.'

She pressed her handbag, patted the table twice in quiet little acts of displacement.

'And you survived, didn't you?' she said. 'In fact, I think you've turned out rather well.'

'Is that so?' I said.

'Yes it is.' She gave a brief parched chuckle. 'You've always struck me as rather fearless. Don't let growing older diminish that.'

Unaccountably, I felt that I might cry.

'You might be a little kinder to yourself though, perhaps,' she said.

'If you mean do exactly what I like, like David, well that's hardly possible, is it? Or right.'

'I'd rather assumed you were already doing what you liked,' she said, with an acute look. She felt for her long wooden beads and I saw something different then, in her steadiness; a kind of tenacity. I thought, I could take this moment. I could simply tell her. I realised she would be difficult to shock; that she could take my disgrace, if it came. She might even call it by a different name.

'I am,' I said. 'I'm fine.'

'OK,' she replied and tapped the back of my hand. 'Anyway.' She gave a light smile. 'What else is news?'

'Well, we're having a party for Frieda in a couple of weeks' time,' I said.

'Of course. Fifteen. My goodness me.'

'It'll be at home. The whole family,' I said.

'That'll be nice. Just tell me when.' She stood. 'Don't worry about this. My treat,' she said, though it wouldn't run to much more than twenty pounds. She wandered off towards the till but was distracted on the way by a rack of expressionist postcards. She gave me one, in a paper bag, as we walked towards the exit.

'For you,' she said. 'Just a little something.'

We left the museum together.

'Bye-bye, Nancy,' she said, in the street, squinting up into the daylight. 'You know I love you, dear.'

We held hands as though we were about to dance and the V of skin between her thumb and first finger was loose and webbed and softer than seemed human, like a trimming of silk. Then off she set, keen to miss the rush hour, her satchel tucked high into her armpit. 'Send my love to the children, won't you?' she called and bent into the weather like someone in disguise, a witch in a fairy tale dispensing her blessing or curse. I felt the old familiar ache of separation and it took me back.

~

We were at the airport, David and I, Mum's goodbye still hot in my throat as we crossed the terminal like some weird kind of hostage exchange, the space between her and Dad empty and risky. I turned for one last wave and the long brave kiss she threw at me, and the way she moved towards the escalator, focused and resolute, was about the saddest thing I'd ever seen.

We were to spend a week in Albufeira, with Dad, Ape and their brother Charlie and his kids. There had been a falling out, but Charlie's wife had died of cancer just that year and so Dad and he were trying again. I spotted our uncle easily enough; he was big, like Dad, and ridiculous in khaki cargo shorts above huge hams of calf, but I couldn't see anyone who might be our cousins. They were twins, a few months younger than me, and it had been years since we'd all last met. Then David gave this chuckle and I followed his gaze and found that it ended on a girl. He had been leaking trouble all that summer and the sound, a burble of glee as though he'd just been proved right about pretty much everything, should have told me how it would be, but I missed it, because I was stupid and I loved him and had spent my whole life defending him.

I chose to see that he was laughing at the way she chewed – the Hubba Bubba he was addicted to by the holiday's end – and the magazine she held, that he had previously judged naff. 'Give her a break, sis,' he said, when I pointed this out later. 'Don't be so quick to judge,' ruffling my hair as he said it, though I was sixteen to his fourteen, but he was taller by a foot, and already had many secrets whereas I mainly worried and hadn't yet kissed a boy and somehow he seemed to know all this.

Dad's brother called it right, though, when his daughter blinked David into focus under electrified blue lashes and gave off an answering heat. He dropped a hand onto her shoulder and she shot her face around as though his touch had burnt. I felt sorry for him; his love looked painful and misdirected. Then everybody watched as David approached. A lanky streak of piss, Dad used to say, which wasn't kind, but David was so beautiful, and knew it, that the insult became something else; an attempt to moor him to the rest of us, so earthbound and ordinary. And space and time did that thing they talk about in love stories and we all felt a whisper of their first touch, the steadying fingertip on the top of her smooth pink arm as he bent to kiss her on each cheek, a ridiculous affectation back then, and for a boy of his age.

'Layla, remember?' she said, and he replied, 'I do. Like the song,' though he remembered no such thing.

I think Dad spoke his name then, hissed between his teeth like an insult and the adults tried to defuse it with chatter and pointless laughs and David's smile was brilliant, all teeth and pleasure. When Dad introduced him again to his brother, David held out his hand. Could he have called him 'Sir'? That's how I remember it. The little shit.

Where was I? Off to one side. Stranded again, in the wake of his latest disruption. I caught the other child's gaze, the boy, Luca, but he curled his lip to tell me that he and I were not the same at all. Aunty April smirked, her hands quick and aimless. She worked her fingers before her as though she was mixing breadcrumbs; she loved chaos, Ape, and also sex, and was realising, now, that it might be a decent holiday, after all, that which had previously seemed nothing but difficult; the attempted rapprochement of her brothers when it suited her so much better for them to be apart.

I see all that from here, but at the time, there was just my isolation. Even now, the first feel of sun on unaccustomed flesh, and the smell of coconut in cheap foreign sun cream prompts a slippery unease.

We were staying at our uncle's time-share, 'a new build,' he told us, proudly, which explained, perhaps, the unfinished concrete around the pool which skinned my toes and the odd trimmings of plastic we kept finding in the joints of things; slivers of packaging that nobody had bothered to remove.

The sun was blinding, thrown back at us from the surface of the pool and the plate glass that was everywhere. Ape walked straight into the patio door one afternoon, despite the sticker, a big red exclamation mark in a triangle above something Portuguese and the impact slammed the door in its casings, making a sound like gunshot. When we opened our eyes, each of us had rolled up on our sun loungers like woodlice. A tray of drinks had exploded on the stone and for a minute, I thought the sangria racing across the tiles was blood, but Ape was fine, apart from a cut on her nose and one black eye. From then on, there was only plastic outdoors. I walked down the baked, rutted lane to buy my first pair of sunglasses.

The shop had once been a house. Lilos, donuts and dinghies swung from a scaffolding pole at the front, tied with brown string in loose bows. On the terrace were racks of shoes, balls and beach sets. A boy about my age worked through an A4 maths book in English at the till, next to a counter dressed with fridge magnets, comedy pens and a cardboard sheet of Lypsyls. I passed into the room beyond and stopped at a great tray of silver jewellery arranged against black sponge, the rings tucked into slits and necklaces suspended on circles of pins. And right at the back, in amongst the sweary T-shirts, I found David, with his hand wedged down Layla's shorts and her head resting sleepily on his shoulder. He jumped when he saw me and said: 'Nance, it's only you!' in amusement and relief. And when I think of my first time, which was later that year with a ghastly boy, the events are somehow conflated and it is the terrible pulsing of cicadas I hear and the pasty throat ache of too much Lemon Fanta that I taste and a sicky little twist of shock in my stomach.

Needless to say, I kept quiet. There were the grown-ups to think about, the ebb and flow of Dad and Charlie's dislike, which peaked at about three each afternoon, bringing lunch to a close, and then surged again, late at night, as I listened from my bed. April watched them like the tennis, back and forth, with evident interest and no apology. She stepped in occasionally, to adjudicate, when their antagonism tipped into explicit disagreement, or she felt she had a relevant point: 'Now now, Bill. You shouldn't say that. That's not fair,' or

'Don't forget, love, your brother's been through a lot.' It always seemed to be Dad she pulled up, though it was he and she who were close.

Still, on the final afternoon, as we walked amongst the dunes, there was the feeling that ground had been made. I walked behind with Layla – she was actually OK; kind, and occasionally funny, despite being so obvious – and April had her arm through Dad's (she couldn't stand to walk alone) when Charlie, on her other side, pulled close enough that she could thread her hand through the bend at his elbow, too, and for a moment they travelled as a three, in an unbroken line.

Then: 'Isn't that your David?' Charlie asked. There was a boy climbing out of the sea, edged in silver. I raised a hand to shield my eyes. He started to run and then, from inside the next wave, launched a girl, arms outstretched as she broke through its surface, sleek as a seal. She caught her footing and sprung after him in a low sprint, shaking off splinters of water and light. She caught up easily and from a stride away, jumped high onto David's back. He tripped and they both rolled, laughing and tumbling in sand and grass, and though Layla was beautiful, this girl was something else again, with her lack of care, her hair clumped round her face and her musculature, her shorts that might have been a boy's, and the light dusting of salt that made her look frost-tipped.

Layla tensed, calling to mind the time between hurting yourself and the arrival of the pain. It came, I assume, for next she staggered, one long weak step, and began to wail with such conviction that it must have been more about her dead mother than David and the girl. Her father bent to her and I saw his tenderness and anguish but also his reticence and how much that would gall, pre-empting her furious bat of his hand. Charlie stepped away and looked around him dumbly but then his pain contorted into rage – I saw it, that distance travelled on his face – and he moved to Dad and roared and Dad threw back his shoulders and roared back. Ape laid a hand on each man's chest and I watched her buffeted, like a woman facing into the wind on the prow of a ship, though they observed the distance that she marked out between them. Next to me, the brother, Luca, cried silently, and David looked on, while the other girl turned cartwheels on the scorched sand behind him.

This is not one of our golden tales. The breach between Dad and Charlie proved final and we never of spoke of it again, not even Ape, who loves to press a bruise. Still, what does it reveal? Little that I don't already know. David in the middle of it all. Incandescent, selfish and cruel. Dad, fists clenched, made impotent by rage. And me, the spectator, standing on the side line, itching for a role. Each of us fixed, forever, into our spots.

19

'Come in, Marie, sit down.'

She walked soft-footed across the carpet. I held the jug and her glass; bent to them at my desk.

'I haven't been telling the truth,' she said.

I have had this moment only once before.

'Please. Carry on. I'll just grab my stuff.'

I scrambled for my book, a pen, and sat across from her. Her hair was two weeks old, now; a difficult age. Where it had grown, it flicked out at the ends, following the curve of her neck. She turned it back between two fingers but it wouldn't submit. She was silent. She looked around the room as if it were new.

'Take your time,' I said.

'I hated it as a child.' She gave a loud, aggravated sigh and moved her eyes past my face to the painting behind me.

I felt something close to triumph. I had thought she had the mark of the bullied, the stillness of a rabbit, those racing eyes.

'What did you hate, Marie?'

'All of it. All of the time.'

I heard contempt; I saw a childhood of restriction and control. Maybe worse.

'Tell me more,' I said, sitting back, creating space. She kept her eyes on the picture.

'Home. My parents.'

'What was it like? At home?' I asked. I took my voice upwards and tried to hide my appetite.

'I just— You know. This is hard.' She watched me closely.

'I do. But you can say whatever you like in here.'

My stomach hopped and I felt my responsibility.

'I don't want you to think badly of me,' she said and leant towards me, closing the gap, and in that moment I felt that it would come, some confession, and that perhaps I could deliver her from it.

'Marie, I won't. You need to believe that. And you must not blame yourself for anything that happened to you.'

'Oh, no,' she said quickly. 'Nothing happened to me. It wasn't like that.'

Her book twitched on her lap and she rolled the barrel of her pen between her fingers.

'It wasn't them at all,' she said, in a tight voice. 'It was me.'

'What do you mean?' I asked.

'I just wanted to get away,' she said. 'Always. Even when I was small. I couldn't wait to leave.'

'And why was that, do you think?'

'Because it was tiny there,' she said.

'In what way?'

'There was no air,' she said. 'I couldn't breathe.'

'And yet you lived at home until you were twenty.'

'Yes,' she replied.

'That must have been hard.' She dropped her eyes and shrugged.

'The way I feel is not the same as what I do,' she said. Then: 'I think that's why all this is happening to me.'

'It might very well be,' I said. 'That's hard to live with, that kind of fracture. And you're recently married, which can prompt a re-evaluation of the past. There can be a concern about repeating mistakes.'

'I don't mean that,' she said and her look was wretched now. 'I think I'm being punished.'

'No,' I replied, though I told myself to go carefully. 'No, Marie. You've done nothing wrong. What I'm hearing here is shame. Shame at your difference which meant you didn't always feel you fitted in. And as for leaving, every child has to leave. It's harder, perhaps, if you're an only child, but it's natural. And your relationship with your parents is good. You see each other. You play your part.'

'Shame,' she said, in a kind of wonder. 'I am ashamed.'

'And shame is a defence, a first-base emotion that shields us from feeling something deeper and more difficult.'

'But I don't feel anything,' she said in a dreamy tone.

'Not yet,' I replied and in one of those odd moments of exchange, I felt it, suddenly, for her; my ribs scarcely containing an anguish, vacuum light and ravenous, threatening to lift me off my feet.

'We need to locate that pain, Marie, and name it. Then we can begin to move beyond it,' I said. 'That's what we're doing here. That's what this is all about.'

She felt for the chain she wore beneath her shirt.

'Do you have a faith?' I asked her, suddenly.

'Faith?' she replied. 'Oh, no,' and gave a faraway laugh.

When she was gone, I sat on the floor by the wall and listened for Adam, but all I could hear was his client's needling tone, his voice reduced to a background murmur. I left the office before he was done.

There was a note when I got home: *At the park!* then Lou's signature smiley face. Upstairs, I noticed Frieda's door ajar and found her at her window, her forehead on the chilly pane.

'I thought you were out. What are you looking at?' I asked, in a high, bouncy voice. There were parked cars on both sides of the road. A stop-start stream of traffic, trying to cut through a rush-hour Monday. Her phone lay on the windowsill, charging.

'Aren't you supposed to knock?' she said.

'Sorry. I didn't know you were here.'

'Oh and that makes it OK,' she replied, but she had no bite.

'How was school?' I asked.

'All right.'

I sat with her on her bed. She smelt institutional, boiled greens and hand-wash and a tang of metallic bus handrail. She seemed so worn. Crumpled and grimed, from top to toe. London all over her. She had taken off her socks and I saw the city's tide-mark around her ankles. I wanted to bath her like I had when she was small; cross-legged, straight-backed in a couple of inches of warm water. A natural sponge and No More Tears shampoo. She would slap the surface with a flat palm, astonished at the noise. I used to end up soaked.

'Any more weirdness with Clemency?' I asked, not that she'd told me the nature of it.

She looked at her nails, snagged and streaked in metallic blue.

'Not really.'

'Good. Girls can be a nightmare,' I said, but she didn't smile. She dropped her head on to my shoulder.

'How is your piece coming along? I can't wait to see the performance,' I said. She gave the slightest lift of her shoulder in response.

'Are you looking forward to your party?' I asked. She shrugged. 'Are you OK, Frieda?' I said and pulled away to better look at her face.

'Oh I'm fine, Mum,' she replied. 'Don't worry,' and I knew I'd struck the wrong note. You cannot solve your child's every problem, I would have told a client, nor should you try and yet she suddenly seemed so opaque to me, so impossible to see. She slid down her bed limply.

'Oh right. Good. Well, if there's anything you want to talk about?'

'I'm tired,' she said.

'Tired?' I felt her forehead.

'I'm fine. I'm just going to have a rest. I'll be down later,' and when I got to the door, her eyes were already closed.

'OK, sweet. Not too long, though, or you won't sleep tonight.'

~

Downstairs, the others were back. Stefan and Louisa played Guess Who?

'Stef. Is Frieda all right?'

'Does yours have any accessories?' he said to Lou.

'That's not a fair question! What do you mean?'

'One second, Nancy. Hats, sunglasses or jewellery.'

'Yes!' Lou replied.

'Frieda's fine,' Stef said to me.

'Any news on Uncle David?' Lou asked.

My anxiety was a high note in the room. I went through to the kitchen and stood at the back. Outside was black now, wet slaps of wind against the glass. Stef followed me. I kept my eyes down as the kids will when they don't want to be reached.

'This response, Nancy. It's out of all proportion. You tell me there's no problem, but I'm worried.'

He leant against the counter with his arms crossed, pulling his biceps tight in the sleeves of his T-shirt. Where he stood under the panelling of the side return, the freckles on his face, in gradations of tan, were thrown into relief.

'I try and talk to you and you just close down. I get that this is disorientating but you can't let yourself be derailed,' he said. 'We have a family now.'

'Oh don't exaggerate, Stef,' I said.

'Are you kidding? I've given you a lot of space, Nancy, but this mess,' he said. 'David's mess is spilling into all of our lives.'

'What are you talking about? You call this a mess? This place is bloody perfect.'

Every surface gleamed, shoes and bags were stowed, each item or appliance that was not beautiful was hidden in its designated place. Even the soap by the sink worked with the kitchen's larger concept.

'You're being facetious. You know what I mean. We're not functioning right now,' he said. 'We need to put in more time.'

I let the dog out and he began his huge looped figure of eights, nose to the ground.

'If I'm not at work, I'm here,' I said. 'There is no more time.'

'Well, we've got to ask ourselves why Frieda is spending her afternoons in somebody else's home.'

I turned.

'Yep, she was there last week and went over to Tara's again today and I guess there was a mix-up of some sort, I don't know, but Tara wasn't there and the husband sent her home which is why she's in that mood—'

'What's up?' said Frieda, in the doorway, one earbud in, the other dangling down her front. Tucked under her arm was the huge frayed envelope she carried everywhere. Scripts from Tara. 'Why are you shouting?' she said. 'I was trying to get some sleep.'

'Ah. You're here,' I said. 'Your dad and I have been talking and we don't want you going round to Adam's any more.'

'Hey. Nancy,' said Stefan. 'Back up. That's not what I was saying.'

'We don't get enough time together as a family as it is—'

'No way,' Frieda shouted at me, viciously. 'I love it over there.'

She followed me with her eyes and I saw her plan to hurt me.

'It's not like here, you know,' she said, slowly, with careful enunciation. 'Tara isn't stressy all the time.'

'You're being ridiculous,' I said. 'They're no different to us.'

'Oh yes they are,' she said. 'It's calm there. You can think.'

'Because they've got no kids,' I replied.

'No, Mum,' she said, 'because they're happy. That's the difference.' She started towards the door.

'That's rubbish,' I called after her. 'They're the same. They just don't show it. They're hiding it from you.'

'Mum,' she stopped and turned back. 'Why do you have to control everything? Oh I know, you just want me to "be safe",' she said, with finger quotes and rolling eyes. 'This is safe. It's helping me with work. There's no reason for me not to go other than you don't like it.' Her point made, she left. I swore less quietly than I should have.

'It's the wrong fight, Nancy, I've told you,' Stefan said. He gave a huge frustrated breath and moved towards the hallway.

'Come on, guys,' he called. He stretched his arms above him and gripped the frame of the door and I saw the waist band of his pants, the name of a brand I'd never heard of embossed in black cotton and a utilitarian font. 'Let's go out for pizza. Five minutes. Grab your stuff.'

Jake thundered up the staircase. I looked around for my bag.

'Not you, Nancy,' he said. 'Stay here. Have a bath or something.'

'I'm sorry?'

'Just get yourself together. I want some easy time with the kids.'

'Where's Mum?' I heard Louisa ask as she fastened her shoes.

'She's busy,' he said. Louisa didn't reply. 'Free. You fancy pizza? Or something else? You choose.'

'Sushi, then, I suppose,' she replied, crossly.

'Sushi it is,' he said.

'Gross,' Jake yelled. 'I'm not eating that,' and the argument tumbled off down the road.

20

We had lunch the next day, Adam and I, a picnic of bread and cheese on his office floor.

'What's this?' he asked, when I came in with the bags.

'A treat,' I replied, not an apology, or salve, or misdirection, though it was all of these things too.

I laid down a couple of tea towels, stained beyond salvation, and he bent to unpack the food. His hair has thinned into a widow's peak in the time we've been together and the skin there looked new and exposed. I ran my thumb across that place and he raised his head and kissed me with an intent I hadn't expected. We ate later; a perfect meal. The crust of the baguette gave with a hollow crack and the bread inside stretched to half its length again before pulling apart in reluctant twisty fingers. The butter was rich and yellow and there were crystals of salt in the cheese which we ate with a tart chilli jam. A bright patch began in a far corner of the room and we moved across and took the bottle, a plain white burgundy, crisp and cold. I laid my head on his lap, my cheek raised to the heat. He turned an apple in his hand above me and peeled off the skin in one long bouncing curl then passed a slice down on the tip of the knife, which I took in my teeth and was so acid that it pulled shut one eye. Each mouthful in high definition. We talked about when we might next get away, where we'd go, but it felt arbitrary and flimsy to me, just a hope.

'I've told Frieda not to go to yours any more,' I said.

'OK,' he replied. 'You didn't have to.'

He looked strange from below; I could see the work of time on his face, the loosening of his skin, gravity's pull. Proof that none of us have forever.

'Do you see much of her when she's over?' I asked.

'Not really,' he said. Then: 'Do you think she's like you?'

'People say so but I've never seen it. I've always felt she's more like Stef.'

'The way her laugh begins is exactly yours,' he said. 'When I first heard it I nearly dropped my cup. I was completely disorientated for a moment.'

'How odd,' I said. 'I've never noticed.'

'And there's something across her shoulders. I don't know if it's anatomy or body language but you're just the same,' and I recognised that in the drop of her school cardigan, in her bony little chest.

'Did you like it, then?' I asked. 'Having her around?'

'Like it?' he said. 'It's absolute torment, Nancy. I mean, that's no reflection on Frieda, I'm nowhere near knowing what sort of person she is, but it's torture, living with these shadings of you. I should keep out of the way, but I can't help but look for what I can find of you in her. It's impossible.'

'I'm sorry,' I said.

'Don't be. I can't imagine it's been easy for you either.'

'Are you happy, Adam?' I asked him then. It wasn't planned. 'Before— You once said that being with me made you happy.'

'Of course. It does,' he said. 'I am. Why do you ask?'

'I mean— With the situation. With how things are.'

'Why? What are you thinking?' he said, and there was a change in him, unmistakably. A tension through the muscles in his thighs beneath my head. I felt his anticipation. I chose my next words with care.

'I suppose— I just wanted to check that you have what you want,' I said.

'What I want?' I watched his throat bob, the mechanics of his swallow. 'Well, I want everything, Nancy.'

I raised my thumb to the hairless patch of skin beneath his chin. The moment when I should have replied came and went. I felt miles away.

'Everything you're willing to give, that is,' he said. 'Nothing else is worth having,' and I would have liked to thank him for that, for his elegance and his compassion, but instead I started to babble: that I was his completely and loved him with everything. That I knew he understood – it was the children – how could it be any other way? And whilst all of this was true, still I was hiding from him, crouched behind each stock phrase. And he listened to me kindly and as I watched, his expression reset into a subtly altered shape and I thought, that laugh of his must have been a cover. A lame frail mask. His face was built for sorrow, after all.

⁓

I left him and went to Louisa, who had an inset day and was spending it with April in the park. It was warm and there were bluebells, scentless, bunched together in the shade. Lou trampled a clump in pursuit of the dog and Ape said: 'We should pick them, Nance. They'll look lovely on your island. They'll only die.' The stems were thick and hollow and crunched when I snapped them, then oozed heavily. Ape gave me the tissue from up her sleeve and I wrapped the ends. I only had an hour and tried to find some pleasure in springtime, family, fresh air.

'Have you heard anything from David, sweetheart?' April said, as we walked.

'Of course not,' I replied. 'I'd have said so if I had.'

'I've been wondering, do you think he's gay?' she asked.

'What?'

'David. Do you think he's gay, love?'

'No, Aunty Ape.'

'Because your dad's not so old-fashioned as all that, you know.'

'He isn't.'

'And it's in the family. Bet no one told you, did they? There was a cousin, a long while back.'

'It's not that,' I said.

'Ah well,' she replied, and there was forbearance in her tone. 'I suppose we'll have to let him have his head,' as though we had a choice. April is a woman who cannot be surprised by a man.

The sun came and went. She held my arm and I looked down at her, small as a child. Her skull seemed narrow and underdeveloped. Her hair, intertwined like metal filament, sprang up from a thick white parting. Her face when she turned it up to me, was creased and beaky, something last century in it.

'You don't seem yourself, Nance,' April said. There was a drop in her shoulder when she led with her right foot, which was her bad hip playing up. 'Your dad says he hasn't seen you for a a while.'

I felt a deep, weighted apathy.

'I'm busy, Aunty Ape.'

'Aren't we all?' she replied.

We watched Louisa cartwheel on the grass beside us, again and again, in last year's shorts.

'She's growing up,' April said, with pleasure.

'She's a baby,' I replied. 'Much younger than the others at that age.'

'Well, I don't suppose you can see it,' she said, 'being up close all the time.'

'Watch me,' Louisa cried when she saw us looking, and this time, as her hands took her weight she snapped her legs together and there was a moment of stillness as they pointed up towards the sky, then she was moving again, carving a beautiful backwards arc to standing.

She came to us a touch bow-legged, the skin of her legs scuffed and bruised.

'Ta da,' she said, throwing her arms apart gawkily. 'What did you think?'

'Brilliant, Lou,' I said, which it was, although I'd seen it a hundred times before.

'Stand up straight, sweet,' said Ape, 'like in the proper gymnastics.'

'See, you're as tall as me now,' April said with a sly look back at me. Then: 'You're freezing, love.' She rubbed at Louisa's bare arms. 'Where's your jumper? And those shorts. Get your mum to buy you something new.'

April started on her legs, working Lou's thighs fast between two hands with an intimacy I wouldn't have risked but Louisa wore a patient smile and leant her hands into April's shoulders. An ice-cream van was parked on the path and played a couple of speeded-up bars.

'Please, Mum,' said Lou, turning to me now, hopping from foot to foot. 'Can I have one? It's virtually the holidays,' and she did seemed outsized suddenly in her rainbow T-shirt and I wondered why we hadn't started those same careful chats that I'd had with Frieda at about this time.

'OK,' I said. 'I'll get them. You two go and sit over there in the sun.'

'She's got her head screwed on, that one,' April said, as Louisa sprinted off lankily. 'Chocolate, please, Nance. With a flake if he's got one.'

The queue was already long and I watched the pair of them as I waited, my aunty tipping up Louisa's chin and establishing the drop of her bob with quick rough strokes. She had done the same to me when I was a girl and I remembered the amplified sound of her touch and then the surprise of her fingertips, abrasive and thick-skinned, when she caught the turn of an ear. I wondered which unsuitable story April was telling. She loved to shock, and I could see Lou listening harder, Ape still worrying

198

away at her hair. It would carry a kink in it for the rest of the day.

I stepped back to let a cyclist through, a toddler strapped loosely behind, asleep and lolling, and I shared a smile with the person in front at the picture they made. The line moved forward and my soles slid a little on the synthetic uppers of last summer's sandals. Across the path, Louisa gave a sudden laugh and I saw April pull her nearer, in that grabby way she has, love and spite all tangled. The dog lay before them, on his back, with his wide hound smile and his legs kicking up. The van played its notes again, fast and anxious, and I imagined leaving all of this behind. It felt possible, though wrong. Then I thought of carrying on without Adam, but the concept seemed beyond my grasp, too complex and unknowable.

'Come on, Mum. Hurry up,' Louisa said, in front of me, suddenly. 'Why are you standing there?'

'I'm not,' I replied. 'Take this over to your aunt.'

'What's the matter?' she said.

'Nothing. I'm coming.'

'Are you ill?' she asked, her face alert.

'No, I'm fine.'

'Get a move on, Lou,' April called across the space, at a volume that got people looking. 'What are you waiting for, girl? They'll melt.' She began to push herself up stiffly.

'You don't look very well, Mummy,' Lou said.

'Louisa, please,' I replied and she started back to April at last, watching the ice creams as she went, the weight of its flake threatening to tip the most top-heavy cone. I binned mine and left, with a view to finding Adam and a promise to get home as soon as I humanly could.

Back in the office, though, and he wasn't there. Lynn couldn't help and so I sat at his desk, feeling for his things, trying to divine where he was and what he might be thinking. The door went and I rose but it was not Adam but Tim, who gave a wry little laugh when he saw me, and said: 'Well, this makes things a whole lot easier, I suppose.'

'What's that?' I replied.

His top lip twitched as if tugged by a line. 'Well, I was actually hoping to speak to Adam,' he said, 'which is why I came into his office, not yours.'

'But he isn't here, as you can see, so you might as well speak to me.'

'Probably for the best,' Tim replied. 'He might have tried to dissuade me, being the softer of you pair.'

'Can you come inside?' I asked.

Another short laugh which broke open into a snarl that showed his gums. He made a throaty sound of repression. 'You're worried about privacy, are you? Or profession-alism?' he said. I'd known Tim for a decade, a person of uneven temperament outside his work to whom I'd chosen to give a second chance. I wondered if he should even be practising.

'What is this?' I asked.

'Hold on a minute,' he said. 'I'll be right back.'

He crossed reception with a bounce in his walk. Lynn, spellbound, turned her head to follow. He reached his office and she woke up, spun her face to me, a study in frozen panic, but then he was out again and her look was drawn back to him. He entered Adam's office fast and kicked the door shut with the back of his heel. He tossed an envelope across the desk and I read the letter in seconds, a template, brief and formal.

'Can I ask you why?' I said, fighting the urge to throw it back at him.

'Personal reasons,' he replied.

He'd given notice on his room, we had agreed at the outset on a month.

'If you've got something to get off your chest, now's the moment,' I said but he turned instead to leave.

'Did you have some message for Adam by the way?' I asked. 'Before you go?'

'Tell him I wish him the very best of luck,' he said, his fist on the handle. He slammed the door behind him, definitively this time, which gave me some small gratification. If he'd allowed himself full rein, I think he might have hit me. I heard him to speak to Lynn through the wall, spitting contempt, and when he'd gone, at last, she came in with a timid knock and a tea trembling in its saucer.

'Are you OK, Nancy?' she asked. 'Oh my goodness. Wasn't he cross.'

She went back to work and when the phone rang outside, answered it quietly, so as not to disturb me, convalescing at the desk.

21

Next day I stayed at home. Stefan was out, presenting visual identities to a luxury riverside brand aboard a boat – his idea – and so I was alone. The house drooped without the kids. It seemed unfamiliar, settled into some earlier shape, our updates just surface and temporary. The paint job looked drab and the dialogue between our modish furniture and the house's old shell – intended to be witty – just fell flat. I felt a kind of tenderness towards our own best efforts and then did what I always do and set about trying to re-establish us.

I shook out a grey wool blanket with tapered stripes like a backgammon board and laid it on the back of a chair, then lit the chain of fluorescent letters we have strung up along a wall. There had been *Fun* and *Love* and *Dancing* on the website but we bought *Ciao* in the end, because we liked the way it meant one thing as well as its opposite and the cursive was looped and elegant. It looked good, in the winter months, when you switched it to blink – it stretched out Christmas – but it was spring-time now and the light outside was brutal and outshone the fairground bulbs. I made a drink and watched the dog claw the blanket back down. He pulled it to the floor with his teeth, he circled and stamped. He kneaded with his pointed toes then flattened it out behind him with quick rabbity kicks, pulling tiny snags in the wool as he did it, but I love to watch him demonstrate his true nature and didn't have the heart to spoil his fun. At last he settled and was sleeping, instantly. I drained the ancient mug, which bore a rude joke – a gift from my son – and went back to the house and its inevitable demands.

I filled a bag with warped trainers and outgrown clothes. I threw out a load of old jars. I stood at the hob, the window in front of me fogged thickly, dripping steady tears, and I was thinking that outside could be anything: alien invasion or the end of the world and neither one of them a disaster, when the landline went, and it was Frieda, asking for her dad. I said he wasn't there and heard panic break in her voice and then her efforts to smooth it away.

'But where is he?' she said. 'Why isn't he there? I've been trying his phone.'

She needed an essay from her laptop which she'd left in her room.

'Don't worry. I can do it,' I said. 'Thank goodness I was in.' My tone was bright. She knew I'd heard her preference for Stef and I wanted her to think I didn't mind. I wiped an oval clear of condensation and his shed came into view. I could see him, usually, through his window, with his headphones on, listening to the music that Frieda recommends, but today the lights were off.

'That's true,' she said. 'Thanks, Mum.'

Still, her instinct was good, for Stefan would never have

203

done what I went on to do, but he is hamstrung by his morality. Do we not, above all, bear responsibility to keep our children safe? He'd drag them from a burning car, but it is me who would have to raise the bat to an intruder if it came to it. Stefan is squeamish and he always thinks first.

'Mum, you will— Respect my privacy. Won't you?' she said.

'Sweetheart. Just tell me what you need.'

My slippered tread felt sneaky on the stair.

The essay was on her hard drive and I was to load my email account on her screen and send it from there. I opened the laptop, bringing the keyboard upwards too; Stef's old Mac, creaky and overused.

'Hold on,' I said. 'I need to put the phone down for a sec.'

I eased the stiff joints apart and her screensaver appeared, a picture of her and her two best girlfriends dropped on to a beach they'd never visited, cheeks pressed together, fish faces and their arms and legs out star-shaped. Her password was an obscure mix of letters I didn't recognise but felt artful; I sensed method in there somewhere. In between, the date of her birth, reversed.

'Say it again,' I said, 'I got it wrong.' She did, and I wrote it down on one of her oversized post-it notes with a pen that had a pom-pom set on its end.

'Shut it now, please,' she said after I'd sent across her work, and then, in a tiny voice: 'Do you promise?'

'Done,' I told her, and I even pulled the screen down, imagining she might hear a tiny whoosh of displaced air or some resistance in the hinge, a metallic twang.

'Right, I need to get on, now, Free,' I said and she

believed me. She was away, leaving me there amongst her things.

It was odd to be in her bedroom without her. There was the faint animal scent of her sleeping self and the sweet clay of the lidless make-up arranged along the windowsill, all gouged and claggy. She had been burning her candles, something unusual, a smoky tea or burning pine, but I smelt mostly dead air, warm and slow, the room returning to its uninhabited state. Dust had settled gently; enough already, on her desk, that I could draw the outline of a heart, visible in a block of sudden sun. When she was small, she drew hearts everywhere, and moons and stars in glitter-pens and I gathered the pages to put aside for nostalgia's sake, but it made her cross – my efforts to give her drawings weight. Her infant self was still so present to me, in the brief flare of her upset, the knock beneath her eye that had left a mark, that I hadn't had to turn to those old things yet.

So I began. I stuck my fingers in the pen jar but there was nothing but old memory sticks, an ink-mulched rubber and a half-wrapped chew. There was a drift of discarded paper which I moved with my foot, disturbing a long string of bobbled fluff. Copy after copy of her essay on *Lord of the Flies* with minute amendments marked in red. 'Ralph and Simon are both good, what are the differences in their goodness?' The bed was loosely made, her water glass half-drunk and starting to bubble. Every plug socket was on, and most trailed chargers. There were clothes all over, of course, and a self-conscious display of photos around her mirror, of girls who I may or may not have known. I checked her drawers – nothing of note but a worshipful arrangement of sanitary products and a slightly racy paperback. I looked under the mattress, at the back of her high shelves, behind a poster. I opened her computer and there was her face again, but it didn't pull me up. I spent an hour pawing through. That she didn't use her email much was clear, seven thousand lay unread, broken up with the odd one she had starred (bless her heart) from me or Stef. Her documents were neatly arranged and contained what their titles implied. I clicked on her history but it had been cleared, which I assumed was just good sense; Jake had brought home a story of a boy who left his laptop unguarded at school, and when he whispered to the others what was found, it was enough to make Louisa blush and Frieda slap his arm.

At the bottom of her wardrobe was a box. I knew this box; it had once contained a gift from me, but now she used it to store her special things. There was no secret about it. She would leave it unattended, though she no longer took me through the contents as she used to, an inventory of every item, a justification for each choice. I flipped a corner of the lid, bent away as though braced for a bang and it was then, as I leaned back in, that I asked myself what I was doing here, what I was hoping to achieve, and the answer was simple and sad, that I just wanted to know her again.

On top, I found a tiny gift, beautifully wrapped in a thick red paper. A ribbon had been wrapped twice around the package and tied in an extravagant bow, wider than the box. The ends were snipped into clean points and a card was tucked underneath. I worked it free. *Happy Birthday and good luck on the night!!* it read, in an even inked hand, effortfully adult.

The knot of the ribbon gave with a fibrous creak that I felt at the back of my teeth. The wrapping was so glossy that the tape eased away with the merest application of a nail and sprung apart entirely creaseless.

The box inside was nondescript, a rough recycled cardboard and I felt both dread and anticipation as I opened it. Inside, I found one tiny earring, a delicate gold cuff made of wire as fine as a paperclip and bent into the shape of a triangle. Sweet, adolescent and blameless.

So I straightened the room. I hid my presence. I bent for the dressing gown I'd knocked from her door, full of a fear that one of them would come home and catch me at it. I was in the wrong now; finding nothing had made me culpable. Then I laid down my head on her pillow, blotched with milky shadings of her spit, and slept a long deep sleep.

Louisa woke me. 'Mum, what are you doing in there?' she cried, from the doorway, her voice high with disapproval. She leaned across the threshold but seemed reluctant to step into her sister's room. Free's rules held in her absence, for Louisa at least.

'Get up, Mum,' she said. 'Why are you being so weird? The house is all dark.'

I scrambled through my apologies and led her back down, my eyes thick and my hair mussed up one side. I twisted dimmers as I went and the house shook out its skirts and raised its best face up to us. A bank of happy photos woke under their lights, the cushions on the sofa picked out a colour in the rug, and on the radio Big Ben chimed the news. The dog leapt from his bed and trotted a couple of perimeters of the room.

'Pasta,' I said, 'don't you think? Fetch me down the big pot,' and when Lou brought it across, her face was smoothed once more by certainty, repetition and habit. Then Jake arrived, delighted by a huge new bruise he had earned in a rough game of rugby. He dropped his trousers to show us, a perfect studded print on the teardrop-shaped muscle above his knee, and he laughed when he saw it again, even darker now, he claimed, and pressed it all around until he found the sorest part. He took a photo on his phone which he sent to friends. I made a bolognese with pancetta added to the onions and a handful of fresh oregano ripped from the pot, which brought the kids across to the pan, and then again later when I added the wine.

I gave it an hour, but still no Free.

I called her number but the phone rang out. I fed the others and asked them did they know where she might be? Could they remember any arrangement? But neither did. I texted Stef, but he was still in his meeting and would be for at least another hour. I looked in the diary and at the board we had long since stopped using and there was an itch at the edge of my memory but I couldn't pull it into view. I poured myself a glass, which fuzzed my worry at first, then sharpened it. I moved around the kitchen and Louisa eyed me subtly, looking away when I caught her.

'I'm popping out,' I said, already wearing my boots.

'Why?' she replied. 'Where?'

'I'll be half an hour, OK? We can all watch some telly when I get back.'

'Where are you going?' said Louisa. 'I want to come.'

'Lou, it's much easier if you stay. Your brother's staying.'

'But he's on his screen,' she said.

'So get ready, then. You need to be quick.'

'I'm not getting out,' she said, settling herself into the front seat in bedsocks and old leggings, grimed and loose at the knees. 'Where are we going, anyway?' She flicked through the radio stations looking for a song. She'd brought a soft drink and a snack.

'Off to get Frieda,' I told her.

'Have you remembered, then?' Louisa asked.

'I have,' I replied and pulled out into the road.

I'd driven to Adam's in the early days, those times of sleepless yearning when I couldn't rest or eat or hear any other voice but his. I'd never met him at his home, but I knew where he lived and liked to drive by, my foot easing up and down on the brake as I passed, or simply park up and watch, just for ten minutes or so, yoga my alibi, a bag of untouched kit in the boot. Most often I saw no one but still it hadn't felt like a wasted trip. To be in his environment gave me comfort.

I never saw Tara, though three times I spotted Adam. The first, he was walking down his road, his long feet flapping, his face raised skywards with a sanguine look and a twist to his smile and I just knew that he was thinking about me. It took everything, then, not to run across the road and embrace him.

Next time, I saw him in his window as he pulled the curtains to at the turning point of dusk; heavy old things, I could see that in their drag across the runners, and he looked so carefully left and right that I wondered if he sensed me out there. I imagined ringing, seeing him raise his phone to his ear and then leaving that warm yellow room behind and coming to me, in the chill, where we would make love in my car, not giving a damn who saw.

Then there was a Saturday. All three children at home, a TV talent show on, gin and tonics and the dog unchallenged on the chair. We shushed for our favourites, texting in to cast our votes and then some young girl hit her note, the crowd roared, and my throat was full of a rising sob; I felt a true desperation. I claimed an allergy, hid the Piriton and left.

I arrived at Adam's at the same time as his early guests, a couple who looked like no one I had ever known. Established yet bohemian. Right-thinking and inherited and certain. When Adam opened the door, I heard the strange and gorgeous music that he preferred, some melancholy aria which moved me, but I couldn't understand. The next pair hopped off the bus with two bottles of champagne that she took out of the shopper on the doorstep and finally two women, who laughed as they pushed aside his gate as though they'd never felt doubt. I watched them all for a while, the party unfolding in the window, and then went home. Lou and Stef stood up when I came in. They asked how I was. I said the medicine made me sick and went to bed. On Monday, Adam had looked tired. I asked him about his weekend but he took my face in his hands and said: 'You weren't there,' and I forgot what I had seen. I never told him, nor went back, though I felt how easily it could become compulsion.

This time, though, I didn't wait outside. I pulled in right before his house in a space that felt like it had been left for me and walked straight up the path. I rapped the knocker, something Regency, in brass. Behind me, Louisa rolled her window down. A light went on in the pane above the door.

'Nancy,' said Adam, and took the top of my arms. He wore old cotton pyjama bottoms of the sort that I had imagined him in.

'Louisa's in the car,' I said.

He looked over my shoulder and dropped his hands. 'Are you OK?' he asked. 'Why weren't you at work? Come inside. Bring Louisa.' I saw him attempt a smile at her. The reflex lift of a hand that he cut short.

'Is she here?' I said.

I tried to form an impression of his home. The hall was large and square and painted a current shade of aubergine. I saw an old grandfather clock next to the stairs with a moon dial above its face, a semi-circle of sapphire sky dotted with tiny incandescent stars. I found it beautiful and that surprised me. I supposed it had been passed down the line.

To my right, a rack of hooks held their coats and outdoor things. There was an old cardigan she would have worn around the house, a tissue worked halfway out of the pocket. She had the same high street parka as me, or similar; a bit too young for both of us. I was aware, for the first time, of my incursion. It struck me like a tiny wonder.

'No, she's still at work,' he said. He looked away and gave an incredulous little burble. 'I can't believe you're here, Nancy,' and lifted his hands towards me once more, briefly, weakly. 'Come on,' he said. 'Let's get Lou in. She must be cold. Tell me what's happened,' and I saw his excitement then, in his fidget and the curl of his mouth. His readiness for what he thought must be this next phase. There was something almost obscene in it.

'I meant Frieda,' I said. 'I thought she was with you.'

'Frieda?' he replied. 'No, why would she be?'

'She's not at home.'

'What is this? Are you worried?'

'Mummy.'

I felt a cool hand on my arm and found Louisa there.

'Lou, I'm sorry.' I smoothed her hair across in a way I knew she would barely abide. 'Frieda isn't here. I made a mistake.'

'Hello again,' she said, looking up at Adam.

'Oh. Hello Lou. Louisa. Yes. We met at your mum's office, my office, didn't we? The other day?'

She didn't reply. Her gaze slipped off behind him.

'Can I stroke your cat?' she said, and I saw it at the back of the room, a saunter in its step, its only acknowledgement of us a shivering at the tip of its tail.

'Of course. He's Bob,' replied Adam and bent down, clicking his tongue. The cat stopped and watched, but didn't come any closer.

'My feet are damp,' Louisa said. 'And you've got carpet.'

We all looked down. She had come out shoeless from the car and her socks, bunched around her ankles, showed a dark rim of wet.

'Here,' I said. 'Take them off.'

'Don't worry. Really. Don't worry at all,' Adam said, still kneeling awkwardly, but she pulled each one off cleanly, straight from the toe, and laid them, like pelts, across my arm. She walked past Adam and sat before the cat. It lowered its head to her and she scratched it expertly about the ears.

'He likes you,' Adam said, coming to stand. Louisa didn't reply. 'So, Frieda,' he said. 'Is she—? What made you think she was here?'

'Oh I don't know. I was expecting her back. I'm sure she told me. I just couldn't think.'

'She's home now,' Louisa called from across the hall. 'She texted. You must have got mixed up.' She pulled my phone from the pouch in the front of her hoodie and held it towards me. I took it and read: *At home Mum. Been at rehearsal. Duh.*

'For God's sake, Louisa, why didn't you say?'

'I just did,' she replied. She brushed the cat's back now and it bowed its spine into each long stroke.

'Louisa, don't be rude. I'm sorry,' I said to Adam. 'She's not usually like this.'

'Like what?' Lou said. 'Be careful, Mum.'

'What?'

'You're very close to this cat. She's allergic, you know,' she said, twisting her head towards Adam, her eyes still on the animal. 'She shouldn't go near them at all.'

'Oh dear,' he said. 'I didn't. Will you be OK, Nancy? Maybe come inside a bit. His basket's just there. Shall I get you a tablet?'

I followed him into their kitchen, a little cluttered, rather folksy. He switched on a lampshade resting on the countertop and poured me a glass of water from the tap. Two cocktail glasses drained next to the sink. A huge flat oval lapis ring lay on the windowsill. Magnets attached the corners of a child's drawing to the fridge's door. A face rendered in violent crayon strokes.

'Nancy,' he said, in a whisper, and took a step towards me. From the hall, I heard Louisa's mutterings to the cat. Adam's face showed loss.

'I don't understand you in this place,' I said.

'I love you,' he replied.

'I love you too.'

He pressed his forehead to mine and I closed my eyes.

'I need to go,' I said, and he nodded. We left the room but the hall was empty now.

'Lou,' I called, higher and shorter than I'd intended.

'In here,' she replied lazily. 'I followed the cat.'

'Is it—? Can I go in?' I asked.

'Oh, Nancy, of course,' he said, hopelessness in his tone.

I found myself in a beautiful room, an almost gothic space of colour and texture, of statement and counter-argument. It was full; layer upon layer of things, carefully accrued. I saw meaning and sentiment everywhere. An anecdote behind each piece. I felt my own threat to this place. I was a bomb in the house.

Louisa stood at the back before a large set of bay windows, her hands clutched behind her like a child from some old painting. Two wingback chairs faced each other across a spindly-legged card table. There was an old tin ashtray on it, a butt wedged down into one of four grooves.

'Who smokes?' she asked Adam.

'Louisa,' I said.

'It's me,' Adam replied and she nodded and moved on slowing, looking everywhere, taking inventory. She seemed to borrow some sort of assurance from this room. I wanted to drag her out of it but suddenly felt afraid.

'Is this real?' Lou asked, pausing at a box set into the wall.

'Don't touch the glass,' I said. 'You'll leave a print.'

'It is,' replied Adam.

'Yuk,' Lou said.

'Do you not like owls?' Adam asked.

'Not in boxes, I don't,' Louisa replied.

'We need to go,' I said.

She crossed the room now, her feet deep in a thick cream Berber rug. I could see her toes flex and dig into the pile as she went, the pleasure travel up and take its place on her face. Her walk was different here, too.

'I like the way this carpet changes,' she said, and she was right. Where I stood, a loose honeycomb pattern had been picked out in black, but it ended at the midpoint and just two thin columns of hexagons travelled on to the rug's far edge. The effect was unmade, as though the weave had come unpicked. Now and again were short, straight lines of black wool, like offcuts of the main design, and splats of mustard, orange and blue. Louisa hopped from one burst of colour to the next, her free leg tucked behind her, until she landed, with a bounce, on a chaise. She dropped on to her knees.

'Is this the dress-up trunk?' she asked.

'No,' he replied. I heard his fingers drum on a console table behind him.

'Frieda's told me all about it, you know,' she said, looking up at us through her tatty fringe.

'That's in Tara's room,' he said. 'I— We don't go in when she's not here.'

'So what's this, then?' Louisa asked.

From the hall, the clock began a busy whirr. A sequence of clicks and grates and it finally chimed.

'It's a tuck box,' Adam said.

'What's that?' she asked, although she knew full well from books.

'It's for children when they're sent away to school,' he replied.

She viewed him with a brief new interest and turned back to the box. She lifted the old brass latch and let it drop with a clank.

'There's nothing inside,' he said.

'Is that your name? ABR Fitch?' she asked.

'It is.'

'What does it stand for? Wait. Let me guess,' she said.

'Louisa. We're going now. Your sister needs feeding.'

'Adam Boris Rupert,' Louisa said. She got up to her feet.

'No,' replied Adam.

'Adam Benjamin Robert,' she said. I put my hands on her shoulder blades and moved her on.

'Closer,' he replied.

And then from somewhere in the room came the noise of material ripping, a long, slow teasing shriek.

'What's that?' I said, and felt a terrible, illogical culpability, as if my malice had somehow found form and vandalised the room.

'Oh, Bob,' said Louisa.

The curtain, a thick rough linen, trembled, and the cat came down to land at its foot. The last half-metre was shredded, fibres everywhere, the bottom torn and jagged like something left over from Halloween.

'Don't worry,' Adam says. 'He does that.'

'And you let him?' Louisa said, looking from him, to me, to the tattered fabric in plain astonishment. I finally got her out.

'Cheerio,' called Adam, at the front door in his best and brightest voice. 'Bye, Louisa. See you tomorrow, Nancy. At the office, that is. Be safe.'

On the path, she shrugged off my touch roughly.

We drove home in self-conscious silence, Louisa humming a tune I couldn't recognise. She played with her hands inside her hoodie's pouch, then took to grooming herself, tweaking skin from the sides of her fingernails, pulling down the vanity mirror to examine her face. I didn't believe a second of it.

22

Marie in her chair, in her suit, looked bland and non-specific, in disguise for the workaday week, or maybe me. I'd fought with Adam before she got there and wished I'd lit a candle. The room was thick with bullshit and old problems. I'd have liked to start again.

'Can I take your jacket?' I said from somewhere off behind her, delaying the moment when I'd have to sit down under her stare. I felt distracted and unprepared, her issues distant and complex.

'I'll keep it,' she replied, 'I feel the cold,' and gave a little tremor to prove it.

'Oh I do, too,' I said, which wasn't true. I felt her watching me, inquisitive, like a bird might from its tree.

A row broke out in the street below. 'You're kidding me,' a voice said. A car door slammed, hard enough to shake my window in its fittings. 'Yeah just fuck off,' the man called again, over the sound of fast wet tyres. He must have kicked the car as it moved away, for there was a tinny kind of clunk, a cartoon noise that must have disappointed the kicker. We shared an acknowledgement of it, Marie and I, and something loosened between us.

'OK,' I began.

'Actually, I've got a question,' said Marie. 'Something I've been thinking about.'

'Of course,' I replied. 'Go on.'

'I've been wondering how much happiness I should expect. How much is reasonable, for someone ordinary, like me.'

She pushed herself deeper into her chair. I looked down into my notebook where I'd plotted the arc of last week's discussion.

'Keep going,' I said, to buy myself time.

'I mean, how do I know if there's more?'

'If you made different choices in your life?' I asked.

'Perhaps,' she said.

'Well part of that is coming to recognise your own wants and needs. I think we touched on that before. Can you think of a time in your life that felt particularly good?'

'Not really,' Marie said, thoughtfully. 'Not long periods, anyway. There were moments, I suppose.'

'What sort of moments?'

She watched me carefully through the sides of her eyes.

'Times when I'd done well.'

'Give me an example.'

'I won a prize at school for reciting a poem in French. I had to go up and collect it on the stage. Everybody clapped.'

'So you're someone who is motivated by achievement but also, perhaps, by recognition from others,' I said.

'You're making me sound shallow,' she replied.

'Not at all. You know, you need to give yourself permission to want things,' I said. 'For yourself. That isn't wrong.'

She gave that nod I'd come to recognise, a scepticism not quite hiding a curious girl.

'I want us to look at this page together,' I said, on a hunch.

In my drawer was a slim file of worksheets. I reached into it, straightening an old photo of David and me, come un-wedged from the casing of my computer screen.

'We call this the Personal Bill of Rights. Have a read-through. Some of the statements might seem odd at first, but we're working towards an acceptance of each of them. Let's start by picking out any that seem interesting to you, in whatever way.'

She began to read. 'Number one. *I have the right to ask for what I want.*' She paused. 'Well, yes, I suppose so, but that doesn't mean I'm going to get it, now, does it?' She gave an awkward laugh and ran her finger down the line.

'So we're always told,' I said.

'*I have the right to express all of my feelings, positive or negative,*' she said.

'You do,' I replied. 'Those are the rules in here, of course, but it's about taking that idea out of this room—'

'*I have the right to change my mind.*'

Next door Adam laughed, the sound reaching me easily, the tumble of it, even and rhythmed, like something out of nature, the collapse of a mountain or an approaching storm. I wondered if I was attuned to it, like a dog and its master's whistle. The air thickened in my throat.

'*I have the right to make mistakes and not have to be per-fect.*' That one made her laugh.

'How about we start with the statements that—' I said.

'Oh here's a goody: *I have the right not to be responsible for others.* You're a mother, Nancy, how does that work for you?'

I had a sudden flash of my children, a tiny vision of each, tucked into their creases of London and the efforts and subterfuge it took to merely hold your place each day.

'I think, to be honest, the idea there is more about—'

'*I have the right not to give excuses or reasons.* Really? So it's a question of just doing what you want, then, is it? This reads like a psychopath's handbook, Nancy.'

I glanced down at my copy. The ideas seemed to have changed in her mouth.

'Well, if that's your response, then we certainly need to do some more work in the area of assertion—'

'*I have the right to change and grow.*' Her voice bounced through the syllables now, openly mocking. 'Where does everyone else fit into this? Because it all impacts on others, doesn't it?' she said.

'Well, as I'm sure you know, before we can really succeed in relationships, we need to take care of—'

'Oh Nancy,' she said. 'Stop pretending, will you? We none of us live alone.'

She turned her face away. In profile, she was beautiful – I hadn't seen it until then – beaked and elegant. I pictured her sometime after the war, at a fireplace, in a grand house, with a cocktail in a hand-blown glass. She held that position and I wondered if she knew her face from that angle; if this impression was her intent.

'*I have the right to be happy.* Do I though?' she asked. 'Do any of us? Is that really a right?'

'Well, you tell me,' I said. 'What do you think, Marie?'

'Do you live by all of this?' she said.

'This is not really the environment—'

'No. I know,' she said. 'I know. Don't worry.' A new, tired smile. 'Isn't time just about up?'

'Almost. It's fine. If you get a moment—'

'Yes,' she said. 'I'll look through them again at home.'

'I understand this process can feel frustrating, Marie. It's not unusual and it often peaks just before some kind of breakthrough. Next time—'

She took a long slow breath in and her eyelids bounced shut just for an instant.

'It's OK, Nancy,' she said, and when she looked at me again, her face had resumed its usual aspect, her disappointment tucked away. She stood, though there was ten minutes to go, holding the page in a pinch at its corner and when she turned, a freak breeze from the window pulled it back towards me in a languorous ripple and I wanted to reach out and snatch it from her. She moved away slowly and her shape, in her tailored skirt, her fluent, unhurried movement, the weight of her shifting from one side to the other, was oddly provoking.

'You're not God, you know,' Marie said, at the door.

'Of course not,' I replied. And yet you've come here, I thought, to be absolved, haven't you? To be told that you can start over.

'See you next week,' she called back at me. 'Take good care.'

~

I watched the weather from the train. A sudden massive dump of water then the first sun in a long time, flashing snags of light at me off the wet fronts of everything; shop windows, cars and hyper-green leaves. When I got off, the rain rushed in a helix through the gutters with a noise that seemed too huge, and at the storm drains, where it should have poured away, it surged up onto the pavements, soaking my shoes. At home, the effort showing on the face of our house – its apple-pie smile shining out from between our shattered neighbours – seemed somewhere between dishonest and an out-and-out lie. Inside, like some weird extension of that thought, I found Jake, Free and Louisa arranged up the bannisters, sit-com style. Only the dog told the truth, acknowledging the artifice with a fixed and anxious swiping of his tail.

'What's this?' I said.

'Date night!' cried Free, in pitch-perfect American high-school. 'To cheer you up, Mum.'

Lou held one of my old handbags. 'Take this,' she said.

'Where did you find that?' I asked. Inside were a long-lost lipstick and an ancient theatre ticket.

'And these shoes,' she said. The Jimmy Choos I'd worn on our wedding day and later dyed so they'd get some use. They looked dried up and wonky, one heel tip gone.

Stefan stepped out from behind Jake, halfway up the stairs, with a little show of presentation. He smelt newly showered and wore a fresh-pressed shirt.

'I thought we could get out?' he said. 'Just an hour or two. I know you're knackered.' Behind his standard smile showed hope, a little doubt.

'And I'm in charge!' called Free, flinging out one arm.

'That's so not fair,' creaked Jake, in his recent adult's voice. Lou bent to his ear, presumably setting out the advantages of flexible bedtimes and un-policed treats.

'And when was that decided?' I said.

'I'm nearly fifteen, Mum, you know,' Frieda replied, her enthusiasm making her seem younger. 'One week to go!' She was humouring me; in no doubt that her daddy's word would be upheld.

'This feels like an ambush,' I said, though that was unkind; they were only trying to be nice. 'We'll be local, I suppose. I need to shower. Give me five minutes,' I said and they scattered.

He had tidied our room while I'd been out. On my bedside table, the books were neat and a clutch of daffodils leant their weight against one point of the vase. I snipped the string with nail scissors and shook them out in a little burst of drips. The week's un-homed clothes had been left, folded, on the end of our bed and I knew he would have moved them from the armchair where I drop them each night and wondered again, why I did that when he had asked me not to, because he felt it as my indifference and that had to hurt.

The chair was his favourite piece, a gift to me: 'An original, you know,' he had said, when he brought me upstairs, hands over my eyes, the seat already settled in its spot. It was mid-century, of slim-lined oak with a thick burnt-orange cushion. 'The frame, I mean. I got it re-upholstered. Do you like it?' he asked. He crouched by its side and ran a finger up the shallow slope of its arm. 'The lines are beautiful, don't you think?'

I hadn't been sure, at first, and then began to notice similar, in magazines or in the background of the right type of television show. I got there, in the end, my own taste moving into line, though it felt a bit learned by then. The chair was never used – what adult spends their time up in their room? And so I buried it in discarded clothes and he mentioned this, for a while – asked me to stop, could I not find somewhere else? – but I didn't, the habit calcified, and he let it go. So I sat there this evening, after my shower, and tried to enjoy its promise of a view. I watched a manic dog zigzag through a rhombus of scrubby park, though I had to lean forward to do it. The angles of the chair were set at an unnatural tilt, they tipped my gaze straight into the sky. I got up and changed into an age-old dress and the shoes that Louisa had chosen.

'Mum, you look lovely,' Lou said, when I came down. Then: 'Why don't you always wear stuff like that?'

'You know the last time I saw you in that dress?' Stef asked and although I did, I told him no, for this was one of the ways that he showed me his love.

It had been a party, a splashy agency do before he set up alone. Lots of brief, aborted conversations and needy men sharing the same restless energy. 'We got out of there, though, and went for food, do you remember?' he said. Dim sum in Chinatown which Stefan loved but made me squeamish, more wine but mostly smugness as we took all the other guests apart from safe inside our functioning marriage.

'Guys. Through to the kitchen, now, please. I'm going to make eggs,' called Frieda, to her siblings, in a parody of Mum. She'd even found a pinny.

'Bye, Mummy,' said Lou, trailing her fingers through my skirt as she passed. 'Don't forget to have fun.'

'Come on. Let's get out of here while we can,' Stef said and slipped his fingers between mine, that snug familiar fit.

'Shall we go the long way?' he asked; a line from our past. When we first met I was living with Mum, and Stef had a flat share with a group of boys he hardly knew. We got to know each other in public, in cafés, pubs and parks. He was outdoorsy and we left London for the weekends. I bought my first pair of walking boots and a proper coat.

'Where are we going?' I said.

'I don't know. Anywhere. Come on. It's cold,' he replied, and it was; a low abrupt wind and rain in the odd spiteful handful. The park was empty now.

'You take my scarf,' he said. He stopped and one end uncurled from his neck in a sudden gust. He caught it and threw the loop over my head and I saw him think of pulling me to him, but he turned instead and we walked on.

I had married pregnant, like my mother before me. Our union had the blessing of serendipity. I met him on my birthday, queuing for a round when he came up and said, 'Hi, I'd like to know you,' with his straightforward look and his hand held out. I chose to read it as a sign. We married three years later to the day. 'Only somebody very certain should marry on their birthday,' Stef had said. 'Nancy the Brave,' I replied, my father's words, but it hadn't felt like a risk. I had believed completely in our chances of being happy. David, when I told him we were engaged, feeling shy and excited and malicious, said: 'Fair enough, sis, you couldn't hope for a better guy,' which left me surprised and I realised, after, a little let down.

'Let's get a drink first,' Stefan said. 'How about here?'

We turned into a new bar and crossed the dark empty floor. A young girl in a vest with an armful of tattoos laid down her phone and asked us what we'd like. We sat on stools.

'Martini?' he said.

'On a week night?'

'Live a little, Nance.'

We observed the ceremony of the drink. She seasoned the shaker and assembled the elements competently. It tasted good; frosty, oiled and brined. Like petrol, briefly, at the back of my nose.

'You guys local?' the girl asked.

'Oh yes,' Stef replied.

She turned the music down a fraction, and eased the lighting up. We laughed at that; at the truth that we were getting old. At the far end of the room, outside was just a rectangle of dun light, dimming fast. He misinterpreted my attention and took my hand.

He began to talk about Free's party, just a week away. His thoughts for the night, how we might marry the needs of our daughter and friends with that of the family. He observed that she was growing. Her need for independence. Did I think some of them might smoke? What was our policy on booze? He had the idea we could splash out on a marquee.

'She's growing up great, though, Nance. Don't you think?' he said, shiny-eyed, but he didn't wait for my reply, borne away on the idea of our family's perfection.

We ordered a second. This one was smoother, easier. Another couple came in, tentative and possibly under-age. When their request for beer was granted, they relaxed and began to kiss, aggressively, at a table a little way away.

'This place is weird,' I said. 'Do you think we should try somewhere else?'

The girl behind the bar was bored. She passed us olives and I speared one with a cocktail stick and raised it towards my mouth. Stef leant forward and closed his teeth over it.

'Anchovy,' he said. 'Saved you.'

The girl watched and I saw her respond to him. His appeal has sharpened across the years, perhaps because his aesthetic has become current but there is also his decency, which is only more valuable over time. Men could over-look him, but he doesn't care, and that puts him further ahead again. Stef is a patient man. A man who carries his load without question. Our family gives him joy.

We talked about Lou. Her curiosity and her kindness.

'She's shrewd, too,' I said, but he made no comment and I didn't expand. Didn't mention her manipulations. The clever ways I'd seen her exert control. Why rain on his parade? Stef is, after all, an excellent mate; respectful, present, true.

When he turned to Jake, he chuckled.

'Such a boy, though, don't you think? It's so funny.

Those conversations about gender and then you have a child—'

'He's wonderful, of course, but he can be mean, Stef. I've heard him. On the computer. With his friends.'

'Sure, the banter and so on, but he's a good kid. He's got a good heart. That's the thing.'

'He can be cruel,' I said. 'I've seen it. You must have too.'

That pulled him up.

'What are you saying—?'

'I'm saying nothing. But none of them are faultless. That's all I mean. Nobody is.'

'I wasn't suggesting they were. I was trying to enjoy, for tonight, our children's—'

'I know,' I said. 'I'm sorry. Forget it. He's a great boy. He is,' but Stef didn't want to talk about them any more. He tipped his drink, setting the last dregs of liquid rolling round the steep banks of the glass. When he spoke again, his voice was even.

'So, I've been thinking about David,' he said.

'Oh Stefan,' I replied. I noticed his arms, my favourite part of him, muscled from all that time in the gym, thick with light springy hair and freckled knuckle to elbow.

'It's just not right what he does,' he said.

'You don't say,' I replied.

'Which is whatever he likes and then hey, screw the rest of us.'

There is something mildly comical about Stef's English when provoked. He can choose the wrong word, slightly retro or tonally askew. I fought the urge to laugh.

'You do everything for your family, Nancy. Your parents,' he said. 'Us. The kids.'

'I don't know about that,' I replied and dropped my eyes, though he read it as modesty and went on.

'And then there's David.' He shook his head at the thought of him. 'I mean, what does it teach the girls? The way he behaves?'

'Well, we can hardly protect them from every difficult thing in life,' I said, on firmer ground now. 'That's not realistic. It's not even desirable—'

'Of course not,' Stefan said, and it was rare for him to interrupt me and I felt, then, his conviction, and the possibility that this evening had some purpose. 'What I'm really talking about is the way that you endorse him.'

'That's just not true,' I replied.

'It is. You know you do. And so it will continue when he comes back, this week, or next, and slots straight back in. Everything forgiven.'

He shook his watch on his wrist in a little declaration of frustration. The other couple ran through ringtones on a phone. Behind the bar, the girl cut a lime into thick wedges with a short sharp knife.

'He's my brother,' I said. 'I love him.'

'But that's not enough,' Stefan replied. 'He doesn't deserve it. He loses the right when he does this stuff. And I'm sorry, Nancy, but he doesn't love you back. If he did, he wouldn't act this way.' He gave a little puff of distaste.

'He's— There's a weakness. Or something. I don't know,' I said.

'You say he isn't depressed.'

'Well, there was no formal diagnosis. Nothing we've been able to put a name to.'

'So what are we left with then? That he's selfish. A baby.'

'Oh Stefan, you see things too simply.'

'You know, you always say that about me,' Stef replied. 'And I do, sometimes. I realise that. But not in this. I don't recognise you in the way you deal with David. The excuses. The denial. The way you obscure the truth of it. You're better than that.'

'Stefan,' I said. 'That's just not fair.'

'You lose your mind around him, with his charm and that handsome face.'

My only resistance now was silence.

'What I'm saying is that I don't want that for the girls. That template,' Stefan said. 'It's not healthy. You know it,' and I remembered that though his judgement was rare, when it came, it was absolute.

'So what are you suggesting? That I simply cast him aside?'

'It's got to change. For God's sake, Nancy, acknowledge what I'm saying.'

The barmaid watched us now, with little glances up through her eyelashes.

'OK, I understand,' I said. 'Just let me think. This is sudden.'

'Thank you,' he replied. 'That's all I'm asking. 'This—' he groped around before him in search of the word. 'This uncertainty. The tension all the time. I don't want it in my life.'

My phone went and we both jumped. The screen read *Home*. It was Louisa. She was OK, but Frieda had burnt herself on the hob. We were to come straight back.

'What on earth's that noise?' I asked, in panic. 'Have you called the police?' but it was Jake, somewhere behind them, on *Grand Theft Auto*.

I gave the phone to Stefan who asked for Free. 'Nothing to worry about, sweetheart,' he said, the middle T sounding as D, in a faint echo of my father's London inflection. 'We'll be home soon.'

The dog, at the door, showed his stress with his strange phlegmy pant, *ack ack ack*. They had done well with a tea towel and a bag of frozen peas. Frieda bore a sickle-shaped brand on the soft flesh of her inner arm, rather beautiful, and her eye make-up had resettled in gentle drifts on the bones of her cheeks. Nobody had eaten. It took ten minutes to sort, then, mouth metallic, my head tinny from booze, I settled with my family, crammed onto the sofa we'd long outgrown. Blankets, squabbles and repeats on the TV.

23

I woke straight into a memory. Matthias Coombes, a narrow child; thick white hair with a vintage wave and a lackadaisical bearing undercut by light nervy eyes. No bottom at all, his trousers at the back were limp and sorry. He was a little sod. Thanks to David, he very nearly drowned.

We were visiting with Mum, as we did each July, a dutiful trawl of her old county friends and every year the space between us and them grew wider, more rock-strewn. We always met at Matthias's home, which gave him an advantage and a slightly make-believe quality. He never felt quite real, as though he might not exist beyond the walls of his garden, or would vanish into a wisp of smoke if caught in the full glare of a day unfiltered by the leaves of an ancient tree or a slab of Georgian shutter.

My primary emotion on those trips was shame. Ourselves as living evidence of our mother's decline, with our London accents and modern clothes and minds full of chat and pop, yet when we got there, it seemed that we were the ones who were out of time. Where could that idea have hatched? It wasn't Mum, resolutely cheerful, bandying round treats all the way up and full of snarky observations in the dark on the fast road home. Monica, maybe – Matty's mother – with her dead smile; for a while I had admired her cut-throat charm. But there was something about the set-up that made David cross. He must have been around ten.

They had a pond, deep and brown and fed by a fast snaky stream. It was a distance down the garden but we were allowed as we were all strong swimmers (were we, though? Ten sessions in the council pool) and if you looked back up, you could see one white corner of the house, composed like art behind a lawn of parakeet green, and sometimes the outlines of the mothers in a window, depending on how the sun fell on the old thin glass. We used to get the dog in – Pooter, a horrible animal, barrel-shaped and stinking – but it was fun to throw sticks and watch her wiggly swim and the way she scrambled out, three or four goes at the steep slippery bank until Matthias bent down and dragged her by the collar.

He had a medal with him, this time, an oxidised bronze disc on a thick ribbed mustard ribbon that his father had won, though he wouldn't tell us how. He swung it in huge circles, the ribbon turning around a finger, and then yanked it back into the flat of his palm. He patrolled the bank and the movement and the thwack were distracting. I saw it cutting into David's focus as he tried to hit a rock with a volley of little stones. There were funny vibrations in the air and I felt anxious but also curious as to what would happen next.

David turned from the water and grabbed a branch of the tree above him, swinging a couple of lazy arcs, a tense band of stomach revealed beneath his shirt. He pulled his legs up between his hands and turned a circle around the bough to come to sitting. Someone had hammered metal hoops deep into the bark and he set off up the tree as loose as a monkey. It was a large elm, stretching halfway across the pond and the very best thing about that place.

Matthias watched, absorbing the challenge and flung up his arms. I saw straight away that he had dropped the medal, though he hadn't seemed to notice. David did. We both watched as it fell into the thick soft grass at the base of the tree where the mower couldn't reach. The disc vanished instantly, though the ribbon lay flat and light on a bed of fat blade tips. David jumped down, feigned a stumble and snatched it. I saw him shove his fist into the pocket of his shorts and the jumping of a tendon stretching up into his wrist as he felt it there. In a while, Matthias came down too, nothing left to prove. He landed with an inelegant thud and stood, breathing hard.

David showed me a metallic flash and I probably smiled. I looked back to the boy and for a second his face was clear but then his eyebrows dropped and his right hand began to open and close. He raised his palm up and looked at it, stupidly, and then felt in his pockets and began to walk, down-facing, in panicky little circles, kicking at the grass.

'What are you doing?' David said.

'I've lost my medal.'

'Oh dear. When did you have it last?'

'I don't know. Up the tree?'

'Go back to where you've been,' he said, and for a moment he was trying to help; that's what Mum would say and it nearly always worked. Though, of course, he had the medal himself, hot in his pocket.

'Perhaps it fell in the water?' David said.

'I didn't hear a splash.'

David walked across to the bank and peered. It is possible I sniggered.

'I think I can see something,' David said. 'In the pond. There.'

He tipped onto one knee.

'Where?'

'See that shiny bit?'

Matthias took a step and as his full weight hit the heel of his shoe, it slid up in a surprising arc. His leg stretched into blank midair and he came down on his bottom, hard, on the edge of the bank. Down he bumped with a splash into the water and then turned at once, as we had all been taught, and grabbed a tree root that had grown out into the pond. He seemed obviously safe and it was funny and we laughed. But Matthias was already crying.

'Please get Mummy, it's freezing,' he said. His chin was shaking from side to side in a way you couldn't copy if you tried.

'Is it deep?' David asked.

In the shade, the liquid around Matthias looked thick and black. He was very still and I had the idea that he was stuck in a smooth, well-mixed tar. But when he raised a hand, the river's properties shifted, water racing off him in the sweetest of candy pinks.

'What?' I said. 'Have you cut yourself?'

He turned his arm before him in a kind of wonder.

The tears had stopped and his face was stiff. There was no visible wound and he dropped his arm. The water took it.

'Matthias. Are you hurt?' I called, on my hands and knees now. I remember David, standing off somewhere behind me, saying nothing.

Then Matthias let go of the root and took a long step back into a slice of brittle sunlight.

'What are you doing?' I called.

The water rose up, nearly to his chest, and a slow deepening red bloomed around him. He took another step, though I was calling his name, and laid his head on the surface of the pond as though it might take his weight. I had the thought that he would lift up his legs and simply float off down the river, like Ophelia, but then the window went, and I wondered why we hadn't called for them before and there were the mothers' voices, climbing as they came across the lawn. We stood aside and they both jumped in, unhesitating, as though it had all been arranged.

They dragged him out easily; in his wet things he was tiny and collapsed. They laid him on the grass, his mother by his head, slapping his face in time to some internal beat. 'I need your shirts,' Mum cried. David and I undressed. The cut was on his calf, deep and neat and already dead-looking around the seams. Our mother placed his foot up on her leg and wrapped my T-shirt around it and I watched the cotton fill steadily with his blood.

'I was looking for Dad's medal,' Matthias began.

'What on earth were you doing with that?' his mother said.

'I dropped it. David saw it in the water.'

237

Mum gave David a sharp look and began to unlace the wet boy's shoes.

I turned to my brother. A triangle of ribbon rose out of his shorts pocket, natty as a folded handkerchief. He covered it with his hand and I felt the danger of his situation.

Matthias started back to the house, feeble in his pants. Mum ran ahead for towels. And David threw the medal towards the pond, high and looping. It made a terrible plink as it hit the water and then the whole thing was gone in a sudden heavy drop.

He gave me that wink that he'd just perfected, vaguely suggestive. Raised a finger to his lips and mouthed shush, long and low. He squeezed my hand. We never spoke of it again.

I went downstairs to my laptop and emailed him.

Dear David,

It's a month this weekend since you left and I've got to thinking about the old days. Matthias Coombes, do you remember? I'd almost forgotten him, which can happen when it's easier that way, but then this morning, all of a sudden, he was back. I kept my word, you know. I didn't tell.

Which led me to another weekend, years on, when Mum left us at home and we had that party and the dog ate your gear. You were tripping, so I had to drive her to the vet, miles over the limit. I've been meaning to ask, were you praying on the way? I recall you mumbling in the passenger seat beside me but I said nothing – I was concentrating on the road. They gave her an injection that made her sick and we cried and laughed all the way back and the party carried on. I used the money I'd saved to go away to pay the bill, do you remember? I was stuck in London all that summer, so it must have been the year I carried half your pills into clubs in my sock every weekend, to stop you from getting done.

Not that it was all one-way. In fact, I'd like to thank you for taking me to the clinic when I found myself pregnant, the guy already forgotten. That was a weird one for a brother, I know, but I didn't have anyone else and it's that I circle back to, as much as anything else. I've never made the kind of friends I'd hoped for, I don't know why, but no one seems to have stuck. All of them, pretty much, wanted to shag you and you often obliged and I have to say, that didn't help. Years ago, of course, but habits set, don't they? Although my work claims they can be broken.

And you're not so different. It wasn't easy, pulling your fortieth together, tracking down all those people you've tried to lose. Most of them said yes, though, out of curiosity perhaps, but you were always popular and your beauty helps. I imagine they wanted to know what had become of you; you were, you remain, the very definition of unfulfilled potential.

Does it still feel like something might happen in your life? Or not, any more. Is that why you ran? On the night of the party, there was no coherence in the room.

When I looked around at all those faces, I couldn't find a pattern. It didn't combine to anything. Did you feel the same? Do you even care?

I wonder if this email is making you cross, but you don't really do cross, do you? I see it starting, behind your eyes – you're not so unreadable as all that – but when I look back it's gone. I'd want to explore that, if you were a client. You rolled your eyes when I was training and I asked if I could practise on you. 'You know everything about me, sis,' you said, 'everything worth knowing,' which pleased me at the time, and so I chose to believe it.

I feel I miss our conversations, though we didn't really talk lately. Sometimes I wonder if I imagined it and ours is just some twisted fictional romance, or each of us a foil, simply reinforcing the other's stereotype. I talk with my clients about relativism. The difficulties of absolute truth and how other people's versions have their own logic and demand respect, but sometimes a lie is just a lie. So, we'll need to talk about your job. I hear you're going away, so do you travel now? Oh, and why did you give Skyler my dolphin ring? And I want to know: how do you turn your face away from the damage you cause? How do you put yourself always so definitively first?

You'll recognise my tone. It's that last blast before I give up – start to cry, or make some demand that you'll agree to but never meet. We exist, we have always existed, in tandem. You leave, then you return. So come back now, David. I need you. Always and forever. N X.

24

I was ten minutes late and had to race to school. Inside, a bell had gone and I moved against the traffic. The corridors were wide and high-ceilinged and the calls of the children cannoned off the walls. I dipped my head against the smell of them; deodorant sprays, sweets, the alliums in last night's dinner. The doors to the main hall were shut when I got there and the glass panels papered over for privacy. When I pushed them open, Stefan turned. He had saved me a place, and bought instant coffee from the machine. I took my seat; aware, suddenly, of my pulse. The headmistress spoke a few words, and the smaller children began.

'Did she tell you what she's doing?' I whispered. Frieda had been practising for weeks behind the closed door of her bedroom but I heard only her intonation, which was strong, and carried.

'She wouldn't say,' he replied.

We watched a boy perform a two-hander, taking a huge step and turning to face the space he'd emptied every time he switched role, and then Stef nudged me and it was Frieda's turn.

In the rafters, someone switched off the lights and there was a moment of darkness. Then a beam hit the stage with a sound like a popped bulb and a bright circle appeared, dim-edged at first and then sharpened until the edges were crisp and cruel and perfect. There was nowhere to look but at the harsh white ring, each nick and splinter in the floorboards revealed. Nothing happened for long enough that I started to think something was wrong and I held my own hands for comfort.

Then Frieda came, stealthily and in utter silence. The first I knew of her was her foot breaking open that circle. A naked foot, bleached bloodless by the light. She stepped inside, blacked out by clothes, just hands and feet and her fierce little face and the yellow of her hair. She squinted at the lamp's full glare and then something above her changed, the light was softened or a shift made to its angle and her features emerged, the bones of her face. I watched a slow swallow travel down her neck, then she drew her feet together and loosened her arms. She looked poised and empty. She began:

'"Love after Love" by Derek Walcott.'

'What?' I said, in a reflex and the woman in front of us half-turned. Stef gave me a mild look of reproach. On stage, Frieda spoke, lightly and with certainty:

'The time will come
when, with elation,
you will greet yourself arriving
at your own door, in your own mirror,
and each will smile at the other's welcome,

and say sit here. Eat.'

242

I was in bed when Adam had first read me those lines, from a volume pulled down off a hotel bookshelf. 'Oh God, not a poem,' I said and hid my face in the pillow. 'Just listen,' he replied. 'It's one of my favourites. It's beautiful.' He sat on the end of the bed, squashing my feet, and carried on.

'You will love again the stranger who was your self,
Give wine. Give bread. Give back your heart
to itself, to the stranger who has loved you

all your life, whom you ignored
for another, who knows you by heart.'

On stage Frieda, spoke out into the blackness of the audience. I was transfixed by her, acute to every nuance of her performance, and it was subtle. An adjustment to her stance, a finger's flex became so freighted. The far reach of each pause was almost unbearable. The meaning of this, her up there, speaking these words, was remote and sealed for now. All I could do was exist from beat to beat. Her voice narrowed as she spoke again:

'Take down the love-letters from the bookshelf

the photographs, the desperate notes,
peel your own image from the mirror.'

She took a huge breath and swept her arm out to the side

in invitation. She spoke the last words in a brutal staccato, each syllable biting and distinct.

'Sit. Feast on your life.'

Adam had dropped the book to the bed and lay by my side.

'What do you think?' he said.

'It's a poem about being dumped, isn't it?' I had replied, hiding behind my fatuousness.

'Maybe,' he said. 'But that's not how I read it. I see us in this.'

'How do you mean?

'You've brought me back to myself,' he said. 'Now I can feast on my life,' and his face was naked and exultant and when I looked up at Frieda, so bold up there, her face was the same and I felt the point of impact, the certainty of collision, and the lights went out.

We all clapped hard and there was that little surge of noise that an audience makes to expel whatever it has been feeling. In the darkness I scrabbled for my bearings and then the lights were back and so was Frieda, with a huge teary smile, and her little bird's chest pumping. As she moved to the front of the stage to bow, I saw that she left wet footprints on the stage; two-parted, the splodge of her heel and then the mound of flesh beneath her toes.

'That was awesome. Wasn't that awesome, Nance?' Stef said.

I saw her find him in the crowd and he lay his palm over his heart. Her smile got bigger and he blew her a kiss. The drama teacher came to us as we waited outside the hall.

'I hope you enjoyed Frieda's performance, Mr and Mrs Jansen,' she said, flushed herself.

'We did. Very much,' Stef replied, and shook the woman's hand without pre-emption.

'She really is talented, and that was the perfect reading,' she said to him. 'I'm so glad you approved it.'

'Did we approve it?' I said, vaguely. 'Did you approve it, Stef?' I was struggling to order my thoughts. The teacher's face closed.

'All pieces are approved. There was a form you will have signed,' she said.

'Yes, of course,' I replied. 'I'm sorry. Of course,' and then Frieda was coming, brilliant and terrible at the head of a great swell of children, jostling and crying out, and I ducked my head at the sight of her.

'Well?' she said.

'That was amazing, my darling,' said Stef. 'So wonderful. We are very proud of you.' He took her face in his hands and she shone up at him.

'Mum?' she said. I dared a look at her. She was tucked compactly beneath Stef's arm, their faces so similar side by side. She was damp around the hairline, expectant, a little bashful. Her frank gaze made me cower.

'It was fantastic. Yes. As your dad said,' I replied.

'Mum, what's the matter with you?' she said, and there it was, her voice sharpened into a point. It struck me that this might be a test. She could never confront me with her knowledge outright. We would be locked into this exchange of signs and signals for ever.

'I'm just— I'm feeling. I'm not particularly well,' I said. Then the buckle of her face made my previous idea seem insane.

'Are you OK?' she asked. She stepped forward and hugged me and I was like a child in her arms. I could feel her heart thumping hard, still processing the last chemical traces of adrenalin in her blood. I slowed my breath and hers steadied in response. I felt her love, her succour, and I knew with a certainty that our contract still held.

'If you're feeling weird, we can go home now, if you like,' she said.

I raised my face, frail and light-headed.

'God,' she said. 'You do look a bit pale.'

'No, it's fine Free. Go say hello to your friends.'

'OK. Dad, look after my bag,' she replied and nudged it across the floor to him. Sticking out of the top was her envelope, ragged and dog-eared now, in which she carried the scripts she had been working on, these past weeks, with Tara.

'Hold on a minute,' I said. 'Where did you find that poem?'

I pictured Tara in that room of hers that Frieda had described, a temple to her mediocre achievement, offering up these words to my daughter like a gift, with its oblique message to me hidden inside.

'Ah,' she replied, stretching the word out long. 'So you get it at last.'

'No, I don't. Just tell me, please,' I said.

'All right,' she replied. 'No need to be like that.'

A darker vision rose then, of Adam and Tara sharing these words, many years before and her passing them on to my daughter in innocence, in love.

'Please tell me, Frieda,' I said, again. 'It's not so very hard.'

'Mum, what is with you right now?' she said, coming closer, snapping the end off every word.

'Did she give it you?' I said. 'Was it Tara?' My own voice rose up towards shrill.

'What are you talking about?' she said.

'Nancy,' said Stefan, 'take it easy. I mean it,' and for the first time I had a sense of him as a threat.

'It was for you, you idiot,' Frieda told me, thrumming with anger. 'It's your stupid poem. Don't you even remember?'

I had gone back to the book while Adam was in the bathroom. I looked at the bindings, thinking of pulling out the page. 'You don't have to,' he said. 'I know it by heart.' A slick of hair at his temple, heat coming off him from the shower. But I am not like Adam. I like to see things before me, hold them in my hands and so I bought the book the following week, a newer edition, and kept it at the bottom of a stack by my bed.

'Oh of course,' I said to Frieda. 'I'm so sorry. I'm just— I'm not myself.'

'Let's go, Free,' Stefan said. He picked up her bag and took her hand and they moved off, pushing through the crowd of ecstatic children. She turned her head back once and cast me a savage glare. I followed them from a distance.

I had read the poem to the girls one late afternoon when we were in my room wrapping Jake's birthday gifts. Lou had picked up the book and wondered at it. 'Bring it here,' I said. 'I'll read you something. See what you think.' When I began, the moment seemed to have become important. My voice trembled and I felt exposed under their evaluating gaze, but when I was done, Lou simply turned back into the room though Free gave a little 'hmm' of consideration. I'd been glad to let it pass unremarked.

'You're nuts, Mum, do you know that?' Frieda said, in the car. Stef had offered her the front seat and she took it. I sat in the back without comment, my feet deep in old water bottles and empty packets of snacks.

'Just don't worry, honey,' said Stefan, his hand on her knee.

She turned the radio up and looked hard out of the passenger window.

'I don't even know how to be around her any more,' she said.

25

I met Adam the next morning at his mother's, who was abroad, though he said she wouldn't have minded anyway. It was a wide Victorian semi a long way down a treeless street in South Ealing. Four storeys of red-brick, all right-angles and huge sash windows, with just a square of paving and a short dense hedge keeping it back from the road.

The house was well-kept but unadorned. She hadn't tried to domesticate it with name plates or little pots of greenery; it was simply itself – a solid pile of sand and lime – enduring and uncompromisingly London. I found the number on a council bin in thick green paint and paused a moment, but Adam, in the front room, raised his head. We met at the door.

'Come in,' he said and pushed his hand through his hair. 'It's weird. I feel a little shy, bringing you here,' and I felt it too, the difference that context made.

The house smelt of stove-top coffee and ancient radiators burning old dust. I followed him into a narrow hall, a round paper shade swinging easily above us. He took me to the kitchen at the back, a high-ceilinged room with white laminate cupboards and a chequerboard floor. In one corner stood a round table under a plastic floral cloth with four nondescript chairs pushed beneath it. She had pinned photos and cards in no sort of order between two large windows on the far wall, and I wanted to go across and look but felt I needed an invitation for that.

'So you grew up in this house?' I asked.

'From aged about five,' he replied. 'It was pretty much exactly as you see it now.'

I saw the top of his head, bent to homework in one of those chairs. Damp hair, still, at his temples from where she'd only just called him in, his feet still twitching for the ball. But he'd told me he wasn't a sporty boy; it was my own son I was thinking of, or my brother, perhaps.

'Wow.' I said. 'She's kept it well.'

'She has.' He felt a cabinet's warped corner as I said it but nothing a spot of glue wouldn't make right.

'Do you want to look around?' he said.

'Yes, please.'

We moved off and I felt a strange formality and a greedy kind of appetite as though I was looking to buy the place. It was Stefan's dream, a house like this, whose face you could wipe clean and then start again. It had struck me as a discrepancy of personality at first, but all these years on, it made more sense.

'Do you remember much about your dad?' I asked.

'Not really,' Adam replied.

In the sitting room, I saw where the family had shrunk. The armchairs were configured for a group but only one seat showed any signs of occupancy with its scattering of effects: a pile of magazines, chemist's spectacles, and a half-finished embroidery frame; she hadn't struck me as the sewing type. Beyond that, the room was just ambiguity. I could find nothing in that space to hang an impression on.

The walls were cream and empty, save for a still-life of fruit in clotted oils and an expressionist print of summer flowers in a field, I think. There was a rattan bucket filled with logs by a green-tiled fireplace and a huge red Persian rug with a thin straw-like pile. The furniture was mismatched; a seat in tobacco leather, then a long woollen sofa of a similar shade, and the chair in dark velvet paisley with subtle twists of silver and metallic purple, that the mother clearly preferred. It was the only item in the room that showed any comfort or care, placed in the best spot, overlooking her yard and the short hop of hedge before the pavement. Across the road were tubed railings of the sort girls like to roll around, bordering a stretch of social housing. I could see six netted windows and wondered if she sat and watched the lives going on behind them. I know I would.

'It's a huge place to live in alone,' I said. 'Or even for two.'

A brass carriage clock, a crystal owl – all glinting rainbow planes – and a clay horse that struck me as Chinese, were arranged on two squat rows of skewed pine shelves. I had never been in a house so inconsistent, so uncontrived, so unimproved.

'Ah, but it wasn't just us,' he said. 'Not when I was growing up. We had lodgers. Did I not say?'

'No,' I replied. 'Wasn't that strange?'

'Not really,' he said. 'They were students mainly.

Older ones from overseas. She must have been on some kind of list. So it was busy, which was good, because she always worked,' and at that the house fell into a different shape and I saw a woman who, although she was alone, had built a broad life of many influences for her son. I thought of the sealed-shut unit of my own little tribe. This felt like a home with no expectation. I thought, what an easy place to grow up.

'And she never considered selling?'

'Not that she said. It might have had something to do with Dad. And it was an investment, of course. Come up here. Let me show you my room.'

The runner on the stairs was worn in a thin dark trench up the middle. The landing floorboards adjusted noisily under our weight and when we reached the top, I saw a glimpse of the bedroom ahead, Vivien's. A pair of practical sandals, huge – still, she was tall – and as we passed, I noticed a strip of her wallpaper, too. It was a deep, dark cobalt broken up by silver lines that seemed to run down the wall, opening up, now and again, like water flowing round stones. I wondered what it would be like to sleep in there, in that river of a room. The choice seemed bold and romantic in the face of the rest of the house, and I adjusted my perception of her once more.

His room was up a final twist of staircase.

'She redecorated, of course, after I was gone, but the bed's still mine.'

It was chilly inside, painted Elastoplast pink, and the single bed of Adam, the boy, had been pushed into a corner, its length against the wall. He sat and put his hand up to the plaster.

'There was a girl next door who I thought I was in love with and I used to press my ear to a glass and try and hear her voice. I suppose that sounds creepy now. It felt like the height of devotion at the time.'

Can another's face solve your problems? Their mere proximity? Then there is his hair which makes a joke of him. In the murk of his room, his eyes had dimmed to puddle.

'Lie down with me,' he said.

We were close in the central sag of his bed, his arm under my shoulder, our heads just touching.

'It must have been cold, in the winter, up here,' I said.

'But nice in the heat.' He turned a section of my hair around a finger.

'Are you leaving me?' he said.

'I can't carry on.'

'So come with me.'

The cotton of his duvet had been worn to a newborn softness. I pushed my cheek down into it, but he didn't turn his face.

'Do you doubt we would be happy?' he asked.

'Not for one moment. But the rest would crowd it out.'

'They would recover, you know. All of them. Your children.'

'But how can I wilfully hurt them?'

He pulled his arm out from under me and rolled onto his side.

'I think they're your excuse, Nancy. I think you use

them to avoid the job of making yourself happy. You say, I am a mother, I am needed, and you step down from it.'

'Well that's easy for you to say—'

'Yes, of course. Because I'm not a parent. But I was a child and the best thing my mother did for me was to leave me free of responsibility for her choices. She made some for me and others despite me, but I never felt that I was the architect of her happiness.'

'Touch my forehead,' I said. 'Do I feel hot?'

'There's nothing noble in playing the martyr, Nancy,' he said. 'No one will even notice,' but I could hear that he was losing heart.

'What would you say to your daughter?' he said, 'if she came to you with this?' but I'd stopped listening by then.

'I have to go soon,' I said.

Downstairs the letterbox went and a package hit the mat in one sharp clap, and then a second with a slower, cushioned slither.

26

Some time in what felt like the early hours, there was her touch. I knew it as I rose up towards wakefulness; her scent, perhaps, the special way she has of stroking my cheek, that particular give of her skin. I opened my eyes grateful. I had thought we were too old for all this.

'It's today,' she whispered and her breath made my nose twitch.

'It is, sweet.'

'It's my birthday,' she said.

'I can't believe it. My little girl fifteen.'

'Yay!' Frieda cried.

She had been kneeling on the floor by the bed and hopped over me, then, in her striped long johns, coming to land lightly in the space between Stefan and me.

'Are you going to get in?' I said. 'It's not even six.'

'Daddy.' She sat cross-legged, facing away from me, her spine curved like a bow through the cotton of her vest.

'Daddy.'

She shook the top of his arm.

'Wake up,' she said, and then he roared and she shrieked and thrashed and shunted me to the edge of the bed.

'Shall I make us some tea?' I said.

'Thanks, Mum,' she called after me.

'That's all right, birthday girl.'

Downstairs was chilly, save for the greeting of the dog. On the island lay a great landslide of gifts that Stef and I had wrapped last night. The fridge was crammed with food, the family was due and the mood of the house was giddy and volatile. It felt like a rehearsal for Christmas. I heard Jake's tread on the stair, struggling with the notion of somebody else's day. He spoke to his X-box, which replied, and I left them to it. Louisa, upstairs, called: 'Bring the presents up, Mum. Free says I can open one, if she chooses which.'

There was cooking later; a neck of pork that had been marinating in the fridge. Disgusting, the girls declared, when I hauled it across, then set to massaging it viciously through the plastic, tipping up the liquid collected in various pockets and working it into the flesh. We opened the bag to a huge slab stained an artificial red, a number 8 marked out in pricks of ink on the skin like a child's join-the-dots. Free traced it with a finger.

'Poor pig,' said Lou, as I tipped it into a tray.

'It's food,' said Free.

'Didn't used to be,' said Lou.

'It's organic,' I said. 'It had a good life. Now rub in the butter, someone. Lou, you can start on the veg.'

She began, humming quietly in her tuneless voice, retreating to that interior place.

'Pay attention, Lou,' I said. 'Or you'll cut yourself.'

Frieda toasted cumin in one pan, which smelt of unwashed shirt, and pumpkin seeds in another. She got hot and blew her new fringe up off her forehead. Stefan in profile, with her wide cheekbones and that flat, straight nose.

'Who wants to separate an egg?' I asked. Both of them did.

The dog came in and sneezed twice, conclusively, which made us laugh. Then a song began which we all three liked and when it was over, Frieda played it again and I risked an arm around each girl, which they allowed, and I wondered if it would always be like this from now, the taint at the back of every happiness. The bone in the mouthful, small enough that I could have been dreaming it, a temporary tickle at the back of my throat, or something worse, something lodged, doing slow, steady damage. And next, I thought: I know this feeling and it is not new, it is as old as I am. It was there before, it has always been there, apart from that brief period when Adam chased it away.

'Oh no,' said Free. 'It's started to rain.' She lifted her head. The panels on the roof of the side return ran. She moved to the back of the kitchen and pressed her palms against the glass. We seem to slide so easily into gloom these days. My unhappiness is the largest thing in the room. If I let it, it might swallow up the world, but I will not. My children are my only hope of reprieve.

'It's pouring,' Frieda said.

'So what?' I replied. 'The party's inside.'

'Suppose so.' She came across slowly, dragging her feet in huge furred slippers.

I turned the music up, spoke of more gifts to come, made an unsolicited offer of sweets and the mood began to reverse.

'Are you looking forward to tonight?' I asked.

'Kind of,' Frieda replied. She wore the jewellery that I had found in her bedroom, a tiny triangle of wire that fitted the upper curve of her ear perfectly. She touched it again; she couldn't leave it alone.

'That's pretty,' I said. 'Birthday present?'

She swerved away from my hand.

'Look, I'll keep the family in the kitchen, I promise. We'll have a couple of hours before your friends arrive and then we'll leave you to it.'

'Can I come in, Free?' Louisa said, morose, already, in advance of the answer.

'No,' Frieda replied. She whisked oil into the egg, flicking gummy splats up her front with each turn of the fork. 'Uncle David won't be here, though,' she said.

'That's true,' I replied, 'but I'm sure we'll cope. Come on. Let's get the sitting room sorted. And after that, time to get dressed.'

I'd bought something new to wear and hung it on the back of my door, where it pleased everyone but me.

'Like it, Mum,' Jake had said, swooping the skirt up as he passed. When he dropped his arm, he took the dress along with him caught on a rough edge of his big cupped hand. It puddled on the floor but he continued, oblivious. This new phase of Jake calls the toddler back to life. He is curious, impulsive, clumsy; often in need of a hug, but unable to ask. His efforts at separation make him foolish, but it is better, surely, than the next bit, when he is gone. To Jake, though, the dress was just a dress. The others tried to read it.

Stefan approved. 'Nice,' he said, a man who feels attention to appearance signals self-esteem.

Next Frieda stopped by: 'Why did you get that?' she asked and I knew she was thinking of the moment of attempted reversal that can happen about now, the Botox or the boob-job. The sudden, directional hair.

'Oh I don't know, sweet. Do you hate it?' I said.

'No, it's pretty,' she replied. 'Will you wear it to my party?'

'If you like,' I said.

'You OK, Mum?'

It was mid-afternoon, after all, and I lay in bed, curtains shut, our separation still knife-fresh, just days old. Adam had left the office and Lynn cried in my arms when he went. He'd bought her flowers as a thank-you and a box of chemist's smellies, but I hadn't loved him for his taste. It won't be hard to fill his room, or Tim's. The rent is cheap for London.

'I'm fine. I've got a headache, that's all. Won't be long,' I told her.

'Would you call it red?' Louisa asked. She had come to find me when she heard that I was ill. The dress was of a mid-weight, well-lined silk with a round neck and wide sleeves that finished on the elbow. It fell loosely, and its success lay in the drape; it hung as it was cut, irrespective of the body beneath.

'Garnet, perhaps,' I said, 'like Granny's old brooch.' My mother had already given the girls her jewellery. 'Why wait until I die?' she said.

'It makes me think of autumn when I look at it,' said Lou. There was the sudden ruck of flesh above her eye. She had found the melancholy in my choice.

'Me too,' I replied. 'Just give me an hour, Lou, would you? I need to rest,' but I was up again after ten minutes; the children needed dropping places, there were things to do. I couldn't just sit in the dark, nursing my tragedy.

The party began at four. April first; handbag high, all exclamation.

'Hello, hello. Are the youngsters here?' she said, her little hands snatching at me by way of greeting. 'I've been so looking forward to it. A bit of life. Lovely to see the youth,' she said, her voice scratched and gleeful.

'Not yet, Ape. I told you. We've got a few hours first. You look smart, Uncle Pete.'

He snapped his heels together, a square of shine on each toe. I wondered who had ironed his shirt, put that crease down the front of his trousers. Not April, that was for sure.

'I'll keep it just now, thanks, love,' he said, when I offered to take his jacket. 'Where to?'

'Straight out the back. They're in the kitchen.'

He passed me, leaving a strong, frank cologne in his wake.

'And you too, Aunty. That's a lovely dress,' I said, although it wasn't. She looked like an old-fashioned child in her patterned nylon frock of blues and greens, long-sleeved and gathered in an elastic ruff at the wrists. Her collarbones and the steep fall of her chest were prominent above the neckline and she wore a thick out-dated foundation that gathered around her pores, and a lipstick of a bright inhuman pink.

'And where's the birthday girl?' she called. Then: 'Is your dad here yet? Ah, there she is!'

Frieda appeared at the top of the stairs and came down gingerly. She wore DM-style boots, laced across the foot although the eyelets around her ankles were empty and the leather gaped. Above, her little legs emerged in thin black stretchy jeans, I'd thought, until she got closer and I realised they were leggings, with the detail of the fly printed on. They finished high, way above her belly button, making a deep curvy shape of her where there usually was none. She'd picked a short, trapeze-shaped shirt, sleeveless and buttoned to the neck, as her dad wore his. Since I'd seen her an hour before, she had sprayed her hair in thick stripes of peppermint and mauve and wore a couple of strings of long plastic pearls, her eyes lined in Winehouse flicks. Otherwise her face was quite clean. There was a discordant elegance to her, some kind of play with proportion and femininity. It was new and mindful and rather grown-up. And I prayed, as I looked at her, let this feeling sustain me. Let this, which is so very much, become enough. And I wondered, when had I got so greedy? When had I started to think that I was due still more?

'Is it OK?' she asked.

'Absolutely beautiful, my darling,' April said. 'Just look at her.' She took Frieda's shoulders and twisted her, a little, left and right and I knew she was admiring her shape; I remembered it from my own childhood, the pleasure Ape took in our development, as if womanhood was some kind of achievement or prize.

'Peter?' she called. 'Come out here and look at Free.'

'Gorgeous,' I said, straight into her ear, as we moved along the hall.

Stefan passed me a gin and tonic in a bowl-shaped glass on a long thin stem with an eighth of pink grapefruit in it and a shaving of orange peel. 'Just as you like,' he said. I look a long deep drink. The gin was tart and dry and sucked the moisture from my mouth.

Dad next, though it was Justine's voice that reached me in the kitchen, asking Stef about the parking. Did we have a permit? She couldn't be doing with the text. I got up and moved straight past them to Dad, who stood on the path, waiting like a pet in the thin suspended drizzle. I stepped down onto the tiles in stockinged feet. His smell was dry and talcy, my tights sucked up the wetness from the tiles, my glass, behind his back was slippy with condensation and nearly popped out of my hand. I embraced him for a long time, which brought a brief kind of rest down on me, and then I thought of raising my head and telling him everything. I wondered what his daughter's shame would look like on his face, the collapse of his vision of his number one girl.

'Nance,' he said. 'What's up, love?' but that question wasn't real. His voice held bewilderment and also an appeal. A plea that I keep silence, leave his fragile redaction of the world intact. He hasn't long to go and he knows it. He's far too old for change.

'Nothing,' I said. 'I'm just glad to see you, that's all.'

'You too, love,' he replied, in relief, and he squeezed me breathless as he had when I was tiny, the very best that he could do. We walked through to the kitchen, hand in hand, the rest of them arranged around the island now, cleared of crap for the day, a row of tea lights running its length, picking out the details of the concrete like pox scars or the outlines of burst bubbles. April ahhed at the sight of us. Stef came forward, and I watched Dad try to stifle his response to him, but it was there in his half-mast arm, which failed, as usual, to deflect Stefan's hug. Weight tipped back to keep it brief. The scolded drop of his gaze. It was Stef's difference, of course; the name at first: 'Steve? Steven, d'you say,' Dad had misheard, for the first six months.

'Mum,' Lou called, in horror. 'Your tights. You're leaving marks.'

'Oh don't panic, Louisa,' I said, 'I can always get changed,' and I laughed in a strange euphoria that would worry her still more. 'Chuck me a tea towel, someone,' I said and toed off the wet. In a weird kind of reflex, I looked around for David.

Mum arrived about this time, with her best friend Alison, making little impact. She gave a vague eye-contactless wave around the room and accepted a fizzy water along with her glass of wine. With both hands full, our greeting was brief. She wore her usual wide-legged trousers, in oat or stone or beige, under a shot silk tunic in a surprising cerise.

'It's a kameez, you see,' I heard her say, 'and the scarf that Alison is wearing is a dupatta. These are the Indian terms. That's where she got them from. Alison travels a lot.'

She pressed her cheek to Dad's dryly when he passed by, later, unavoidably, on his way to the loo and I watched them for a bit: Alison doing all the talking, Dad hunched and apologetic, working hard to respond in the right ways, and Mum looking between them quietly, holding the end of her thin loose plait. Then she said something I couldn't catch, just tossed it at him and the way she tipped her cheekbone and he quickly raised his gaze made the two of them, just for a second, seem possible. I wondered, suddenly, if he had loved her all along, and then from across the room came Justine's laugh, loud and full of anguish, for she had seen it too, and her love for him was teenaged, all temper and jealousy. She tapped a nervous little run against the back of a chair with her shellacked nails and I enjoyed the sound of it and the brief possibility of chaos. Then Dad returned and he kissed Justine, restoring order in the act. She closed her eyes deep into it.

And finally, there was Madeline, frantic with apology, fresh from some task both stressful and important. If David had been there, he would have taken her in his arms about now: 'Come on, sis. Forget it. You're here.'

Ever since she was a child, when he held her, she fell into a kind of swoon like a girl in a story book.

'This'll help,' I said, to Madeline. I had made her one of the gins and another for myself.

'Yum yum,' she said.

'Nance,' said Stefan. 'Isn't it about time we started with the food?'

We ate late. My appetite was shot and I couldn't taste for seasoning but I had laid the table earlier with vintage linen and packed four stubby vases with hydrangeas, the blue ones, cut short, so it looked nice, at least.

'They've come round again, have they?' April said. Then: 'Oh right,' as she noticed the pile of plates and heaped cutlery. 'Eating off our laps, are we? I see.'

'You can sit at the table, Ape, if you like, but we're thirteen, so we won't all fit,' I said.

'Thirteen, is it?' she replied, and began to count down names on her fingers.

'Don't start all that again, love,' said Peter. I saw her remember David, and stop.

'Sit down, Ape, please,' I said. I pulled out a chair.

'Don't bother on account of me,' she replied. She wore a pair of drop earrings with a stack of black and red stones that stretched the piercing in her lobe into a keyhole. She looked like a saloon-bar madam and I failed to stifle a laugh at the thought of it.

'New earrings, Ape?' I said. 'Don't think I've seen those before.'

'New?' she replied, raising her hands to them.

'Why don't you sit up here at the counter with the birthday girl, Aunty,' Stef said.

'Yes I think I will,' she replied. 'Free, come up here with your old Aunty Ape, will you?'

She gave me a haughty look, rehabilitated by Stefan's attention, and Frieda came across, moving through the kitchen with the slow acknowledgement of her own importance that she seemed to be assuming for the day.

'Be nice, Nancy,' Stef said, quietly, as he passed.

The meat was shredded on a huge oval dish, with a garnish of coriander and red onions that I'd pickled in lime.

'Lovely bit of roast pork,' Peter said, skimming his serving from the plate's edge. 'Any gravy with that?'

'Mum, do we still get Dominos?' Frieda asked, turning her fork through her coleslaw and looking glum.

'Yes, of course. Later,' I said. 'But there's this, for now.'

Jake sat at the table in his headphones, his expression mobile and eccentric.

'Should he be allowed to do that?' April asked but I pretended I hadn't heard.

'It's all delicious,' said Mum, who ate standing, with just a fork. 'Very authentic, dear. Have you been to the Americas, Alison?'

The pork cooled quickly and set into a fibrous kind of nest. Nobody wanted seconds, but there was pavlova next, which redeemed things.

'Here we go,' Peter said, stretching out the vowels and

rubbing his hands together as I brought it to the table. It gave us all comfort, that pudding, rising up on its porcelain-footed stand, peaked and princessy, so blessedly familiar. When I cut it and crunch gave way to marshmallow, April clapped like a child. The cream was so thick you could stand a spoon in it – Jake did – and the fruit on top was raspberries – Frieda's choice – plus a little slick of coulis, just berries and a sugar syrup pushed through a fine mesh sieve.

'Lovely,' Ape said, all forgiven. 'I don't know where she gets it from. Do you bake, Kath?'

My mother looked up, surprised to be addressed.

'No, April,' she replied. 'Do you?'

'Is there any—? Oh, here we are.' I passed April the jug of single cream that I know she likes. There was cheese, too, the Camembert already sprawled across its slate, with oatcakes for Mum and the Swedish crispbreads that Stef prefers. I was past food, myself; I stuck to wine.

The doorbell went, although it still seemed far too early. I looked up at the clock which was vintage and unreliable. It read ten to five. I watched it for a while. The zero in the ten is my favourite number – in that font, a kind of war-time Gill Sans, it looks all crushed and stunted – but just as I felt sure that it had stopped, the hand jerked by.

'Is that right?' I said. 'Has anyone got the time? Who's seen my phone?' I was drunk by now, and observing things from a distance, my pain hard and tinkling at the edge of it all.

'Wake up, Mum,' Free yelled across the table, in panic. 'Who is it? Why are they here?'

I was just getting to my feet when Jake burst in.

'It's some weird guy,' he cried. 'I saw him coming up the path.' The bell rang once again. 'That's him!'

'I'll go,' I said.

'No, I will,' replied Stef. He shut the kitchen behind him and I sat down, feeling weightless and suspended. We all listened. There was the timbre of a man's voice but it was impossible to make out what was said.

'Who's that then?' April said, gaping, agog. Then Stef was in the doorway. 'It's for you, Nancy,' he said, unreadable. I stood. The skirt of my dress had gathered at the front in two jagged fistfuls.

On the doorstep stood a man I'd never seen before, a handsome man, ten years younger than me at least, with the overdeveloped look of the gym-goer; bunched thigh muscles that pulled his jeans out of shape and a mound of chest rising above the neck of a thin white T-shirt. His hair was short and neat and he gave off a gentleness and capability like some kind of idealised army recruit.

'It's the weekend,' he said. 'I'm sorry.'

'I'm not sure we've met before.'

'We haven't,' he replied, 'though perhaps you know of me. I've come about Marie.'

Mark, then. Unrecognisable from her account or my extrapolation.

'I'm afraid it is not appropriate for you—'

He shifted on his feet and flexed his hands.

'I know. I just wanted to talk to you for a moment.'

'I'd have to speak to Marie about that first. But either way, you shouldn't have come to my house.'

'Please,' he said, 'I don't want to disturb you or you family—' Still, he looked so strong. 'I just need you to help me understand.'

I took a step towards him. He was surprised and his heel tipped back off the path. The outside light came on and he startled in its glare, his leg struck out to the side like a dancer. I'd expected trainers, but he wore lace-up shoes of a thin brown leather, narrowing to a squared-off toe. Their delicacy at the end of his thick blunt body make him look unbalanced. I wondered if he'd chosen them for me, for this meeting on my doorstep in the wet.

'You need to go,' I said.

He was pathetic in the rain, the cotton of his top drenched instantly.

'Please,' he said again, 'I'm only asking for five minutes.'

The front door opened. 'Is everything all right?' Stef called over my shoulder.

'Stefan,' I said. 'It's about a client. I can deal with this.'

'She was pregnant,' Mark said. 'Not any more.'

'Oh my God,' Stefan said, 'I'm so sorry.'

I felt the weather too, then, a swipe of moisture on my cheek, the wind take up my hair.

'I know nothing about that,' I said and thought of her face, the way she had seemed to have an idea ticking behind it. 'And I'm sorry too, but you have to leave.'

'Nancy,' Stef said, in a short shocked voice. He pushed past me into the rain. 'Can I drop you anywhere?' he said to Mark. 'Is there somebody we could phone?'

Mark pulled his eyes from me to Stef in a kind of benign confusion.

'Go now, Mark,' I said, 'or I will call the police. You can tell Marie to ring me, if she needs to. She has my office number. I can pick up calls.' I heard the school-marmish strain in my voice.

Mark gave an incredulous little laugh and raised his face up to the wet. I could see Stef turned to me, his deep disapproval, but I knew he wouldn't speak again.

'But she must have— Surely you—' Mark said.

'No,' I replied. 'Not at all.'

Mark went then, without fuss or aggression, and I listened to the tap of his surprising shoes as he crossed the street; their high, hollow sound. He got into a car and I saw the swivel of his head, one way, then the other and back again, just as they tell you to do for your test. He pulled out carefully and was gone. The light on the path went out and Stefan spoke to me in the dark.

'That was harsh,' he said.

'There are rules, Stefan. For very good reason.'

'And there is behaving like a human being,' he replied. His tone was chill. 'Did you not hear what he said?'

'Of course I did.'

'And did you know?' he asked.

'No,' I replied and I hadn't; I had no inkling. 'And if I did,' I said, 'I wouldn't tell you anyway. My office is a sealed space, you're fully aware of that.'

'A sealed space?' Stef replied. 'It strikes me things are leaking.'

'I'm going back in,' I said. 'This is Frieda's day. I won't have it spoiled.'

I went upstairs and called the office answer phone but there was no message. I thought of Marie. The fierce grip of her gaze. That look of hers locked on like a bite. Where I'd seen challenge, perhaps I should have read fear. Was it all defence? I thought of that slim chain she wore, the way she felt for it as I talked, smooth under her neckline, out of sight.

'Nancy,' Stefan said from beyond the bedroom door. 'Are you coming out? I can do this by myself, you know.'

'I'm coming,' I said and tried to pull all this down off my face.

'Whoa, Mum,' said Jake, when I joined them. 'What the hell was that?' A cluster of bright blemishes had risen on his neck across the day.

'Don't swear,' said Stefan.

'That's not swearing,' replied Jake.

'It was nothing,' I replied. 'Just work.'

'Thank God,' Frieda said, with a huge theatrical exhale, her hand on her heart. 'I thought, like, everything was going wrong for a moment. I'll wait upstairs now. And can you keep that door shut please?'

'What's the matter?' said April, after she left. 'She ashamed of us?'

'Come on, Ape,' Stef said, in a larky voice he'd borrowed from someone else. He threw his arm around my aunty and she wiggled deeper into it. 'Jake, find some music please,' he said. 'I know. Who fancies a game of cards?'

'Oh yes,' April replied. 'Rummy, we could do, or twenty-one? Shall we play for cash? Who's seen my bag? And I'll have another drink, Nance, while you're up. Go on. Whatever you're having,' she said. 'Surprise me.'

27

The girls arrived. Who first? Who else, but Clemency and Jude.

'Oh sorry,' Jude's mother called down from the cabin of her boxy car, 'are we too early? I thought the invite said six.'

'No,' I replied, 'you're fine.' My cuticles were stained pink with achiote paste and one sleeve was rimmed with grease.

'I won't get out.' She leant her forearms on the fat stitched circle of her steering wheel, a stack of gold up to the knuckle of one finger, the broad stupid face of a Labrador looking out at me from the boot.

'Be back for them about half-ten,' she called. 'Good luck!'

Clemency and Jude, bouncing off each other as they staggered sillily up my path. They fitted their names, all grace and eccentricity, and seemed to put the other girls down implicitly, merely through contrast. Their arms were threaded, the padding of their jackets huge. I couldn't see where one of them finished and the other began. Their intimacy was a subtle form of aggression; a smiling, scatty, spite.

'Hi, Mrs Jansen,' they called. They are not my favourites,

Clemency and Jude, though just like Frieda, I would have wanted them for my own.

'Frieda,' I shouted, 'your friends are here.'

There was a clatter from beyond the kitchen door and Ape's pissed titter.

Frieda appeared at the top of the stairs.

'Hi,' she cried maniacally, but she didn't move, waiting for their cue. She looked down, the pair looked back, then something broke and the girls bounded up.

'Who was it?' cried Ape.

'No one you know,' I replied.

I kept my phone in my hand like one of the kids, refreshing and refreshing, alert to every ping and buzz, but no one called.

The rest arrived across half an hour. 'The names!' Ape said, when Stef returned each time and told us. 'Don't they come in, Nance? Don't they at least pop in to say hello?'

There were Beatrice and Hannah. Emily, Sydney and Cait. Nic and Savannah – the final pair – arrived alone. They'd walked from the bus-stop, and each carried a loaded rucksack, the straps pulled tight across their shoulders, the body of the bags slung low.

'You know the rules, girls,' I said. 'No alcohol. Did your mothers say?'

'Yes, Mrs Jansen,' the children sang. They each wore a thick fishtail plait that began above one ear and ran around the back of the hairline, coming to rest heavily across the opposite shoulder.

'OK,' I said, 'Upstairs.'

Mum and Alison left, and the whole room breathed out.

'Are you all right, darling?' my mother asked, when we were alone in the hall waiting for Alison to find her scarf. 'I mean what with your client. My gosh.'

'It'll be fine, Mum,' I said. 'Don't worry. Off you go.'

Back in the kitchen and: 'You don't think? I mean, the two of them? Surely—' April began, but no one finished the thought.

'Nance,' said Peter, come back from the loo. 'I'm not being funny, but there's a strange smell out there. Like alcohol, or something.'

Upstairs, I found that Nic and Savannah had emptied their bags. A towel was spread on the floor and a girl rested back upon the knees of another. One painted finger-nails, one toes, each removing old polish with a swipe of acetone. A pile of discarded pads lay on the carpet; beautiful, really, a slick, on each, of a fashionable shade. As I watched, Sydney dropped a little constellation of stars onto Hannah's cheek and licked the tip of a cotton-bud which she used to alter their placement. Someone else sat crossed-legged, sorting hair accessories into piles: clips and bands, flowers and jewels, nets and hunks of artificial hair. By this girl stood a huge canister of value spray. I had to smile, at their innocence, their effort, their application.

'Mum,' Frieda screamed, when she saw me at the door. 'Get out.'

April got her wish; they all came down and showed themselves to us when they were done, walking a circuit of the kitchen and accepting our praise. 'What beauties!' Uncle Peter cried. A number of them blushed; not yet so grown. Frieda, I thought, looked largely unchanged, though her nails were done in alternate greens and someone had clipped in a couple of fluro plaits.

'Shall we go into the sitting room now, Mum?' Frieda asked.

'Yes,' I replied. 'Say goodbye to Ape and Peter, then you can all go through.'

Our theme was Moroccan, our colours turquoise, fuchsia and gold. The windows were hung with layers of gauze and chiffon, altering the light, and we had covered the furniture in old sarongs. On the floor lay a rug that Stef and I had had shipped from Marrakesh a long time ago, and I'd bought two hammered brass trays and a couple of Moroccan tea sets with fluted metal pots and henna-patterned glasses.

'There's mint tea, girls, in this one, and a rose cordial over there,' I said. Lou and I had candied petals in a spare half-hour the previous day and laid one in the bottom of half the glasses, a mint leaf in the rest.

'Look through here, though, look through here,' Frieda cried and flung back a drape at the far end of the room. Behind the door out to our tiny front garden, stood a squat tent, hired for the night; a scarlet curtained pergola, lit by souk lanterns and piled with pillows. The girls began to scream in various tones and pitches until the sound seemed to come together in one brief wavering note.

'Girls. You can't make all that noise. There's neighbours,' I said but then they had stopped and each circled the space in silence, her phone held high before her.

'Out the way now, Mum,' Frieda said.

'Happy?' asked Stef, back in the kitchen.

'I'd say so. Yes.'

When Stefan next checked, they'd turned up the lights and were playing 'Let's Dance'.

And finally the boys, and these children were new to me and their mothers too. They came to the door and made conversation, reluctant to deliver their sons, who looked down as we spoke, toeing the floor, fingers flexing around their devices. The girls were silent, also, in the room beyond, the squealing over, the atmosphere ominous and I felt all their difficulty as the first boy went through. This was Ollie; next came Toby, then Ethan. There was Caleb, Kyle and Jos. Zac and Ty and Ryan but it was Brandon whom I recognised, with a mother who loved him too much, who couldn't take her eyes off him, much less her hand, a boy who met my gaze and smiled: 'Hello, Mrs Jansen,' and if a real-life smile could ting, his would; a cartoon glint, a square of dazzle off those big white healthy teeth. And I saw that the way he tucked his T-shirt in one side was no accident and that his hair was longer and less effortful than the rest. He had charisma, this boy. A boy of luck and shine. He made me think of David.

'Bye, Mum,' he called over his shoulder and I lost her attention to him for a moment. 'Are the guys in there?'

The family left and I went through to my desk. The room was cold, largely unused and stored the mahogany chairs and table of my girlhood. I found my workbook and turned to that last failed meeting with Marie, but there was just her name and the date, prim and underlined at the top of the page and a scribble I'd made, further down, of a catherine-wheel, perhaps, or a lolly.

Then the door went and one of them – Clemency? No, it was Jude – took a long weak step inside, a gulp of a sob and abandoned herself to crying into the neck of her friend.

'Hold on,' I said. 'What's this?'

Clemency gave a tiny scream. Jude detached herself quickly and the two of them straightened in some schoolgirl instinct.

I flicked the light switch and they winced at the overhead bulb, girls more used to mood lighting and soft shades.

'What happened?' I asked and Jude's head dropped again, crying more of her sweet, weak tears.

'Speak up, someone,' I said. 'Clemency?'

She gave Jude a furtive glance but there was little to be seen of her but her mass of hair, its great weight tipped forwards, the origins of its height revealed in the snarl of back-comb at the roots.

'Look, we're not blaming anyone,' Clemency said, at last.

'Well, if that's the best you can do I'd better go in and ask somebody else.'

I was up and past them before they grasped what I meant.

'No, Mrs Jansen, please,' the girls began, snatching for each other and me, cowering and supplicant and I understood that they were never spoken to like this, their feelings an irrelevance, nor an action taken without due discussion and regard.

'Let's hear it then,' I said and Clemency began.

'The thing is, Brandon and Jude. I mean, it's not like they were together but they message, literally, all the time, and he likes everything she posts. Straight away. And he does not do that with everyone. Anyway. So I think she's a bit upset.'

'About what?' I said.

'And it's not as if it was a secret, either. Everybody knew. Of the girls, I mean. Jude showed us all of it. We talked about it like every day.'

'So where's the problem?' I said.

'Well, I guess she's just disappointed, I suppose, seeing as how things have turned out.' Clemency's wrist was thick with friendship bracelets and festival wristbands. She twisted the frayed cotton ends into a nib and looked at me carefully. 'Now that he's with Frieda,' she said, with a tiny lift of gratification in her voice.

Frieda, in her room, morose. That far-off look. Today's face, stripped of colour, an appeal to somebody else's taste. It suddenly made more sense.

'That boy?' I said. 'This is about that boy?'

Under the hair, the sobbing gained pace.

'Er, it's more the fact that Frieda knew, and still—'

I chuckled. Clemency gasped.

'Girls,' I said, 'let me reassure you. That boy is vain and spoilt. He is no loss. Clemency, please don't look so alarmed. Jude, you will survive, more than that, you will thrive. You people always do.'

Jude raised her head, sending tributaries of glittered tears off down her face. The two girls gaped at me with twinned bafflement.

'How about I get Frieda out?' I said. 'Perhaps we can clear things up before your parents arrive.' Jude wiped her nose in the crook of her elbow, bursting the inky streams into a phlegmy smear.

'OK, Mrs Jansen,' she said.

'Are you going in there?' Clemency asked, in a high fast voice of shock.

'Well, yes,' I said.

She gave a short excited giggle. 'I think it might be an idea if you knocked.'

At the door I caught them exchange a look, goggle-eyed and twitching, an impression of me, I assumed.

Frieda, when I pushed open the door, did not protest this time. She didn't move from where she sat; legs folded beneath her on our velvet button-backed chesterfield revealed now that its throw lay at their feet, trampled in a complex tangle of discarded shoes. She looked heavy-lidded, relaxed, luminous. Brandon was by her side, very close, no apology in it and Beatrice, on the other, pressed almost as tight, moonstruck too; in awe of her friend's success.

'Hi, Mum,' Frieda said. Brandon, whose arm lay across

my daughter's shoulders, lifted his fingers off her and waggled them.

'Can you come out here, a moment, please?' I said. 'Did you notice a couple of your guests are missing?'

At the sound of my voice, an anxious couple scrambled out through the mouth of the tent.

'Oh dear,' Free said. As she pulled away, he let his finger-tips run the length of her arm and she cast a strange blind look back at him, drunk on the pleasure of it, either the boy or her win. There was only that; not me, my shock or opinion, or the hurt girl next door and her friend, and the danger they presented with their telling of events.

'Where are they?' she said, with an ambiguous little tremor.

'In there,' I replied. 'I'll leave you to it.'

I found the broom and swept up a pile of dog hair, party poppers and the foil from prosecco corks. I moved a great pile of belongings to its next stop at the bottom of the stairs. Amongst it was Frieda's envelope, the first time I had seen it out of her grip, and whereas before I might have looked, this time I simply laid it with the rest. And as I did, I saw Tara's message written in a corner: *For Frieda. Food for thought XX*, and I recognised that hand from the gift that I had found, that perfect little earring which Frieda had worn to catch the boy and I supposed that they had talked that through; Frieda, tender and ready, and Tara, wise, warm and credible. I imagined them settled in her actress's snug, the older woman's counsel: first love, its power and its pitfalls. Who belongs to whom, the politics of friends. Sharing the way it had happened for her, so long ago now. What she had learnt and would happily pass on. Meantime, I had been here, hiding, twisted and obsessive, atrophying over my own heart's desire.

The hall was dark and I was alone. My subconscious took its chance and threw up a couple of little reminders: the skewed tooth in his smile, the way his touch was wired into my system, how his closeness brought me rest. I was still there with my back against the cold cellar door, imagining the empty space behind me with a sick satisfaction, the tumble through moist air and the blunt connection of stone and skull, when the girls came out, arms linked, all three faces streaky now. The party throbbed behind its door and they moved towards it, until at the last, Free stopped Jude with a hand at her chest.

'OK?' she asked, seriously, proprietary. She ran her thumb under the other girl's eyes, making the mess far worse and wiped what she had collected there on her jeans.

Jude nodded. The hierarchy had shifted. 'Come on then,' Frieda said. They shared a brief three-way hug.

'Mum!' Free cried, when she saw me. 'You scared me half to death!'

They all shrieked with varying commitment and collapsed against each other in mock fear and relief, their hands in unceasing motion, tweaking hair, pulling at sleeves, running their fingers across the surfaces of their skin, seeking out any fresh imperfection.

'Wrap it up now, Frieda,' I said. 'The parents will be here.'

Then: 'Mummy.'

'Christ, Louisa. You made me jump. What are you doing, sitting up there by yourself?'

'Nothing,' she said. 'Waiting for you.'

She sat cross-legged, her book spread in her lap.

'Bedtime now. Come on.'

'Can I read, though? Just for a bit?' she asked.

'Ten minutes,' I said. 'No more,' and she scampered up the stairs.

It was fathers mostly for the pick-up, who didn't want to double-check that nothing had been left, nor cared how the party had been or what I had gleaned about their children's lives.

The final tidy revealed little of note, a rip in the back of the tent where they had pushed their way out, leaving a handful of fag butts in a considerate little pile and four empty cans riding deep inside a hedge.

Stef ran through his emails. Jake was back downstairs now that the house had emptied and had retaken his spot before our largest TV. Frieda sat in the kitchen, quiet, hugging her knees, high on fresh sex. I picked up my phone and went back through to the dining room.

I dialled Marie's number. She had told me that she didn't sleep. That she liked to be the last to bed. It was only just after ten. The phone rang and I readied myself. She didn't pick up, so there was that middle phase when I waited for the answer machine instead, planning my message, then we had passed that moment too and I saw her, heaving herself up from the bath, or raking through her things to find her phone. I was prepared for her voice, out of breath or even cross and then it came, but it was recorded, and if she hadn't said her name at the start, I wouldn't have believed that this was Marie. I heard, in her accent, that childhood that she'd denied to me, right there, in a bright thread of estuary. The modulation in her voice, its easy journey, and the pitch – much lower than she presented in our sessions; I recognised none of it. Everything was new and I saw that she had been in disguise, those bright blue eyes a mirror, blinding me with my own reflection. I spoke. A cracked whisper, at first, that fitted my status, crouching, wrong-footed, in the dark, which I expanded across the sentences into something better, more true.

I told her that I hoped she was OK, that I looked forward to speaking with her next week. I acknowledged that perhaps I shouldn't have called, but I wanted to reach her and that seemed the bigger thing. That she was in my thoughts. That we could start again on Monday and I would do my best. I rang off and went to the kids. I took Frieda in my arms though I thought she wouldn't take it, but she hugged me back with her eyes shut tight and I felt the risk she'd taken and her vulnerability.

'I'm getting off soon, Mum,' yelled Jake when he heard me at the back of the room. 'I promise you. I just need to do this,' he said, so I left him fighting zombies and went to say goodnight to Lou.

~

She had suffered a strange spate of night terrors a few years back. A floorboard would most often give her away and we'd find her creeping around the house in the grip of her vision. If she saw us, she would scream and flail, panting with terror, so we learnt to let her be and tracked her from a distance, two frightened parents tiptoeing behind, communicating in looks. When the noises stopped, we knew that she had come to rest and Stef would pick her up from wherever she lay and carry her back to bed, bone-light. She remembered nothing the next morning but was changed by the month's end, I felt sure of it. More grown-up, somehow; the experience marked her, though we rationalised the spell as part of some kind of neurological leap.

So when she wasn't in bed, I thought: this again. I tried the children's rooms first, but nor was she there. I did the rest of upstairs – we had found her once asleep in the bath – but still no sign. I set the other two to looking, racing each other as though it was a game, but they came back to me empty-handed.

'She's gone,' I said to Stefan, when we met in the hall, fighting a rising wall of panic.

'Nancy, please,' he said. 'Keep calm. She'll be here somewhere.'

There are other places a sleeping child might hide, so we checked those next: under the table, behind a curtain; our inventiveness was horrible. I began to call her name, which broke the rules – the sleeping child should never be woken – and acknowledged that what was happening tonight was something else. I became more rash, more manic, turning back into the same room again, the children keeping close now; quiet and obedient, their faces changed. I opened the front door and listened. I tuned out my thumping heart. The entire sheet of my skin began to tingle. My hair rose with the effort of it and I felt sure that if she was out there, I would know it; sense some disturbance. I listened for change, for dissonance, but there was nothing and I had the idea that she had slipped through a crack in the planet. Then the wind slammed the side-gate against its latch, bouncing it wide open, and the possibilities this seemed to suggest escalated my fear to the point that I thought I might scream. I heard Stef's voice.

'She's here, Nancy,' he called. 'Out the back.'

I found her in Stef's office, in his swivel chair, wrapped in her blanket that I hadn't seen was gone, white and silent with the mad hair of the recently wakened. Behind her, in an arrangement like a formal family shot, stood David.

'Hello, Nancy,' he said.

'Where the fuck have you been?'

'At Alice's,' he replied. 'How's things?'

28

Alice's house was beautiful, a home of straight-forward London dreams. Brickwork like royal icing, a strip of chequerboard tiles unrolling from the front door and railings lacquered so thick and black they looked like they were dripping. David opened the door barefoot in old jeans and waited for me to say something.

We hadn't talked the previous night. I cried after we found them, a decent stretch of sobbing that motored along under its own steam, and they left me to it. I texted David later to see when we could meet and he suggested this morning at Alice's house, which he described as a neutral space.

'Come in then,' he said, in the end, with a sweep of his arm. 'Welcome to my lovely home.'

I followed him through. The floorboards were bleached, the walls a chalky pinkish white.

'Where is everything?' I asked. 'I thought she had kids.'

'Oh Nancy,' he replied. 'You should see the storage.'

We went into the sitting room, a room too huge for any standard domestic purpose, which had been split in two and decorated identically with pale squared-off sofas and low polished tables made of slabs of varnished tree. At the far end, raw steel screens opened to a couple of feet of balcony and below, I could see the kitchen through the roof of a matching extension. At the end of her garden, a wooden pirate ship had been set into the earth, its prow raised as though it broached a wave. Beneath, a patch of imported sand showed where a corner of tarpaulin had come loose in all this wind.

'Is that actually beach, out there?' I said.

'I don't know,' he replied. 'I've never seen it in the summer.'

'You here is ridiculous,' I said, which was a lie, he looked amazing in that house; born to it, louche and entitled.

'How so?' he replied. 'I'm staying at my girlfriend's for a bit. Is that so strange?'

I walked away from him, into the other half of the room. A massive pop art pool-scape hung above a bare mantelpiece; a woman, face-down on a lilo, the pool a camouflage print of three contrasting blues, her arms and backside pink and mottled and outsized and her face hidden in shade.

'And that is truly shit art,' I said.

He laughed. 'You know nothing about art.'

'I know when something's shit,' I said. 'Where's Alice?'

'At her office,' he replied.

'On a Sunday?' I said, and thought of Marie, tomorrow; her blanched face across my room. I'd heard nothing from her. I remembered my phone, charging in a socket in the hall.

'Do you want a drink?' David said.

On the table lay a book of architect's blanks and the pencils he preferred.

'Been working?' I asked.

'Just scribbling down a few thoughts,' he said.

'So it's new then, is it, you two?' I said. The wood beneath my feet was warm. I could feel heat rising through the floorboards into the wet soles of my favourite flats, reserved for evenings. I should never have worn them to cross town this time of year.

'New?' he said, laughing and evasive. 'Not exactly.'

'I mean, this latest phase.'

'Well, no. We hook up now and then. More so lately. It's been going on for years. I imagined—'

'You imagined what?' I said.

'I don't know, really,' he replied thoughtfully. 'I kind of imagined you knew.'

'How would I know if you haven't told me?' I said, feeling an inkling of failure. 'Don't you think we would have talked about it, David? If I had known.'

'Yes, now that you mention it,' he said. He gave a dry laugh. There is a crease of worry that drops down from one edge of David's mouth. It isn't always there but to pull it onto that careless face has always felt like a win. Proof of love.

'So who else knows?' I said.

'Well, Mum,' he replied, dropping his gaze.

'She knew you were here?' I said.

'Oh no. I mean about the two of us.' I tucked that slight away for later.

'And she had nothing to say? I suppose it went on throughout Alice's marriage, did it? You played your part in that collapse?'

He made a long frustrated sound.

'What do you care, Nancy? What has that possibly got to do with you?'

Something beeped from another room and I laughed spitefully at the thought of his involvement with some sleek domestic apparatus.

'Are you needed?' I asked but he didn't reply. Growing up, he had hated me like this, alert and sensitised and snarky.

'So you're living here, now?' I said.

'Well, it wasn't exactly a plan. Look, sit with me. Please,' he said.

He took a low seat, faintly waffled like natural candle.

'Me and Skyler were pretty much done and Alice had been wanting to give it a go for a while. I wasn't sure, but at the party, when I saw my life in one room, it was obvious that she was the best thing in it.'

He looked up to see how that declaration had landed, but I made no response.

'I woke up the next morning feeling all kinds of shitty and just left. It's grown from there,' he said.

'Off you went,' I said. 'On a whim.'

'I took a chance, Nancy, if that's what you mean. I saw something that I thought could make things better and I followed it.'

The money had rubbed off on him in subtle ways. This backdrop amplified his glamour. He looked like some sort of creative or maybe a chef. I wondered if she'd sent him to her hairdresser and upgraded those jeans. His beauty made me angry. It struck me that perhaps he was just happy.

'I called you the next morning,' he said. 'You didn't answer.'

'Well you could have tried again.'

'I'm sorry but I was taking a break.'

'From what?' I said.

'All of it,' he replied. 'Just for a bit.'

'Including me?'

'Yes, including you. You weigh heavy, Nancy. You ask a lot.'

'I would have kept your secret,' I said. 'I wouldn't have spoiled it for you.'

'Are you sure about that?' he said.

'Of course,' I replied and felt a sharp clean hurt and the knowledge that he was right, I might well have ruined it, or at least had a go.

A cat appeared, the same colour as the couch. A car pulled out of its spot outside and started away with a huge throbbing roar.

'This place is a joke,' I said.

'Probably. I don't care about this place.'

There is a little cuff of hair that shows beneath his sleeves. His hands are rough and designed to build. His face is slick as Hollywood, that wave of liquorice hair.

'I should probably be thanking you, Nancy,' he said.

'I've been wondering, why did you invite her anyway?' His tone was light and curious.

'What?' I asked, to earn myself another second or two.

'To the party?' he said. 'Why did you do that?'

'Why not? I invited everyone I could find,' I replied, and once I might have believed that of myself but it was not true, I had done it out of spite, to shame him in her eyes, or show him what he had lost, how far in life he had fallen. But he knew all that, and for an instant, I thought that he would call me on it but instead he took my hand. I jumped at his touch.

'Not OK?' he asked, looking down at the knot of our fingers.

'Yes. Fine.' I had forgotten this about him, his sudden sweetnesses.

'So what's up with you then?' he said. 'Louisa phoned me very anxious. She says that something's wrong.'

I watched our matching hands.

'Do you want to talk about it?' he said.

'Not really,' I replied.

'So there's clearly someone else.'

'Why would you say a thing like that?' I cried, childish and hostile.

'It's obvious, Nancy. There's something different about you. It's been coming for a while.'

'I don't know what you mean,' I said but that wasn't right; I had felt it too.

'You're altered, somehow. The space you take up. There's more of you now.'

'I don't know about that,' I said again.

'That's pretty rare, at our age, you know. That kind of change,' he said, and I saw an envy on his face, a look I didn't know. 'How does it feel?'

'I can't do it any more,' I replied, in a shrunken voice.

'That's sad,' he said.

'Not for Stefan and the kids.'

'Anyway, I don't believe you,' he said. 'I thought my sister could do anything. Nancy the Brave, wasn't it?'

I tried to read his face for subtext but there was nothing but the old wry smile.

'This isn't the moment to lose your nerve,' he said.

'Just forget it,' I said. 'I want you to forget it, OK?'

Before I cry, my face fills with blood, a sweep of heat and colour.

'Come here,' David said, but I couldn't stand his pity, least of all from this new, privileged vantage.

'I need you to observe my privacy,' I said stiffly.

'Oh right,' he replied, and I laughed with him, a little, at that.

'Come here. I love you. Always and forever or whatever that bollocks was.'

There was a small stretch of comfort to be had in his arms.

'Oh Christ,' he said. 'Have you got the time? I need to pick up the kids. They've been at their father's,' he said, in flagrant challenge, in anticipation of my contempt, which I did not voice.

'So it's you and Alice now, is it?'

'For the moment,' he said. 'She's great, you know.'

'She always was,' I said.

'I have to go in a minute. Will you walk with me?'

I told him that I had to get home.

'By the way,' he said at the door, and his face showed a little tease. 'That business with Matty Coombes.'

'What?'

'Your email. That's not quite how it went, my dear martyred sister. Think again,' he said, and he winked, that wink that was his trademark, and it took me back again, to summertime and the pond.

Our mother had wrapped Matthias's wound. I couldn't stop looking at it, the way the blood filled the cloth.

'I was looking for Dad's medal,' he began to say.

I turned to David. A triangle of ribbon rose out of his shorts pocket, natty as a folded handkerchief. He covered it with his hand and I felt the danger of his situation.

Matthias started back to the house, feeble in his pants. Mum ran ahead for towels. But David, when I looked back at him, showed no arrogance or dare. He was afraid.

'I didn't mean—' he said.

'Shut up. Give it here,' I replied.

'Why?'

'Just give it. Be quick.'

'Are you going to tell on me?' he asked.

'Don't be so stupid.'

He extended his arm and I snatched the medal and flung it towards the pond in an extension of that movement. The throw was high and wild. It made a terrible plink as it hit the water and then the whole thing was gone in a sudden heavy drop.

'Right,' I said. I held my finger close to his face. I seem to remember a single tear. 'Not a word. Do you understand?'

'I'm not sure,' he said. 'Mum won't mind.'

'Yes she will. She'll kill you. You mustn't say a word.'

'Do you think he'll be OK?' he asked.

'I know he will. Now promise me, David. Don't make a fuss. It'll only make things worse.'

It was the summer before the split, everything already badly wrong but me still believing I could fix it through sheer strength of will.

He turned away and kicked a gnarl of root, launching a fan of earth into the air.

'It's not good to keep secrets,' he said. 'Mum says to always tell the truth.'

'Not this time. Promise me, David,' I said, following him round, finding his face again.

'I promise,' he said at last.

'Good. And the very least you can do now, is say thank you.'

'Thanks, sis,' he said, but he wouldn't meet my eyes.

29

Home, when I got back, was the same as always, a muddle of love, resentment and dependency.

'How is he, Mummy?' Louisa asked, washed out from last night's drama.

'Fine,' I said, 'better than fine,' and thought of him debriefing Alice in the filtered atmosphere of that house, over a glass of something special.

'He sends you all his love and he'll be round to see us soon,' I said. 'Did anyone call, Stef, when I was out?'

'No, Nancy,' he replied. 'I'm afraid not.'

'So everything's back to normal,' Frieda cried and threw her arms around her daddy. Just for a second, my cover slipped and I assumed my true form. I withered and shrank, my face matched my heart, but I'd forgotten Lou, who had slid up onto the counter and watched, her legs hugged to her chest, steady and appraising. The tenor of the room changed and for a moment I thought I was about to faint or suffer some other cognitive collapse.

Then: 'Look at that,' Jake said, pointing. 'The *Ciao*'s gone out,' and it had; something must have fused, for every little bulb in all four letters had blown, leaving one side of the room in partial darkness.

'I'll sort it,' Stef said. I unstuck rotting fruit from the bottom of the bowl and he took a pear and ate the unblemished side in quick precise bites, stripping it efficiently. He threw the core in a slow arc into the compost bucket, which woke the dog.

'He shoots. He scores!' Jake cried and high-fived his father. 'Are there any more? Can I have a go?'

Louisa took her chance and tried to slip by – she can be light and silent – but I caught the top of her arm, narrow enough that I could almost close my hand round it.

'Lou,' I said. 'Can we talk?'

She narrowed her eyes. Her hair was wisps around her old-fashioned aristocrat's face. She is an anomaly, Lou; she bears no resemblance to anyone under this roof, her genetic story begins with my mother and flows backwards into that well-bred past.

'Come into my bedroom,' she said, which was a surprise. I followed her up the stairs, righting photos knocked wonky as I went. We both paused in the doorway. It struck me that I was her guest.

'My friends usually sit on the beanbag,' she said. 'But I think you might be better off on the bed.' She took her own place on the swivel chair by her desk. The room needed an update; piles of books she'd long outgrown all over the floor and old framed artwork on the walls.

'Can you come a bit nearer, Lou,' I said. 'I feel like I'm being interviewed here.'

She dug her heels into the carpet and pulled herself a leg's length closer.

'I want to talk to you about your call. To Uncle David,' I said.

She tugged her hoodie over her knees and bent her toes up into it. I saw a huge hole worn through her sock at the pad of her foot, evidence of another tiny failure. Her eyes on me were level.

'Is there something—? I wondered if there was anything you'd like to talk to me about,' I said.

'Like what?' she replied.

'I don't know, Lou. Whatever it was that made you phone David. He says that you're worried about me, or something.'

She swivelled lightly on her bottom, setting the seat of her chair moving left and right.

'You don't need to be, OK?' I said. 'I'm absolutely fine.'

'I thought you missed Uncle David,' she said.

'I did, sweet, but he's back now. And it's not your job to try and solve these adult problems.'

'I thought that you could talk to him. You told me once that he was your best friend,' Louisa said.

'He was— he is— it was very thoughtful of you but—'

'But you're still not happy, are you?' she said. She dipped her head, intent upon her movement, her hair hiding her face.

'Louisa. I don't know where you've got this idea from. It's been a difficult time, that's all. You don't have to try and understand everything. Just let it be. It's fine.'

'I know a secret,' she said, down towards her toes.

'OK,' I replied, carefully. 'And what sort of secret is that?'

'A big one,' she replied.

'And has someone asked you to keep this secret?'

'No. I found it out. By accident,' she said, looking up quickly.

'Do you want to tell me about it then?'

'I thought you said I shouldn't keep secrets,' she said.

'I did. I do. Is it making you feel bad?'

'Yes,' she replied and a flat dread landed on me.

'Then you must,' I said. Lou is a worrier in the abstract, about things that could, would or might. When they do, she is dead calm.

'But telling you might make things happen,' she said. 'Things that I don't want.'

Downstairs, the music of a reality TV show started. 'We're watching telly,' Jake bellowed. 'We're not waiting. We're going to start without you.'

'Please look at me, Lou,' I said, and I knew that this was wrong, that I should respect her boundaries, that she had established this distance to enable herself to speak, but I had to see her, to gain some clue as to what was coming, and when I saw the pinch of her frightened face, I sent out a shameful prayer, that of all the terrible things that she might go on to say, none of them would have anything to do with me.

'It's already happened, Lou, whatever it is. You can't change that.'

'I'm not sure I can say it out loud,' she said thoughtfully, and I allowed myself to hide, for one last time, in the easy fiction that I had been careful, that I had left no traces, but this is Louisa and she is patient and focused and in love with the truth.

'You can,' I said. 'I'm telling you now that you can.'

'But if I don't. If I never say a word, I think it might go away,' she said, 'and that would be good,' and I saw that she was making me an offer, she was telling me she would save me, if I asked her to. My brave and resolute child.

'It doesn't work like that, Louisa. It will never go away. Now tell me,' I said and came down off her bed. I took her hands in mine, knelt at her feet.

'I know that you love somebody else,' she said.

Her look, just above me, was clear and frank and temporary. Its collapse began, and the impulse to stop it by whatever means, to deny it all straight away, surfaced briefly, but Louisa saw that and went on.

'It's that man from your work.'

'Louisa. He and I are friends. I can see how you might— How perhaps— Look, hold on. You tell me what you're worried about and I'll see if I can put your mind at rest.'

She looked at me shrewdly and then accepted these terms with a nod. She sat a little straighter on her chair and I recognised that my youngest was now my opponent. I watched her wonder where to begin.

'I see how you are together,' she said, sullen suddenly. 'I'm not some stupid baby any more.'

'You're not, Lou. Not at all. And yes, we are close, Adam and I. We've known each other a long time. I can see how it might look like something different.'

'You're weird around him,' she said. 'You don't act normal.'

'Well, it might just be that you're not used to me having friends who are men,' I said.

'He uses your words.'

'Well, the things I say don't belong to me—'

'Why did you get so cross about Frieda going over there, Mummy?' she asked and I saw her confidence spike and I thought, is this all you've got? And a little spring of hope arose.

'That's more complicated,' I said, hitting my stride. 'It can be hard for a mother to see her child form a relationship with someone else. It's silly and it's selfish and I didn't behave very well,' I said. 'I'm sorry.' I wondered if that would be enough.

'Then what about this?' she said and pulled open her drawer. She reached in and when she withdrew her hand, whatever she held inside was hidden completely.

'What is that?' I said, watching the bones of her knuckles bulge white through her thin skin. The question grew huge and then she twisted her fist over quickly and opened her hand like an illusionist. Inside lay a bronze Zippo lighter.

'Where did you get that from?' I said.

'Adam's house,' she replied. 'On the table, by the window, when we went over to look for Free.'

'Well, you mustn't take other people's things,' I said, 'what on earth were you thinking?' and I saw her blink, her shame at her own infinitesimal wrong.

'It's got this on,' she said, holding the spine of the lighter towards me, 'the flame, or whatever, just like your necklace,' and I saw her eyes drop to my throat, where the matching image hung, the dream or wish, or whatever it was, and a million evasions began in my head, but I looked at her solemn little face and couldn't lie any more.

'Does Daddy know?' she asked.

'No,' I told her. 'I haven't talked to him about it.'

She nodded and I waited. She watched her feet, her fingernail working at a scrap of varnish left on one toe. The doorbell went downstairs and we both cringed in terror.

'I'll keep your secret, Mummy,' she said. 'You mustn't worry any more,' and she fell into my arms and though she didn't cry, her breastbone pounded as though her heart was trying to break out from behind it.

'You don't have to do that, Lou. I would never ask that of you,' I said.

We took the stairs together carefully and when I saw Stefan waiting at the bottom I thought he must have heard it all.

'Louisa,' he said, 'I need you to join the others in the sitting room, please. Nothing to worry about, though,' and at that, her face flared into horror. 'I just need to speak to your mum.'

He followed me into kitchen and pushed the door shut behind us. In the weak light, he took my hands and I thought of the moment he had proposed.

'Nancy. I've just had a visit. It's about your client, Marie. I have to tell you. She has committed suicide.'

30

I found a night two weeks later. Jake's easy, he is bid-
dable and will go where he is asked. Frieda's willing but
over-scheduled. Louisa, though, needs persuading. She
has these three lanky cats that she likes to rest on a pillow
by her face and feels inhibited in this at any other place
than home. Still I found a date, a Saturday, and crammed
each child's arrangements onto the diary page.

Stef noticed the next day.

'Hey,' he said. 'Am I reading this right?'

I poached salmon to make fishcakes for the kids. Pearls
of orange fat collected on the surface of the milk which
I broke up with a fork, though each time I turned back
to it they had come together again. I lifted the fish out
with a slotted spoon, peeled off the skin and the dark V of
grey flesh underneath which makes the children gag, and
dropped it, calling for the dog.

'What?' I said, although I knew full well.

'A child-free evening weekend after next,' he replied.

Louisa, stretched up at a cupboard for sanctioned bis-
cuits, paused in her groping.

'Is there a plan?' he asked.

'What do you mean?'

'Have you booked anything?' he said.

He had just come back from a run and bent a leg behind him to catch the top of his foot. He eased it towards his flank, his thigh muscle coming into definition. I couldn't see his face.

'Ugh Dad,' Frieda cried. 'That's so gross. You're sweating all over the floor.'

'I haven't,' I said. 'No.'

'I can do it, if you like?' Stef replied, dropping his leg and bending low.

'It's all right,' I said, in a tone loose enough to bring Louisa off her toes. 'Leave it with me.'

He went upstairs for his shower, towelling his head roughly as he passed.

I was at home for an indefinite time; my choice. Only the lawyer disagreed, seems the family sometimes sue in these cases and he felt it sent the wrong signal, but there had been no word and so I stayed inside, waiting. They managed me now, the children and Stef. They handled me carefully. They tried to lubricate my days. Time slid by.

I thought of Marie and wondered if anything she had told me had been true. I wished that I had touched her and been kinder. I wished that I'd never seen her face.

I thought of Adam. I hid behind my book and called to mind the rough feel of the calluses at the roots of his fingers, the way they snagged on my hair. I drank my wine, locked into my spot on the sofa, and dreamt of the whiskery ridge where his chin gave way to throat, the prickle of it, back and forward on my cheek. I took his laugh to bed with me.

Meantime I planned how I would tell Stef. I plotted it out in the hours when I used to see clients. I tried to find the words, I settled upon tone. I let myself imagine the whole thing done. I floated adrift in the family and they let me, all of us loosening, little islands now, eyeing each other across the space.

Then the mother rang. I had a strange premonition when the unfamiliar number came up; not that it would be her, but a sense of something imminent. I answered anyway, grateful for change.

'It's Mrs Bingham,' she said, sounding irritated and officious. 'Irene Bingham. Mother of Marie,' but I already knew; their voices were the same, thin with a sandpaper edge.

'I've got some questions,' she said. 'I wondered if we could meet.'

I heard her effort to elocute each word and saw her at home in a hard-backed chair in the sitting room that Marie had once described. She named an all-day café on the high street and I agreed to see her there.

I arrived early. The place was a disaster, crammed with tiny tables and disco on the radio. I went back outside, took a seat, and watched a decorative ball of plastic greenery swing gently on a tripod of chains in front of the dry-cleaner's next door.

She arrived with Mark; a small woman, an earlier iteration of Marie, a prototype, a rough first draft wearing too many layers and the thick woollen tights of a child. When she reached me, she stopped; her arms packed before her, just like Marie, and looked straight over my shoulder as she told me her name. Mark shook hands and went inside to buy tea. I'd pulled two square tables together and Irene took the seat diagonally opposite me and watched the café door steadily, in silence, until he came back out.

'I'm so sorry—' I began, but she stopped me with two efficient little nods.

'Was it a surprise?' she asked, suddenly, as soon as Mark was sitting.

'Irene has been wondering—' he said.

'She can answer,' Irene replied sharply. 'It's simple enough.'

'Absolutely,' I said. 'A complete shock. I had no idea at all.'

Those choked little nods again. She had plucked her eyebrows to nothing and drawn them back on in two thin identical lines.

'Sealed tight as a nut, that one,' Irene said, 'Always was.'

'She was certainly very private,' I replied. 'I was hoping that, over time—'

'And did she tell you about Luke?' Irene asked.

'No, she didn't.'

'My oldest child. We lost him, just as he came up to ten.' She watched me, now, very closely, but I did not react. Across the years, in my work, I have heard many dreadful things.

'Two years apart, the kids, give or take. A long illness,' she said, her face clenched like a fist.

'She was never able to talk about that with me,' I said.

'I see,' Irene replied. 'I wondered.'

'I can't imagine how that must have been,' I said.

'No, you can't,' she replied, in simple agreement.

'Did she speak with anyone at the time?' I asked. 'Did your family get some help?'

'Help?' she called, with a splintered ill-used laugh. She made the sound again, looking at Mark, trying to enlist him, but his face was locked. 'Help with what exactly?'

'With your grief,' I said.

'My grief?' she repeated, and struck her chest, hard, with her palm. 'Oh I don't need any help with that,' she said and I saw that without her pain she would simply collapse, an old sack of bones.

She got up then. She was still wearing her coat and held her bag pressed under her armpit. 'I was curious about that,' she said. 'I wanted to know.'

'Is there anything else—?' I asked.

'Thank you for your time,' she replied formally. She walked away and came to stop a little way down the pavement, waiting there, stick straight, as Mark worked his thick legs free from beneath the small zinc table.

'Goodbye,' Mark said. 'Marie liked you, you know.'

'Thank you,' I replied.

He shook my hand once more.

'But she struggled with hope,' he said and was off, after Mrs Bingham, striding out to catch her in those same smart dress shoes he'd worn to my house. I walked home myself, as fast as I could, mere survival feeling like a miracle.

We had dinner for my brother that night, though Dad cried off. April and the girls placed him at the centre of the table as he spun a tale about a love that had endured, waving his hands around, slopping his wine. Stefan allowed it. He had made no comment about David's return and I wondered at that. He seemed watchful and apart, but we were all on pause. Waiting out the hiatus.

'Going well, then?' I said, when David came to find me at the stove. His face showed the blind shine of a zealot.

'Really well, Nance,' he said. 'I want you and Alice to be friends again, like the old days.' He took the top of my shoulder, and rubbed the heel of his hand into the sinew at my neck with a touch meant for her. He smelt expensive, dry grass, vetiver and citrus. I saw it would survive. The daylight had made them strong.

'Perhaps,' I said. 'If I get the time.'

'I'm worried about you, Nancy,' David said.

'Since when?' I replied. I felt corrupted and mean.

'You can't keep going like this,' he said. 'Seriously.'

'Can't I?'

'Look, I just want you to be happy,' he told me and I laughed at that, at the reversal, and the gap between intention and effect. I'd said the same to him, and meant it, many times across the years, a pang of righteous sorrow in my chest, and yet the sentiment reached me now as facile and limited and self-serving. I thought, what a pain in the arse I must have been, which made me laugh again.

'Well I guess I'm David-proof,' I said, and was pleased with it. He went back to the table and opened another bottle of wine. In the end Stefan offered to drive him home.

I took a sleeping pill and went to bed.

I walked, I slept, I tended to the kids and then one afternoon Adam emailed, saying that he had heard about
Marie and could we talk? I laid down my glass and left.
I walked to the middle of the park, the wind a shriek
every time I turned into it. When I found a sheltered
place, I called him.

'God, Nancy I am so very sorry,' he said. His voice
sounded close.

'Who told you?' I asked.

'Lynn,' he replied. 'She called me.'

'Has it ever happened to you?'

'No, it hasn't,' he said. 'How are you doing?'

'I'm terrified,' I replied, just realising it. 'I feel lethal.'

I watched a child running face first into the weather,
ecstatic, her arms off behind her and her mouth stretched
wide.

'You didn't have a chance, Nancy,' he said, 'Marie
wasn't honest.'

'But she wanted to be. She came, didn't she? Week
after week.'

'But she couldn't,' he said. 'Some people can't. It's just
too difficult.'

'I should have found a way,' I said. 'Adam, I don't know
if I'll ever practise again.'

'You will,' he said. 'Use it, Nancy. Assimilate it. Allow
it to make you better,' and I wanted to grab hold of that
logic, pull myself, fist over fist, to where Adam stood, on
firm dry land.

'Thank you,' I replied.

'You're welcome. I need to go now,' he said. 'Take care.'

'You too.'

Then the weekend arrived and saying goodbye to the children felt weighted, but I refused to give in to the melodrama of it. They fought for favourite sleeping-bags, packed chargers, slipped in sweets. They bounced their stuff down the stairs and the dog woke, moving fretfully between them. Into each wash-bag I slipped my usual note, *Sleep well. Love you, Mum XXX.* Jake keeps them all, I once found a great scrunched bundle in the corner of his shelf. I kissed them and wondered what they would come home to. Then the last of them had left, and Stef closed the front door and walked back down the hall towards me.

'So,' he said, the way he does when he is about to tell me a story that he knows I'll like. He drew out a chair at the end of the table. I stood behind the sink, dropped flush into the island, my hands in scalding water. I cleaned the last part of his juicer with its special brush, working the bristles hard into the tight links of mesh.

'So,' I said, which is how it often goes.

Stef's eyes are conker brown, complete, with no gradation. It struck me, then, that he was hard to read and that I'd never before acknowledged this because I'd never before thought he might be hiding. He wore a new shirt, slim-cut in a faded Oxford stripe, though the difference between all of them was slight, even on the rail.

'You first,' he said, and at that, I should have simply

begun, but this was not the way I had imagined it and I faltered. I pulled the plug from the sink. The first suck was thirsty and then the flow of water slowed and I made a production of plunging the hole with the heel of my hand.

'Oh come on, Nancy,' he said suddenly. 'You've got something to say. Just say it. I'm not an idiot, you know,' and I realised my mistake, for his voice was changed. It cracked and wavered.

'You're right,' I said. My hands dripped and I groped for a towel. I had considered the phrasing. I wanted to be straightforward. To name it for what it was. Behind me the dishwasher drained and then settled into its low, even chug.

'I had an affair,' I said. The other options had seemed either too cosy or too bald.

'I see,' he replied, very still. 'I'm going to guess—' He crossed one leg high over the other and the shade of his sock made me think of that instant at which yellow and red combine at the mid-line of a Tequila Sunrise. The skin above it, by contrast, was white. 'I am going to guess Adam.'

'Why do you say that?' I asked, which was immediately wrong.

'Is it Adam?' Stefan said, again.

'Yes,' I replied. I wanted to ask him how he knew. Whether he had seen it, that time in the office or at the party. I felt sorry, and also shame, but a kind of gratification too, as though Stefan's recognition gave our love materiality, form.

The dog sensed the mood and circled the island at a trot. He found the tea towel that I'd dropped and took it over to the door, whining. I didn't dare respond, but when he started to scratch at the glass, Stef went across and let him out. It felt better with Stefan moving. I drank water straight from the tap while he was still behind me, then he was back and pushed up onto the island, where Louisa sits, though she's too big for it now, chatting to me sideways as I chop. This close, I saw a popped blood vessel in the white of one eye.

'In your office, then. All this time,' he said, nodding down at his feet which dangled just short of the floor. 'Or beforehand too?'

'Not before,' I replied.

'A year, then. More,' he said.

'Yes,' I replied.

'Why did you do it?' he asked. He cocked his head, squinting as though the sight of me hurt his eyes, listening completely.

'Stef, you know there's no single answer to that—'

'Well, give me one of them then,' he said, 'just to start me off.' So here was bitterness, a brief phase of attack. It felt like headway.

'There was the fact that I knew him from before,' I said. 'I think that's relevant. We got close in a way I wouldn't have let happen, otherwise.'

'So you were unhappy, then? With me? With us?' he asked.

'I didn't think so,' I said. 'I don't know. I felt angry a lot of the time. And compromised, somehow. I'd lost myself.'

In the silence, I became aware of a low electrical hum. The lighting, the extractor, the speakers came together

and as I listened, the sound seemed to narrow and accelerate into one symphonic drone.

'We could have talked,' he said.

'I know.'

'But you wouldn't allow it.'

I said nothing.

'So you fell in love with him and out of love with me,'
he asked. 'Was it like that?'

'No,' I replied. 'Nothing like as binary.'

'Do you still love me then?' he asked. He leant forwards
over the lip of the counter, his weight in his hands, the toes
of his trainers tipped up.

'Of course,' I said, 'but being with Adam feels— More
truthful. I don't know how else to put it.'

'Truthful,' he said, thoughtfully. 'The kind of word you
use with your clients, I imagine, to explain away all their
shit decisions, too. I don't even know what that means.'

'I can't explain it any better.'

'More truthful than your life here with your children?'

'That is something completely different,' I said.

'No,' Stef replied emphatically. 'It's not. That's where
you're wrong. You don't get to pull things apart like that.
You know who you sound like, Nancy? Your brother,'
and he landed that last word hard, as though it were the
worst kind of profanity.

'David's got nothing to do with this,' I said.

'Ah. Well,' he replied and pushed up off the island,
landing with a pitter-patter, a kind of skippity two-step.

'What you've just described to me,' he said. 'It's just so
fucking selfish. Seriously. Do you even hear yourself?'

He moved around the kitchen with a strange sudden energy. The dog, wanting in, gave a rough two-note bark.

'Look, you're in the grip of this. I get that. And then there was Marie. But you're honestly here to tell me that you're giving up – no, destroying – all of this? This effort. This time. Everything?'

'Stefan, please. Just let me tell you what I need to—'

'You've told me, Nancy, OK? It's done.'

At the far end of the kitchen, he paused. He eased his shoulders out in a couple of subtle rolls, loosened his head on the stem of his neck. He turned and took a full breath – I observed the procedures of it – the lift of his chest and then the reciprocal swell of his belly. I watched him wilfully collect himself and start back towards me.

'The deceit is over, all right? And carrying that weight must have been hard. It must have felt impossible. But it's gone now,' he said and at his words I felt a sudden dizzy relief.

He came closer, raised his hands before him and laid his palms high on my chest, quiet and heavy, setting my heartbeat staggering.

'I want to ask you to reconsider,' he said. 'You are not that person, I know you're not. The kind of woman who is like, *I was bored, no one sees me,* all that crap people bring to your office every day. This isn't in the abstract. This is real. We are talking about our children's lives. Are you ready to rip this down?'

'It doesn't have to be like that, Stef,' I said.

'Will you really leave our children?' he asked.

'I would never leave the kids.'

314

He laughed then, a short hard laugh and raised his hands from me.

'Well, what do you think we're going to do?' he said. 'All live here together happily? I'm asking you to think again.'

'Stefan, I know this is sudden, but I'm worried that you're not really hearing me—'

'I'm not in shock, if that's what you mean. I'm hurt. Of course I am. But I've thought about it and I know it will take time, but what we have in this family is more important —'

'Stef, I'm sorry. I don't understand—'

'Oh, Nancy,' he said, in a pitying kind of voice. 'I know,' and for an insane moment I thought: Adam.

'It was your brother,' he said.

'What? When?' I asked.

'In the car, when I took him home. He couldn't wait. I don't know if he thought he was acting on your behalf, I've no idea, I've never understood that man, but, you see, I have had time and I believe, no, I am sure, that we can still make this work.'

Stefan took a step away. He was utterly familiar now. Steady and lucid. Firm and eternal.

'You know me, Nancy. I can put this aside, if that is what is needed. We can start again. No harm done.'

As a child I had dreamt of an old age with my brother, unborn children grown and gone, unmet spouses swept aside. In my vision, I would look after us, I wouldn't ask questions, and he would stay. I pictured fun, and that part was feasible – we have always laughed – but also ease and comfort, as though these were our ways and his love didn't come with teeth. I'd thought that I was wishing for nothing to change, for one strong unbroken line stretching from childhood to the end. But that was a little girl's fantasy. I saw, now, that I had been dreaming of the opposite; a laying down of weapons, of truce.

31

Midsummer and my office was full of a hard white light, sharpened through the wet glass of the pane. Simple refraction – I'd been through it the night before with Jake, who had come to me reluctantly, in need, thanks to a pressing test. I touched the back of his neck, hot and damp, as he turned to his work, and he let me. Louisa seems OK and Frieda is lost to Brandon for now. It will out in its own good time.

I visit them in my old home, a guest, ringing the front doorbell again and again when no one comes, with the anticipation of a lover. I had to bang on the sitting room window the other afternoon; I could see Jake in there, on his feet, with his headset on and a console in his grip, lurching around and calling out. The brief lift in his face when he saw me gave me hope. The girls came downstairs dreamily, their heads still in whatever they'd left behind upstairs.

The house is subtly changed. It is cleaner, for a start. Stef has someone new who comes in twice a week and the place smells strongly of her bleaches and sprays, chlorine and pine. It is neater, too. He seems to have subdued all the crap that I could never quite keep down.

Something was altered at the back when I followed them through, though I couldn't put my finger on it. He saw me looking and said: 'It's the garden. Do you see? I've only just begun, but there's been a lot of cutting back. It's completely changed the light.' And he is right. The eye falls differently; the shape of the room, and its emphasis, has shifted. Even the dog has noticed and moved his spot. It wouldn't support the old life, I wouldn't know how to be in this new space, but that is fine, for I am just a visitor now. Stef took me through his plans and I listened with affected interest. He treats me with a kindly sort of sympathy. I feel like a tolerated but disappointing child. After that, he left, and I was free to enjoy the children as best I could for the hours meted out, though I will see them again tomorrow and on my weekend, which falls in just nine days. Then I will stay two nights in the house, in the spare room that I furnished over a decade ago, stranded in the wreckage of my own outdated taste.

David phones and phones, he wants to see me, at least to speak, but I'm holding him off. He will expect thanks, I imagine; his part in all this to be recognised. He thinks I've learnt from him, at the feet of the master; he doesn't see the cost. He'll be missing our games and will know that he'll never replace me. I am his only worthy opponent. We were so perfectly matched. Not any more, though. He may want to spar but I find I've lost the taste.

Lynn buzzed to tell me that my client had arrived, speaking her name with a roll, like a compere; her most winning habit. Nicola Strode. The syllables scanned beautifully.

I had been back at work for a couple of months. There will be no court case though there was a moment when it looked as if the mother might proceed. Mark became my ally in the end. He saw his wife far more clearly than she or I ever did. I swear I will work harder next time. I will not give up.

I met Nicola at the threshold of the room and we turned inside together, taking our corresponding places in my chairs. I looked at her properly, then, for the first time, my very best part of the process. This is ancient circuitry doing its thing. I've seen the moment that it happens on a screen, the almond shape of the amygdala lighting up with a gentle flickering, tentative and careful, nothing like the absoluteness of its verdict. I sat back and let impressions hit. I am an empty vessel. But the sun was in my eyes and Nicola's face was nothing but a brilliant vacuum. I looked away and refocused on what was close, the bookshelf, the painting, my own naked hand. There was a glare in the room that made everything savage and perfect. Someone slammed a door in a neighbouring room, my coffee shuddered in its cup and I felt like Peter Parker at the first effects of the spider-bite. The beginnings of a change, subtle and monumental.

'Sorry,' I said, 'the light in here's blinding. I'm going to have to shift my chair.'

It was heavy and took a number of shoves. She watched me from her seat. The wheels had left deep rust-stained dents in the carpet, but that could wait.

'Much better,' I said and the room resettled. I saw a young girl, a little face beneath huge hair, presenting cynicism, lip and isolation. She was as brilliant as the day, as exposing and relentless, but there was joy in her too, which leaves its mark as surely as pain or age.

'I have your doctor's referral here, and I can certainly help with your symptoms but what we're really trying to do over the next few months is get beneath all that and understand the reasons why you're feeling the way you are. We need to address the root cause. Does that make sense?'

She nodded, and took a thick wedge of hair and flicked it across.

'They will have told you, too, that everything you say in here is confidential. It will remain between us. So the more honest you can be, even about the most difficult things, the better.'

She wore the same boots as Frieda, I recognised the stitching on the sole.

'I should mention at this point that I'll be off for the next week, which is bad timing, I know, but I won't be away again during our first chunk of sessions.'

I felt her withdrawal. 'Off somewhere nice?' she said, jerking her head towards my suitcase, tucked away as best I could behind my desk.

So, an observant girl. A person who needs to feel in control of her environment. Or somebody attuned to threat.

'It's not a holiday actually,' I said. 'I'm moving.'

'Oh,' she replied, and her attention focused. What kind of woman moves house with one old bag she's dragged into work?

~

'You're not leaving me again, are you?' Adam had asked, when I went to go this morning. 'Not a second time.'

'No,' I replied, 'but thanks for having me. You know it was never permanent.' I turned back to kiss him goodbye.

'Won't you reconsider?'

'In a while, perhaps,' I said.

'Will you write?' he asked. 'Will you call?'

'Come over this evening,' I said. 'Maybe I'll cook.'

'Can I stay over?' he asked.

'We'll see. Bring pyjamas. Just in case.'

My new house is small and unimproved. I got a builder in to pull out the vile fitted wardrobe and found a strange green corrugated wallpaper behind it. When the plasterer stripped that back, there was another layer of paper, satinette this time, a spray of red roses on endless repeat. 'Give up, love,' he said, 'we'll be here until we're old,' and he was joking but when he'd finished with the walls, I sent him away, and now plan to leave the elaborate cornicing and the rest of it, and try to live around these things instead. There are two bedrooms only and we will see how the children feel about this place, but it is not my intention to build a replica home around myself. They have one already, which they love and which works, and I plan, instead, to help to keep that standing. For me, now, this will do.

'OK,' I said to Nicola. 'Shall we begin? Do you want to tell me, in your own words, why you're here?'

Acknowledgements

First and profound thanks to Antony Topping, my agent, who sees where I'm going long before I do, nudges me gently that way and waits patiently while I get there. Also Judith Murray and the team at Greene & Heaton.

Next Louisa Joyner, my editor. She lifted this story pretty much clean from amongst many more thousand words. And Sophie Portas, for helping it find its audience.

Thanks to all at Faber, in particular Samantha Matthews, Dominique Enright, Alex Kirby, Paul Baillie-Lane, Sarah Barlow and Anne Owen.

The estate of Derek Walcott for allowing me to quote his beautiful poem 'Love After Love'.

Then my early readers, Dorothy Hourston, Rosalind de Haan, Shiraz El Showk and Kirsty Negus for their honesty and insight.

Toby Wiltshire, Ollie Waring and Sarah Libbey for advice on matters youth-related.

My writer friends, Jo Bloom and Rebecca Whitney for their wisdom, perspective and company.

Christina Harris, my mother, for emergency child-care and more. And last, Neil, Martha and Archie, for all the rest.